Praise for

Kindred Spirits

I adored the characters in 'Quinn's Blessing'...a charming, uplifting, passionate love story with a timeless message—pure love is the greatest blessing of all. ~ *Queer Magazine Online*

Total-E-Bound Publishing books by Jenna Byrnes and Jude Mason:

Untamed Hearts
Feral Heat
Bear Combustion
Wolfen Choice
Stallion's Pride

Kindred Spirits
Ethan's Choice
Hunter's Light

Anthologies:
Friction: Maximum Exposure
Over The Moon: Trapped
Gaymes: Good Cop, Bad Cop

KINDRED SPIRITS
Volume Two

Alex's Appeal

Quinn's Blessing

JENNA BYRNES
JUDE MASON

Kindred Spirits Volume Two
ISBN # 978-0-85715-403-3
©Copyright Jenna Byrnes and Jude Mason 2010
Cover Art by Natalie Winters ©Copyright 2010
Interior text design by Claire Siemaszkiewicz
Total-E-Bound Publishing

This is a work of fiction. All characters, places and events are from the author's imagination and should not be confused with fact. Any resemblance to persons, living or dead, events or places is purely coincidental.

All rights reserved. No part of this publication may be reproduced in any material form, whether by printing, photocopying, scanning or otherwise without the written permission of the publisher, Total-E-Bound Publishing.

Applications should be addressed in the first instance, in writing, to Total-E-Bound Publishing. Unauthorised or restricted acts in relation to this publication may result in civil proceedings and/or criminal prosecution.
The author and illustrator have asserted their respective rights under the Copyright Designs and Patents Acts 1988 (as amended) to be identified as the author of this book and illustrator of the artwork.

Published in 2010 by Total-E-Bound Publishing, Think Tank, Ruston Way, Lincoln, LN6 7FL, United Kingdom.

No part of this book may be reproduced, scanned, or distributed in any printed or electronic form without permission. Please do not participate in or encourage piracy of copyrighted materials in violation of the authors' rights. Purchase only authorised copies.

Total-E-Bound Publishing is an imprint of Total-E-Ntwined Limited.

If you purchased this book without a cover you should be aware that this book is stolen property. It was reported as "unsold and destroyed" to the publisher and neither the author nor the publisher has received any payment for this "stripped book".

Manufactured in the USA.

ALEX'S APPEAL

Dedication

To my writing partner, who pushes, cajoles, curses and very possibly sticks pins in voodoo dolls in order to get me motivated sometimes. I'm so glad I met you! ~ Jude

Chapter One

"What kind of a crap outfit leaves a customer standing at the door with enough luggage to choke a small army? Lazy bunch of no good…"Alex Brookfield let the rest of the sentence fade into nothingness while he bit the inside of his cheek to keep from laughing out loud.

Across the beautifully appointed lobby, he saw the owner and his good friend, Ethan Roberts, tense. The man spun away from the picture window and faced him, a scowl distorting his normally handsome face. An instant later, the frown faded, replaced by a gaping-mouth look of confusion.

Alex couldn't stop the laughter from erupting. The look on Ethan's face was hilarious. The wide-eyed stare, priceless.

"Well, fuck!" Ethan managed to get out after only a few more seconds of obvious confusion. "Alex, I should have known it was you."

Alex, dressed in his usual suit and tie, strode across the floor, leaving his large suitcase where it was, blocking the doorway. "Possibly, but I'm glad you didn't. I haven't had a good belly laugh like that in months."

With his hand extended, Ethan took a couple of steps forward and grasped Alex's hand, giving it an enthusiastic shake. "Welcome to Whiskers', Alex. It's been too long, my friend." The owner of the inn patted Alex on the shoulder then pulled him closer for a warm hug. "How are you?"

"I'm good. Thanks, Ethan." Alex accepted the hug. For an instant, it brought back memories of college days when he and Ethan had been more than friends. But that was a long time ago, and they'd parted on the best of terms. "Really, to leave a man's luggage sitting by the door. Anyone could walk in and swipe it, you know. And me being a lawyer and all, I'd have to sue." The last words came out with laughter that came bubbling up again.

"Bloody hell, man." Ethan grinned and pulled him towards the front desk. "My luck, you'd do it and claim you've got all the family treasures, the deeds to any property you own and the winning lottery ticket you purchased not ten minutes ago."

"You know it." Alex beamed. Tension he hadn't realised had been knotting his shoulders seeped out of him the further into the inn he went. "So, the place is doing well, I hope."

"Yeah, we're just getting into the busy season. Bookings have really picked up since the beginning of the month."

"Excellent, I'll adjust the numbers when I sue." He tried deadpanning it but managed to keep a straight face for only a few moments. It felt good to laugh.

Ethan chuckled along with him. "Nice. I'm so glad you're a friend, not just my lawyer."

"Kidding aside, the place looks great."

Ethan seemed to glow with pride. "We haven't made many changes. A new coat of paint, added some artwork that I felt suited the place better. Cade keeps the grounds up and does all the little fixes that need attending to."

"Cade? Would that be the same Cade Wyatt who's been here for years?" Alex remembered the man from a previous visit—a hunk if there ever was one, and if he wasn't mistaken, Ethan's special someone.

"Yeah, the one and only." He leaned closer and whispered, "My one and only."

"If I remember the man correctly, and I always remember good looking men correctly, you're a very lucky guy. He's a hunk." Alex pushed down another sudden flash of memory. His own special someone was gone, and he still missed him terribly.

"He's around here somewhere," Ethan said and reached across the desk for the register and a pen. He glanced down the list of names. "Tell me you booked ahead."

"Yes, a couple of weeks ago." Alex leant in and scanned down the page.

"Here it is." Ethan placed his finger on the line. "Logan probably took the call. I have him manning the desk when I'm 'occupied'," he said with a smile and wink. "How long do you plan to be with us, Alex?"

"Not sure, I've got some thinking to do." He took the pen Ethan offered. Bending forward, he signed on the dotted line then tossed the pen aside. Reaching into the back pocket of his suit pants, he pulled out his wallet and retrieved both his driver's licence and credit card. "For sure the weekend. I'll go from there, if that works?"

Ethan checked the registry. "Yes, but give me as much notice as you can if you plan to stay longer. Logan put you down for five days, so a week won't be a problem. I don't want to overbook, though. Tends to piss off the regulars."

"I'll definitely let you know if I plan to stay longer."

Ethan took Alex's credit card and walked around to the business side of the desk. A moment later, he handed back the card.

Alex signed again then pocketed his plastic.

"Done. So, the upstairs corner room you had last time all right?" Ethan started around the desk but stopped almost instantly when Alex didn't move.

"No, I'd like a room on the main floor, if you've got one." His heart raced. He didn't want to even go close to the stairs unless he had to. Memories of staying here with Russ were strong enough without going near their old room.

Ethan hurried around the desk and laid a hand on Alex's arm. "Damn, I'm a dumbass. I'm sorry, Alex."

Taking a deep breath, Alex fought down the pain threatening to overwhelm him. After eight months, it should be easier. "Not your fault. I'm fine, honest." He took a step back, hoping Ethan got the message and would just let it go.

"So, you said you had some thinking to do. Nothing upsetting, I hope?" Ethan pulled his hand away from Alex's arm. He headed for the front door, and the suitcase still sitting there. Faced away, he added, "Damn customers, leaving their crap in the doorway." He peered over his shoulder and winked then reached for the handle of the dark green case.

"Yeah, must drive you crazy." Alex snickered and waited while the owner wheeled his bag towards the hall. A noise from the kitchen caught his attention, and he glanced that way, and did a double take. The young man standing in the doorway was stunning. Blond hair, long lean good looks and muscular in an outdoorsy kind of way. But young, so very young, he sighed. *If I was only ten years younger, I'd be on this one like a dog on a bone.*

"Come on, this way. I've got a lovely room for you at the end of the hall." Ethan's cheery remark dragged Alex's attention back to the present. "So, what was it you had to think about?"

"I've been offered a judgeship," Alex blurted, and even as he said it, wondered if he'd take it on. "It means I'll have to move north. Old Judge Colson is retiring, and it seems I'm next in line for the promotion."

"Hey, that's great news!" Ethan smiled broadly. "Congratulations! *Judge Brookfield.* Has a nice ring to it."

"I haven't decided if I want it yet. Moving, well, it's something I'm not sure I'm ready for."

Ethan stopped in front of the furthest door and stood the suitcase up. He produced a key card from a pocket of his shorts, swiped it then handed it to Alex. A soft buzz sounded, and he pushed the door open.

"Room eight," he said with a funny smile on his face.

"What's up with room eight?" Alex asked as he entered. The sun filtered through the full length drapes, yet the room wasn't hot like he'd thought it would be. He walked towards the window, and a sudden gust of cool air against his face made him shiver. The curtains billowed.

"It was the room I stayed in the first time I came to the inn."

"Really?" Alex looked around the room and smiled. Russ would have liked it, he was sure. It was spacious and airy. Being so close to the ocean, the breeze coming through the window was cool. "You haven't changed it, have you?" he asked, knowing the answer before the man spoke.

"No, it's just as it was. Hard to believe it's been only a year."

"Why mess with a good thing?" He shifted his attention to the window and its view. "It's gorgeous here."

"Yes, it is. I really lucked out on this place." Ethan dragged the bag over to the stand, lifting it onto the sling. "So, this judgeship. Why would you refuse?"

Alex pushed the drapery back and smiled. The waves crashed onto the sand in small curls of white against the vivid blue beyond. "Russ and I lived in that house for nearly thirteen years. I know I need to move on, but somehow, it just doesn't feel like it's time, yet."

"How long has he been gone?" Ethan asked in a gentle voice. He walked to the end of the room where the door leading to the beach stood. It took a moment of fumbling with the lock to get it open, but when he did, another gust of cool air pushed its way in.

"Eight months. But, it seems like eight weeks, or even days sometimes." Alex closed his eyes and pictured the man he'd loved for so long. Dark hair cut short, the cleft in his chin and the deep brown eyes he'd adored gazing into. "I miss him."

Ethan was silent for several minutes, as if at a loss for words. But, finally, he said, "I think you always will, Alex. I just hope the loss becomes more bearable."

Alex faced the man and smiled—a weak one, but a smile nonetheless. "Yes, I do, too. Russ would have berated me as a fool for prolonging the agony."

"So, a new job opportunity. That might be just the thing to get you to move on." Ethan pushed open the door and stepped out into the brilliant sun.

Alex followed, finding himself on a wide expanse of grass surrounded by tall leafy trees he couldn't have named if his life depended on it. They did offer shade, though, and he took a deep breath of the lovely salt tainted air.

"Having a ground floor room, you've got access to the property as well as the beach." Ethan peered around, as if looking for someone. He looked back at Alex and added, "You never know, you might see someone interesting." He winked and took Alex by the arm, guiding him back into the room. "You know the routine here," he said as they crossed to the door leading into the inn's hall. "Oh, we do have a new cook. I don't think he was here the last time you were. Nice guy, got some amazing ideas about how to feed the guests."

Alex cocked his head, remembering the young man standing in the doorway. He was sure he hadn't seen him before. "I can't remember who was on staff. Well, except for Cade. He's one in a million that one."

"Can't argue with you there. He's liable to hear you, and I'd be in for it." Ethan chuckled good-naturedly. He looked at his watch and asked, "It's getting late. Any interest in dinner? Logan's got this smoked salmon that'll knock your socks off tonight."

"Honestly, Ethan, I'm beat. I think I'll pass for now. It was a hellish drive from the coast, and all I really want right now is to lay down for a while. Must be getting old. I'm going to take a nap." He knew he was being an ass, but he really just wanted to be left alone. He'd wander into the dining room later for a bite.

"No problem. Just yell if it's late. If Logan's not here, I'm pretty sure I could rustle you up something to tide you over until breakfast." The man turned and headed for the door. When he'd opened it, he turned and faced Alex. "If you need anything, just give a holler."

"Thanks, Ethan. I'm sure I'll be fine. What time does the kitchen close down?"

"Logan sticks around, usually, until about nine or so."

Alex checked his watch. It was just past eight. He wanted to make sure it was after nine before he went down, so he didn't have to make small talk with anyone. "Thanks, I'll just close my eyes for a bit."

Ethan nodded and left, shutting the door quietly behind him.

Alex went to his suitcase and pulled out the few things he wanted hung up. He tossed his shaving kit into the bathroom, admiring the large soaker tub while he was there. Done, he pulled off his tie and jacket, swearing he'd not put them on again until he had to.

"Shorts, all the time I'm here," he vowed and chuckled. His legs hadn't seen the sun for the entire summer. He'd likely scare folks.

He hung his jacket in the closet, rolling the tie and stuffing it into the breast pocket. Kicking out of his shoes, he sighed with pleasure at the feel of the soft carpeting on his feet. He stripped out of his slacks and hung them with his jacket. Out of the corner of his eye, he caught sight of himself in the closet's mirrored door.

Sucking his tummy in, he grinned. "Not too bad, for forty-two." The hair on his chest was still black and only a touch of grey sprinkled into the dark at his temples gave any indication of his age. His belly was still flat. His chest might not be as muscular as that hunk Cade, but he did the best he could with occasional visits to the gym. He reached down and cupped the nice bulge at his crotch. The soft material of his black jockeys slid over the head of his cock and made him shudder. After giving his package a squeeze, he released himself and went into the bathroom for a quick shower.

In the bathroom, he pondered whether to shower or try out the soaker tub. After a moment's thought, he decided on the shower. Stripping out of his shorts and socks, he tossed them towards his suitcase then went to the shower stall.

Alex didn't spend much time luxuriating under the water spray. He truly was tired and longed to put head to pillow, even for some quick shuteye. He soaped up, rinsed off, and climbed out of the stall. The towel hanging on the rod next to him was thick and plush. He buried his face in it for a moment, before drying off and replacing it.

Some clean jockeys were all he needed. He ran a brush through his short hair, and called it good. Exhaustion, masquerading as heaviness in his arms and legs, seeped through him. He tossed back the covers and dropped into bed. Just before he dozed off, he thought he might be so tired he'd sleep through until morning.

Sounds good to me.

He closed his eyes and nestled into the pillow.

* * * *

It was pitch black when he opened his eyes again. Reflections from the moon, peeking through trees, sent scattered shards of light into his room. Alex yawned. *The moon?* He glanced at the bedside clock and discovered it was 11:30 p.m. *So much for sleeping through the night.*

He sat up and yawned again. The time didn't come as much of a surprise. Since Russ had died, Alex hadn't slept through the night in one chunk. It was bits and pieces, a few hours here, a few hours of fitful tossing and turning there. He didn't like it, but he'd grown accustomed to it.

His stomach growled. Alex looked at the clock once more and wondered if it was too late to scavenge in the kitchen for something to eat. He hated the thought of waking anyone. *A sandwich sounds good.* He could sneak in quietly, make something simple and bring it back to his room to eat.

A plan in mind, he pulled on a pair of shorts and a shirt then slipped into a pair of loafers pulled from his suitcase. Key card in hand, he entered the dimly-illuminated hall and headed towards the kitchen.

The lobby and dining rooms were deserted. He was surprised to see a light on in the large galley and even more surprised to see the handsome blond-haired cook standing behind the counter, stirring something thick and gooey in a bowl.

"Sorry," Alex stammered, one foot in the room.

The handsome hunk jerked around then smiled. "Sorry about what? Sleeping through dinner, so we didn't get the chance to meet earlier?"

Alex's face heated with a blush. He'd been a trial lawyer for many years and wasn't easily flustered. Something about this man made him uneasy—in an interesting kind of way. "It was quite a drive, after a long day. Yeah, I'm sorry about that. I'm Alex Brookfield, a friend of Ethan's."

"I know, he told me. After I pointed you out and asked a bunch of questions." The cook pulled some baking sheets from a cabinet and continued working. "Good old Ethan, he knows I can't resist a bear. I'm Logan Emerson, by the way."

The influx of information confused Alex for a moment. "Are there bears up here?"

Logan stared at him.

It took a second, but Alex caught on to his meaning. His face must have registered his surprise.

The handsome cook laughed. "There are now."

Embarrassed, Alex scrubbed a hand over his brow. 'Bear' was a slang term for a big, hunky gay man. He knew it, just hadn't been expecting to hear it from this hot, young guy. "You must think I'm a complete idiot."

Logan pulled a spoon from the bowl he'd been stirring and slowly licked what appeared to be cookie dough off it. He maintained eye contact with Alex as his tongue cleaned the utensil, working up and down in a steady rhythm. When it was spotless, he tossed the spoon into a large stainless steel sink off to his side.

"I don't think anything of the sort. I mean, I had some thoughts about you. But idiot wasn't a word that came to mind." He batted his long lashes in Alex's direction.

Boing. Alex wasn't sure if it was Logan's words or killer blue eyes that had his cock springing to attention. Watching the man fellate the spoon hadn't helped matters. *Probably a combination of all three.* He needed to change the subject, fast. He looked into the mixing bowl and tried not to lick his lips. "Is that chocolate chip cookie dough?"

"Oh, yeah. I was sitting in my room, jonesin' for it. Finally decided to come in and make some cookies." He got two spoons from a drawer and dipped one of them into the thick mixture. With a sly smile, he handed the utensil to Alex. It was loaded with the luscious tan-coloured confection, overflowing with chocolate chunks.

Alex hesitated for only a moment, then took the spoon and tasted the dough. *Heaven.* No surprise, really. The handsome hunk struck him as the kind of man who mastered everything he tried just about perfectly. "Oh, my god. This is amazing. Will there be cookies, or are we going to sit here and polish off the bowl?"

Logan smiled as he reached for the first baking sheet. "I made a double batch. Plenty of cookies for the inn's guests tomorrow. Enough dough to do something kinky with tonight." He waggled his brows up and down.

Flattered and apprehensive at the same time, Alex laughed. He took a step backwards just to be safe. The last bite of the sweet confection melted in his mouth, and he shook the spoon at the cook. "You're trouble. I suspected as much when I first caught sight of you, but now, I see the evidence first hand."

"Oh, that's right. You're a lawyer." Logan began dropping spoonfuls of dough onto the cookie sheet. "All about the evidence. Hey, I promise, when we're done, there won't be a *lick* of incriminating evidence left."

Alex dropped his spoon into the large double sink. "Ah, well, as...*tasty*...as that sounds, I should get some sleep. It was nice meeting you, Logan."

"Hey, wait." Logan hurried to fill the last sheet, stuck them all in the oven and set a timer.

With a glance at the man over his shoulder, Alex continued out to the dining room. Nothing good could come of his staying. The frisky cook appeared to be a bit more than he'd bargained for.

"You came in for a reason; you must have been hungry," Logan called after him. "I could make you a sandwich."

Alex's stomach chose that moment to rumble, rather loudly, and he paused. He turned back to Logan, standing in the warm kitchen wearing shorts and a ratty, ripped T-shirt. The man obviously wasn't there to work. It'd be too much to ask him to make anything, but Alex *was* still hungry. "A sandwich might hit the spot. But it's late, I couldn't ask you to—"

"You didn't ask. I offered. Besides, I have an hour of baking ahead of me. I could use the company."

Alex hesitated again.

Logan grinned, a sly thing that caused him to look like an impish boy. "To *talk*. I promise to behave. Tonight anyway."

Alex folded his arms across his chest. Despite the devilish look on the man's face, he could tell Logan had backed off the teasing. Suddenly, Alex was ravenous, and not so nervous. He actually felt quite comfortable staying. He could dish it out, too. It'd just been ages since he'd had anyone to spar with. "You make a lot of promises, kid."

"I'm good for them." Hands in the air, Logan shrugged, still smiling.

"I'm sure you are. But, hey, I never wanted to put anybody out. I didn't figure Ethan would mind if I slipped into the kitchen and made a bite."

"Ethan's great." Logan nodded. "But it's my kitchen. I do the cooking in here. Let's see what we've got. You can tell me what sounds good." He opened the big refrigerator and bent over to peer inside.

Alex's gaze immediately went to the man's ass, which looked tight and beautifully sculpted in the skimpy shorts. *I know what looks good.* He tried to drag his mind out of the gutter, but with a long string of months between him and the last time he'd had sex, finding a distraction was easier said than done. He watched the delectable ass cheeks shift as Logan moved, gathering things from various shelves.

"I have some nice ham. Or turkey. You like turkey?"

"I like it all," Alex replied, still staring at the tight butt and well-shaped thighs. The kid was muscular, no doubt about that. But young. *Too young.* The last thing Alex would ever do was rob the cradle.

"How about a club sandwich? Ham, turkey and some fresh bacon." Logan turned around, his arms full of foodstuffs.

Alex's gaze automatically dropped to the man's crotch. There wasn't an erection, but a very nicely shaped bulge outlined in the thin material. He gulped, feeling his own cock thicken and lengthen.

"What do you think? A club sandwich okay?" Logan prodded.

Focus. "Oh, yeah. Sure."

The cook set the food on the counter and went back for more. "You like the works, tomato, lettuce, mayo?"

Alex shifted from one foot to the other uncomfortably. When he'd entered the kitchen, he had nothing but food on his mind. Logan's playful teasing had surprised him. Now it was all he could think about.

"Hey, Counsellor, are you with me?"

"What?" Alex shook his head, chasing away seductive images of the sexy stud bent over, grabbing for his ankles. He blinked and stared at the vegetables in Logan's hands. "Yeah, sure, whatever you think."

With a soft chuckle, Logan set to work preparing the sandwich. When the timer went off, he removed the cookies from the oven and set them aside to cool.

More bending and stretching. Alex's eyes were glued to the handsome, lithe man, and all thoughts of distracting himself fled. *Might as well humour my libido with a little fantasy.*

He moved behind Logan and placed a hand at either side of him on the counter. "You mentioned a little something kinky?"

Logan pressed his back against Alex and exhaled a warm sigh. "Oh, yeah. I was hoping you'd see things my way."

One of Alex's fingers traced the edge of the mixing bowl, gathering some of the sticky dough. He circled Logan's ear, dragging the finger across the lobe and kept right on going over his neck. Alex's mouth followed, licking and sucking the sugary substance from Logan's slightly salty skin.

"Mmm," he murmured, his tongue darting inside the ear and over the lobe. "Tastes good."

"God, yes." Logan shuddered as Alex continued his ministrations. "I'd love to paint your cock with the stuff and lick you clean."

Chuckling, Alex shoved his groin against Logan's ass. "You're assuming I have that much patience. I had something different in mind for my cock, like burying it in your sweet, tight ass."

Logan nodded and groaned at the same time. "Yes, yes. I'm all for that idea, too. There's oil on the shelf behind you. Not exactly the right stuff, but I've found it works in a pinch."

"Oh, you have?" Alex pressed Logan's body against the counter, his mouth still savouring every bit of sweetness from the man's tasty neck. "Do you let many people fuck you in your kitchen after hours?"

"No," Logan answered quickly. "But I want you to. I've wanted it since the minute I laid eyes on you. You're exactly the kind of man I've always dreamed about."

"You're the man of my dreams, too, sweet cheeks. Now bend over, and let me get a look at you."

Logan obliged, clinging to the counter as Alex did the work of lowering his shorts and boxers. Alex dropped to his knees and buried his face between Logan's ass cheeks.

Warm, firm and tight, exactly what Alex expected. He inhaled the man's arousing, masculine fragrance before prying the cheeks apart and tasting the rosebud hole. More delicious than anything from a bowl, Alex dipped his tongue deeper and groaned with pleasure when Logan's sphincter loosened and allowed him in. He tongued the orifice, until his own throbbing cock became too much to ignore.

On his feet, he shucked out of his shorts and briefs and let his erection bob forward. Alex reached for the bottle of cooking oil from the shelf and poured a small amount into his cupped hand. He stroked it over his shaft then realised he didn't have a condom.

He'd be better prepared for the real thing, if it ever happened.

He greased his pulsing shaft and nudged the tip to Logan's anus.

"Oh, yeah. This is going to be a nice fit." Curbing his enthusiasm, Alex pulled back and eased his oiled fingers in first to loosen and prepare the entry.

"Good, so good." Logan pushed his ass against the fingers. "Need more."

Satisfied the man's hole was properly stretched, Alex replaced his fingers with his aching shaft. The tip already oozed pre-cum. He'd be lucky to last a few strokes.

Alex smiled. It was his fantasy. He could go all night if he wanted.

"Take it all," he muttered, driving into the tight hole.

"God, yeah. Give it to me. More. Now." Logan squirmed between the counter and Alex's body.

Alex drove balls deep and paused, savouring the sensation of his cock enveloped in warm satin. Then his primal needs overtook him, and he pounded in and out, climbing towards the first climax he'd had with another man in nearly a year.

"Yes, yes," Logan repeated over and over.

"Fuck, yeah," Alex muttered, balls rising, orgasm imminent. To hell with going all night. He was coming now. He shuddered and shook as his balls emptied into Logan's hot ass. Waves of cum repeatedly shot out in a longer, more intense climax than he'd ever known possible. Alex clung to Logan, who clung to the counter, the side of which was dripping with Logan's spent seed.

"Good," was all Alex could murmur. "Very good."

"Glad you like it."

Alex blinked and stared at the sandwich in his hand, one big bite missing. Logan leaned against the counter across from him. "I, uh, yeah. It was wonderful. I mean, it's great."

"Good." Logan cast him an inquiring glance but didn't ask any questions. He straightened and busied himself removing warm cookies from the baking sheet and adding another round of dough. "Fresh cookies when you're done with that. I might even spring for a glass of milk."

Alex smiled and took another bite of the sandwich, speaking with his mouth full. "You've done too much, already."

Logan glanced up, blue eyes dancing, and smiled. "Anything for you. I mean, any friend of Ethan's is a friend of mine."

There it was again. *That sexual spark.* This time, Alex didn't run from it. He embraced it. A thought crossed his mind and he had to ask, "How old are you, kid?"

"Twenty-eight. How old are you?"

Whew! Not as young as he looked. A relief, considering the wicked thoughts running through Alex's mind. He took another bite of his sandwich and winked. "Old enough to know better."

"Oh, I hope not." Logan cast his gaze down Alex's body and back up again. "Lord, I really hope not."

Alex smiled.

Chapter Two

It was pitch black outside, but Alex was still awake. The sleeplessness wasn't uncommon, but it didn't feel like his usual blundering up from a deep sleep and wishing Russ was still with him. He rolled onto his stomach and buried his face into the warm pillow.

"Hey, hot and sexy, why didn't you take the young guy up?"

"Because, he's too young and I'm…" The words trailed off as Alex realised he was talking to…no one.

He flipped over and sat up, eyes wide straining to see whoever had spoken. "Who's there? Where the hell are you?"

He climbed out of bed and walked to the window, thinking someone had possibly come in through one he'd left open. He checked each of them. There were open, but the screens were in place, undisturbed.

Brushing a hand through his hair, he felt like an idiot. It must have been a dream. The cook, Logan. Alex must have been dreaming about the guy.

Fumbling back to the bed, he climbed in and covered himself. He remembered the stories about ghosts in the inn. Laura, the little girl who many people claimed to have seen. Another one was Ben, an old fisherman who left pools of water in the hall that smelled of fish. He'd never seen or heard any of them, but perhaps, that's what was happening.

Ghosts, how ludicrous. You're definitely too old to believe in spirits. He shifted onto his side and closed his eyes.

"Yes, much too old to believe in ghosts, but hot, sexy young men...that's a different story."

Alex shot bolt upright and peered around the room. "What the fuck! Who's there?"

From somewhere behind him, which put the voice behind a wall, a soft whisper came. "Just me, babe. I can't let you go on like this."

Alex leapt from the bed and turned to face the wall. There was nothing there—no one, no speaker, or window, nowhere for a voice to come from.

"What the hell is going on?" He flipped on the bedside table lamp and peered around the room. Still finding nothing out of the ordinary, he was about to turn it off and climb back into bed when a gust of ice-cold wind swirled around him. The light flickered, and the wind stopped as quickly as it had come up. He spun, trying again to see who or what was making mischief.

"That's enough horse crap for one night," he growled and, after a short search, slipped into the shorts he'd left on the chair and headed for the door. He opened it, but before he could step out into the hall under his own steam, something pushed him.

The door slammed shut behind him.

"That's it." He stumbled down the hall to the front desk, knowing the owner's room was right behind it. Ethan, or his lover Cade, would hopefully be there.

The hall was dark but for the soft glow of night lighting set low along the floor. He hurried past the kitchen and finally strode around the desk. He took a deep breath and banged on the door.

He stood waiting, his heart beating as if he'd run a marathon. That voice, the whispers, had sounded just like Russ. He shook that thought aside and focused on the door. He was just about to knock again when the door opened and a sleepy Ethan, dressed in a pair of baggy sleep pants, stood scratching his head and looking bleary eyed at him.

"What's up? Christ, it's the middle of the night, Alex. What's the matter?" Ethan's eyes widened, apparently realising how rattled Alex was. "You're white as a sheet. Are you all right?"

"Yes, I think I'm all right." Alex suddenly felt like a complete ass for dragging the man out of bed. What could he say, some voice had woken him up?

"Okay, then what's up?" Ethan persisted.

"I'm not sure. I woke up, heard something very odd, then got tossed out of my room." Saying it, he realised how insane it sounded and wished he'd simply gone back to bed—if whatever had disturbed him allowed him to.

"You saw one of our ghosts?" Ethan sighed then stepped out of his room and closed the door behind him. "They don't normally toss people out into the hall though."

Alex thought for a moment then replied, "I don't think this was one of your regulars."

"Say what?"

Turning towards the hallway, Alex was hesitant to go on but knew he'd have to, if only for his own peace of mind. "I've heard of your ghosts, although I've never actually experience one before. This one, well, he was familiar."

Ethan blinked, then cocked his head. "Familiar? You mean someone you know...er...knew?"

"Come and see for yourself," Alex said and strode across the room towards the hallway. Behind him, Ethan grumbled but kept up. The walk seemed to go on much longer than it should have. When they stood in front of his door, he reached into the pocket of his shorts, thankful he'd stuck the key card in there.

The door opened easily enough, and all seemed quiet as the two of them entered. He flicked the light on and gazed around. Everything was in order, except the bedding had been pushed off the foot of the bed and now lay in a rumpled heap. He spun slowly, expectantly.

"Oh my god!" The words exploded from him unexpectedly when his gaze came to rest on the mirror over the dresser. A face, familiar, longed for, loved, desired above all over, hung there. It was Russ. His smile was enchanting, the soft brown eyes captivating, the dimple in his chin and the close cropped dark hair exactly as it had been the last time Alex had seen him. He took a step closer and reached out. Then closed his hand and groaned.

"What's up?" Ethan, who had stayed next to him, grabbed him by the arm. "What the matter, Alex?"

"The mirror, can't you see?" He pointed to Russ. Heart breaking, he took another step closer but stopped after only a couple of steps. "It can't be. He's dead."

"Alex, what in hell are you talking about? There's no one here. Just you and I." Ethan spun Alex around, forcing him to face away from the mirror.

"It's Russ," he groaned and twisted his face to look over his shoulder. Russ was still there, the smile turning to a frown of puzzlement. "He's looking at me, frowning. Can't you see him?" He faced Ethan.

The man looked at the dresser and the large mirror sitting on top of it. Shaking his head, he said, "No, I can't see anything, but the reflection of the room."

Alex shuddered. "He's right there, in the freakin' mirror. You have to see him!" He was beginning to feel panicky. Russ was dead. *What does this mean?* Why couldn't Ethan see him? What did he want? *Christ, am I going crazy too?*

The questions raced through his mind. A chill went up his spine.

"There's nothing there, Alex."

"I have to get out of here." Alex moved towards the door, suddenly desperate to get away from his dead lover's ghost. He grabbed things as he went but didn't slow down until he was standing outside the room in the hallway.

Ethan soon joined him, holding the rest of Alex's belongings. "We've got an empty room at the other end of the hall, closest to the dining room. It's the same, but you might get some noise at meal times." He guided Alex by the arm.

"Anything. I just don't want to stay in there." Alex forced down the fear that gripped him. He'd never felt anything like it before. He just knew he couldn't stay in that room.

Ethan showed him into room number two, and after hanging Alex's clothes and depositing his toiletries in the bathroom, he faced Alex. "Are you sure you're all right?"

Feeling foolish, Alex looked around the room. The atmosphere was totally different, friendly rather than threatening. "Yes, I'm fine." He looked at his friend and smiled sheepishly. "I don't know what came over me. I'm really sorry for bothering you, Ethan."

The man patted Alex on the shoulder, reassuringly, then said, "Don't be. I'm used to this kind of thing. You have to be if you own a haunted inn." He chuckled and moved towards the door. "Try and get some sleep. We'll talk in the morning."

Alex followed him, again thanking him as the man left. After a quick look around, he stripped and climbed into bed. Lying back, he thought about Russ. His irrational fear was gone. Memories of his lover remained and warmed him. Their life together had been special. Russ' death had been devastating. Yet, he knew life would go on.

When he closed his eyes, it wasn't the image of Russ that he saw. A young blond man filled his thoughts and was the last thing he saw before sleep overcame him.

* * * *

Alex thought over the events of the previous evening. Russ' ghost and the fear he'd experienced before changing rooms tore at him. Why, all of a sudden, had Russ come back?

The concept disturbed him. He'd never believed in ghosts. He was too educated, too rational, for any kind of supernatural hocus-pocus. But he couldn't deny what he'd seen, or felt.

He rolled over onto his back and stared up at the ceiling. He was still tired but knew he'd never get back to sleep. He grunted, annoyed that his first night away had been so disturbing.

He recalled an earlier part of the evening when he'd sparred with the cook—the sexy, young blond man who'd been the last image in his mind before he'd fallen asleep.

Thrusting his arms beneath his head, he laid back remembering the fantasy he'd dreamed up while the young chef had prepared a sandwich. Visions of Logan bent over, his sleek firm ass displayed and ready for use, had Alex ready for action in a matter of seconds. His cock pulsed, the head pushing the sheets up into a tent at his middle. He reached down and gave his erection a firm stroke, before the morning urge for a pee hit.

He tossed back the covers and hopped out of bed, exhaustion tugging at him. His night time adventures and the scare of seeing Russ had made his sleep less than restful. A quick look around got his bearings, and he headed for the john.

After a long, hot shower, he felt nearly human and ready to face the world, maybe even a little of Logan's sexy teasing. While brushing his hair, he couldn't help but smile. The young man seemed very eager to find out more about him. Alex wondered if he really wanted to know, or if he was just a horny twenty-eight year old.

"Might as well go find out," he mumbled and went back into the bedroom to dress. A quick glance outside confirmed the casual clothes he'd hoped to wear would be perfect for the weather. He donned fresh underwear, shorts and a polo shirt. After pushing his wallet into his back pocket, he grabbed the key card, wondered if he should get a new one for the new room, and walked out.

Entering the dining room, he glanced around and was surprised it was nearly empty. Only one other couple inhabited the place. A young married pair by the look of them, fawning all over each other. He looked away and spotted the clock over the mantle. Nearly eleven, the morning mob would be long gone, and it was too early for the lunch crowd. He grumbled as he sat near one of the large windows overlooking the inn's garden. Maybe the view would improve his mood.

The tree-lined area was like a haven. Through the evergreens, he could just see the wide expanse of sandy beach broken here and there by large boulders or logs washed up by the frequent storms the coast was known for. People sunned themselves or beach combed along the nearby shore.

"You managed to nearly miss breakfast. And here I thought you enjoyed my company last night."

Alex looked away from the scenery and turned his attention to the sexy young man standing beside his table. Logan's shorts were much nicer than the pair he'd worn last night. His crisp polo shirt had the Whiskers' Seaside Inn logo on the breast and was spotlessly clean, which bespoke a professionalism Alex liked. The relaxed uniform was unexpectedly sexy, which he also found he liked, although he'd never say it.

"Rough night, kid," he muttered, trying not to growl the words out. "Any chance of some breakfast, or are you already into the lunch menu?"

Logan opened his mouth, apparently about to say something smart-alecky, then shut it and cocked his head. "Breakfast if you want it, Alex. What happened last night?"

Alex looked up at him and pasted on a half-hearted grin. "Ghosts."

Logan smiled and nodded. "Yeah, it happens a lot in this place. I've seen a couple myself. Can be damned unnerving."

"You have?" Alex was curious. The kid seemed to be pretty normal. Did he believe in ghosts?

"Sure. Angry Annie has slammed doors around me, and the little girl, Laura, she's scared hell out of me a couple of times with her pranks." He again opened his mouth, as if to add more but closed it. Silence followed, broken finally when Logan asked, "This ghost you saw, was he wearing a white turtleneck?"

For an instant, Alex couldn't remember. Then it came to him. He'd thought only the man's face had been visible, but actually, his upper torso had showed, too. "Yes," he whispered and felt the breath go out of him. *How could Logan know?*

The young man stepped closer and placed a soothing hand on Alex's shoulder. "Hey, it's okay. Honestly."

"But how…?" He looked up at the cook's face and recognised concern in his blue eyes.

"I've seen him. He appeared to me in the kitchen."

"Appeared in your kitchen?" Alex took a moment to gather his scattered thoughts before continuing. "Tell me, what did he look like?"

"Slender, kind of bony, close cropped black hair and a cute dimple—"

"I'll be damned! You saw him." Alex was beyond baffled. How could this be happening? *Why?*

"Hey, hang tough, Alex," Logan stroked his arm. "Let's change the subject for now. What can I get you for breakfast?"

Mind still trying to wrap itself around the strange occurrence, Alex replied woodenly, "Just some coffee and toast."

"Done," Logan stepped away and looked down at him. "It'll just be a couple of minutes."

Alex forced his thoughts away from the craziness and leant back, crossing his arms over his chest. This gorgeous young man drew him, and he couldn't bear to let him just walk away, not yet. "Don't you have a home to go to? I mean you were here until heaven-only-knows what time, and I bet you were back bright and early to take care of the breakfast crowd."

"Yeah, I was. I have a small cottage just up the road. Wouldn't work if I had to travel far." He turned and took a step towards the kitchen. Over his shoulder, he asked, "Sure you don't want a chocolate chip cookie with that breakfast?" He winked and smiled broadly.

The man had such cheek. Alex couldn't help but smile. "Maybe later."

Grinning, Logan nodded and went on his way.

Alex gazed through the window, watching the waves crash on the sandy beach. The tide was in, and those who were sunning themselves would soon have to move or be washed away.

His thoughts turned to Russ. They'd loved each other unconditionally for years, and his partner's death had torn Alex's world apart. He'd thought his life was over. It wasn't. But he'd been at loose ends for months. This offer of a judgeship seemed to be well timed, but he wasn't sure he could tear himself away from his home. *Their home*.

"Here you are." It was Logan again, bearing a tray with his breakfast. Besides the requested toast and coffee, the plate bore a small mound of scrambled eggs and a couple of slices of juicy, fragrant ham. A second plate held two of the largest muffins Alex had ever seen, one obviously blueberry and the other something sprinkled with nuts. *They smell delicious*. So did the two chocolate chip cookies that finished off the plate.

Alex glanced at the chef, amused. "Toast and coffee?"

Logan scoffed. "That's not a fit breakfast. You've probably got a busy day ahead of you, hiking, or beach combing, or lying in the sun in a tiny little Speedo." His gaze travelled down Alex's body and up again, the moment ending with what looked like a wistful shake of his head. "You will let me know if you're going to be sunning in a Speedo, won't you? I'd pay to see that."

Alex chuckled, his face warming with a self-conscious flush. The kid was relentless, but to Alex's surprise, his words were welcome after such a long time alone. "I don't own a Speedo, but if I did, I wouldn't fit into it after eating this kind of food. Are you trying to fatten me up?"

"Nah. You don't look like a stranger to exercise. With a body like that, you must work out a bunch of times each week."

This guy is good. Alex's first instinct was to admit the truth. Between a dying lover and working eighty hours a week, who had time for a fitness routine? After Russ had died, the workload had increased—anything to keep from spending time in a big, empty house.

But this was his vacation, and the handsome young cook wanted to flirt, not hear about his problems. So Alex played along. "Oh, yeah. In between rounds of tennis and golf, I do what I can. And then, of course, there are afternoons at the yacht club."

"Wow." Logan raised his eyebrows. "That sounds great. I wouldn't know what to do with that much spare time."

Huh? Alex could have kicked himself. In a pathetic attempt to sound humorous, he had Logan believing he was some rich, lazy socialite. *I suck at small talk.*

Before he could correct the misconception, a tall, rugged man approached the table. The handsome hunk's blue Whiskers' Inn polo shirt indicated he worked there, while his ragged, cut-off jeans and work boots left no doubt that he was the go-to man outdoors. Tan and fit, he sported a long, sandy-blond ponytail and a face not easily forgotten.

"Cade! How are you?" Alex extended a hand.

The big man shook hands then swept Alex into a hug. "Alex! It's great to see you. Sorry I missed you last night. Ethan's thrilled you're here."

Taken aback but not unhappy, Alex accepted the hug and motioned for Cade to join him at the table. "It's great to be here. The place looks super."

A wide smile on his face, Cade sat and glanced down at the aromatic plates of food.

"Get you anything, Boss?" Logan asked.

"Coffee, please." He sniffed the cookies. "And some of those. I didn't know they were on the breakfast menu."

"Trying something new." Logan waggled his eyebrows at Alex as he left.

Alex shoved the second plate in front of Cade. "Help yourself. Your cook is a bit overzealous. I asked for toast and coffee."

Cade laughed. "Well, that's never gonna fly here. You'll find Logan is an excellent cook and one hell of a baker. He loves to show off his wares."

Eyes glued on the sexy chef as he returned with another cup of coffee and more cookies, Alex smiled. "I have noticed that. Yeah."

"Talking about me, I hope?" Logan served Cade then placed his hands on his hips.

"You wish." Cade grabbed a cookie and took a bite. "Man, these are good. Truthfully, I was telling Alex what a good cook you are. But don't let it go to your head."

"Of course not." Logan rolled his eyes playfully at Cade then turned back to Alex. "I hope your breakfast is all right."

Alex looked down at his untouched plate. "Oh! I'm sure it's great." He picked up a fork.

"Yell if you need anything else. As you can see, I'm not too busy." Logan glanced around the now-empty dining room. "The lunch crowd will filter in soon, though."

"I'll catch you before you get too busy. Maybe we can get some coffee later and talk about our mutual friend."

Logan smiled. "Sure. Enjoy your meal." He wandered away slowly, appearing reluctant to do so.

Alex couldn't resist sneaking a peek at the man's bum when he walked away. The sight gave him an instant hard-on, and he quickly looked back at his food.

"Good guy," Cade commented, sipping his coffee.

"Yeah, nice kid." Alex shovelled a mound of scrambled egg onto his fork and suddenly realised how hungry he was. The ham and eggs had cooled but still tasted great.

"I think he's close to thirty."

"Twenty-eight," Alex mumbled with his mouth full.

Cade smiled. "So, not really a 'kid', then."

"Ah," Alex waved one hand and continued to eat with the other. "What do you know? You're just a kid yourself."

Elbows on the table, Cade broke another cookie in half and ate it slowly. "Sound like you got here just in time, man. You need to relax and unwind. Whiskers' is the perfect place for that."

"I thought so, too. I wanted to get completely away so I could think everything over with a clear head. But after last night, I don't know."

"Ethan told me what happened but said he didn't see anything. Usually, he's pretty perceptive about this stuff."

The memory of his lover's face in the mirror sent a shiver down Alex's spine. "I saw Russ. And I think your cook did, too."

Cade raised his brows. "Interesting. But ghosts aren't uncommon here. You knew that."

"I figured the place just had its own ghosts. The little girl, the door slammer, the fisherman—I think I could have handled any of them. But this one hit a little close to home."

"If there's one thing I've figured out about this inn," Cade shoved back from the table, "it's that you never know what to expect. Strange things happen sometimes, right out of the blue. Other times, it's so quiet and peaceful, you wouldn't believe it." Cade finished off his cookie, brushed the crumbs from his hands then stood. "Guess you picked a good time to come."

"Lucky me." Alex took one more bite then pushed the plate away from him. "I couldn't eat another bite. I'm stuffed. That was amazing."

Cade snatched another cookie and nodded, a smile playing at his lips. "I'd offer to give your compliments to the chef, but I think you might want to do that yourself—and try to figure out why the ghost of your late partner appeared to Logan." He rubbed his chin thoughtfully. "Makes a person wonder."

"Yeah, right. Thanks for the advice." Alex smiled at the tall hunk before Cade turned and walked off.

A family entered the dining room, and the place came to life with noise. Alex wrapped the last two cookies into a napkin and pocketed them as he pushed away from the table and stood. He watched Logan greet the newcomers and waited by the door to the kitchen until the cook was free to talk.

"Hey." Logan finally approached him. "Noon sitting has begun. Did you need more coffee or anything?"

"I'm good." Alex shook his head. "Thanks for breakfast. It was fantastic, as expected. Do you have a bill for me?"

Logan waved a hand. "Toast and coffee is complimentary."

Alex gave him a knowing look.

The cook shrugged. "The rest was my idea. I can't charge you for that."

"Well, it was really good. Thanks again."

"Wait until you see what I do with salmon. See you back here for dinner?"

Alex rubbed his stomach. "I'm not sure I'll ever need to eat again. But I would like to talk. What time should I show up if I wanted you all to myself?" *Did I really just say that? Oh shit!*

Logan grinned. "Mmm, I could go for that. By eight, most of the diners are out of here. If I've got my work done, I could probably eat with you."

"Eight." Alex nodded, a flicker of excitement welling in his chest. "I'll see you then. Oh, and Logan? What I said earlier about playing tennis and golf and going to the yacht club?" A twinge of embarrassment hit him. "That was my poor attempt at humour. I work so many hours every day, I probably wouldn't remember how to do any of that stuff."

"I know." Logan smiled. His gaze followed a couple entering the room, and he nodded towards them. "I should…"

"Yeah. Go get your work done."

He glanced over his shoulder as he walked away. "Oh, it'll be done. Don't you worry."

Alex smiled to himself, thinking how much he wanted to have dinner with the young chef. *If his work's not done, I'll stay and help him finish it myself.*

* * * *

The afternoon sun rose high in the sky. Alex followed a path he vaguely remembered from his last visit to the inn.

He passed a row of stunted fir trees, choosing one of several trails leading from the inn to the water. Before long, the trees opened onto the sand.

A bevy of sunbathers lined that stretch of the beach. To the left, people swam and children splashed in the clear, blue water. He turned right, away from them and towards the lighthouse, a tall pillar of white brick with a shiny red dome at the top. Sand gave way to patchy grass and rocks. Sharp rocks lined this portion of the shore.

'No swimming' signs changed to 'no trespassing' as he neared the lighthouse. The beach path ended with a chain crossing from one cement block to another. Alex stopped and admired the tall structure but didn't have any interest in going further. He turned back towards the inn and scaled the rough terrain until he reached a well-worn trail.

He hiked until he came upon a small, rustic cabin, nestled in the woods. *Could this be where Logan lives?* Alex tried to peer in a window but found all the panes securely shuttered from the inside. *No peeking into this place.* He made a mental note to ask Logan if the cabin was where he called home.

He'd do it later. The round-trip had taken nearly two hours and despite the impression he'd given Logan, Alex wasn't used to the physical exercise. In the past couple of years, when he hadn't been at Russ' bedside, he'd been slumped over his desk or doing research in a musty law library. The longest walks he'd taken had been in the courtroom—from the defendant's table, to the judges' bench, and back. It felt good to stretch his legs. It felt better when he saw the peak of the inn's rooftop and knew he was nearly back.

Alex entered his room through the beachside door. After drinking a glass of water, he dropped onto his neatly-made bed without bothering to pull back the covers. His mind raced as quickly as his heart from the influx of exercise.

The judge's bench. What would it be like to view court proceedings from that perspective? Being nominated for judgeship was a tremendous honour, something he could feel truly proud of. Actually accepting the position was another matter.

Not much intimidated him. He'd faced down some of the toughest lawyers in the province, prosecuted mobsters and criminals so rough, even their mothers must have questioned their innocence. But he'd never backed down, never been the type to worry or fret.

Then Russ got sick. His world had turned upside down. Worry had become the norm. The thought of losing his mate had scared him silly. Yet he'd done it and survived, and after that, nothing else had seemed quite so bad. *Until now.* The thought of uprooting his life, making a major career change and leaving the home he'd shared for years with his lover was the second most daunting thing he'd ever encountered. It was almost like leaving Russ all over again.

The job offer constantly simmered in the back of his mind. Every once in a while, he'd take it out and mull it around, hoping for an epiphany of some kind. When it didn't come, he tucked the thought away for assessment at a later time.

Right then, Alex just wanted to rest. He closed his eyes and forced his breathing to a slower rhythm. *A quick nap might just do the trick.*

* * * *

Alex strolled into the dining room at eight. He was pleased to see the place empty of guests, but he'd expected to see one table set. Everything looked cleared away for the night. A tingle of disappoint ran through him, and Alex knew it had nothing to do with food. He wanted to see Logan.

He pushed open the kitchen door and glanced around. Everything looked clean and shiny from what he could tell with the room so dimly lit. There was one light burning, a small bulb over the stove.

"Hello?" *Had they gotten their wires crossed?*

"Hey, back here," Logan's voice called from the other end of the room.

Alex followed the man's voice and, when he turned a corner, saw a table in a breakfast nook he hadn't even known existed. Two long taper candles provided the only light, but Alex could see the table was elegantly set, and their meal was already there, under warming lids.

"Hi," he said, a little overwhelmed by all the fuss.

"Hello there." Logan smiled at him. "You're right on time. Hope you're hungry."

"I haven't eaten since this morning. Well, there were those two cookies I stuffed in my pocket. I went for a walk this afternoon, and they gave me the sustenance to find my way back."

"I'm glad they did. Sit down." Logan motioned to one chair and sat in another. "Did you get lost? There's a lot of country out there." He removed the lids from their plates.

The pleasant aroma of salmon, a baked potato and mixed vegetables wafted up, and Alex's stomach growled. "I guess I am hungry. This looks great. Smells even better."

"I hope you like it." Logan lifted his wine glass. "I took a shot that Chardonnay was all right with you."

"Fine." Alex tasted the wine then dove into the meal. It tasted as fabulous as it looked, so he ate and talked at the same time. "I didn't get lost, just walked for a long time. I found a cabin not too far from here. That your place?"

Logan swallowed and shook his head. "The cabin is Cade's. He doesn't use it much anymore, but I think he keeps it as a little getaway. In case the inn ever gets to be too much. You know." He grinned.

"I'm sure," Alex agreed. He could easily see how living with ghosts would make a person nervous and edgy. *Funny, considering the inn is supposedly a relaxing retreat.* "I remember Ethan mentioning that cabin. Anyway, I wanted to talk to you about the—apparition—you saw. The man in the white turtleneck. I know who he is...*was.*"

"I figured. But, hey, let's enjoy this nice meal while it's still warm. There'll be plenty of time to talk later." Logan looked at his plate and added, "If we feel like talking, that is."

Uncertainty tugged at Alex. The chef was handsome enough and obviously interested in him. *Am I ready for this?* He'd always known, in the back of his mind, someone else would come along, one day. He'd never expected that someone to be such a strapping hunk—*and so young.* He decided to lay all his cards on the table. "Logan. I'm flattered by your interest, but I'm just not sure this is something I'm ready for."

Logan looked him straight in the eye. "How long has it been? Since your partner died, I mean."

He knows. That was a relief. Alex hated telling the story. "About eight months."

The chef's eyebrows rose. "Really? Damn, I figured you'd be *really* ready for it after all that time."

Alex rolled his eyes, amused. "That's not what I meant. I just don't know if the timing is right."

"Hey, look." Logan touched Alex's hand. "I'm not asking you to marry me. You just really turn me on, and I thought we could enjoy each other's company while you're here. If you're not interested—"

"I am," Alex said quickly, without thinking it out. Thinking brought on more questions, usually followed by headaches. Perhaps it was time to give the brain a rest, and let some other part of the body take over. He shoved the plate with his mostly-eaten dinner back from the edge of the table. "I'm ready."

Logan laughed and took one last bite of food. "Damn, I didn't mean we had to go this minute. But I'm finished if you are. Just let me put these things in the dishwasher, real quick."

"I'll help." Alex got to his feet, his hands instantly dropping to his groin where a sizable erection had formed.

Logan stood to face him and licked his lips. "Don't do a thing to compromise that bulge in your shorts. Wait right here." He gave Alex's package a quick squeeze then picked up their plates and cleared off the table.

Alex's cock and heart both lurched at the same time. He watched Logan's bum as the man walked away and grinned, thinking about the fantasy that was about to become a reality. He grabbed the last of the dishes and met Logan by the sink. "Your place or mine?"

Logan eyed Alex's crotch again. "Yours is much closer. I vote for yours."

"I'm coming around to your way of thinking. Let's go." Alex headed for the door to the dining room.

"Right behind you," Logan whispered in his ear then squeezed his ass. "And enjoying the view."

Chapter Three

Alex was shocked at how eager he was to be alone with the handsome cook. Having the man behind him had his blood boiling.

The walk across the dining room and into the hall seemed to take forever. Alex kept thinking someone would call, a guest would need a meal and Logan would have to bail. He quickened his pace.

"Slow down, sexy," Logan's voice came from no more than a stride or two behind him.

"I'm afraid someone will call for room service," Alex replied but slowed down and wiggled his butt a little more than normal.

"Oh yeah, much better."

The cook's hands gripped Alex's hips and held on, slowing him even further. The hard bulge of the man's cock pressing against his ass had Alex's heart beating like a wild thing in a trap—a lusty, robust, man trap.

He took a couple more steps, all his attention on the erection grinding so sexily into his ass. If a freight train had gone by, he was sure he'd have missed it completely. As it was, the few steps down the hall to his room were a blur. When he stood in front of his door, it was all he could do to dig out his key card and swipe it without dropping the darned thing. His hands shook, his fingers refused to grasp the small plastic card, but he managed it on the third attempt. All the time he fumbled with the key, Logan gently humped against his ass.

"You're killing me, kid," Alex muttered while pushing the door open. He didn't want to move but knew if he didn't, and fast, they'd wind up indecently exposed in no time. He shuffled forward, a chuckling Logan on his heels.

"Yeah, I know," the cook whispered then leaned closer to plant a kiss on Alex's neck. "And you love every second of it, right?"

He thought about it. Did he really love it, or was he just horny? Remembering how they'd clicked every time they were together, he decided it was more. "Yeah, I do. But if you don't get in here and shut the door, we're liable to get tossed out of the inn."

"Move your ass then, sexy," Logan teased, again grinding himself against Alex's backside.

"You mean like this?" Alex stuck his bottom out and swayed it from side to side. He reached down and slid his palm over his own raging hard-on, giving it a squeeze. The shaft pulsed, and he found himself biting his lower lip to keep from groaning out loud. He staggered a step forward and wasn't surprised to feel Logan shuffle along with him. And, it didn't surprise him when the man's hands moved from his hips around to his crotch.

"Hey, I want that," the young man griped, pushing Alex's hand away.

A moment later, Alex couldn't hold back the groan he'd fought to suppress as Logan's hand slid over the erection trapped inside Alex's shorts. He squirmed with pleasure. The guttural moan turned into a sigh. When Logan's fingers wrapped more tightly around Alex's shaft, Alex's breath caught and his hips jerked.

Alex shuffled forward, then turned enough so he could reach out and give the door a shove, closing it with a soft slam. He tossed the key card on the table and looked into the deep blue eyes of his guest.

"Last chance to bail, youngster."

Logan looked at him, lips slightly parted, a darkness in his blue eyes that spoke of lust and hunger. "Are you insane?"

Chuckling, Alex reached out, wound his hand into the short blond hair and pulled the cook's face close. "Yeah, probably. A little insanity isn't a bad thing, though."

"Kiss me then, crazy man." Logan leant forward, pulling the hair Alex still held, until their lips met. Softly at first, the kiss quickly intensified, and Alex's grip loosened. Instead of holding the man at bay, Alex used Logan's hair to guide the kiss, to press their lips even tighter together. Finally, he released his hold all together and wound his arms around Logan's waist.

They kissed until Alex couldn't catch his breath and pulled away. Lightheaded, his thoughts raced. *It's been so long. Will I measure up? How fast can I get this guy's clothes off?*

As if Logan could read his mind, the blond stepped back and reached for the hem of his polo shirt. He pulled it up, revealing washboard abs and a muscular chest before slipping the material over his head then dropping it to the floor.

Alex's mouth watered. The taut muscular chest and tiny nipples perched like titbits of candy drew his attention. His mouth soon followed. Leaned forward, he flicked his tongue across one puckered treat.

Logan inhaled, his breath hissing.

That tiny bit of encouragement was enough to urge Alex on. He circled the nipple with his tongue then sucked it in, brushing its rounded edges with his teeth. Another sharp hiss from the man made Alex smile.

Raising his head, he looked into Logan's eyes for a moment. Long lashes swept over the man's deep blue eyes. A deep flush coloured his cheeks.

Alex bent again, moving to the other side of Logan's chest, but also reaching for the button and zipper holding up his shorts. While he fumbled with them, Logan's slid his hands along Alex's back and sides. As Alex pushed the man's shorts down, his own shirt was being tugged up over his back and shoulders. He let the shorts go in order to strip off his shirt. Naked from the waist up, he gazed at his lover's body.

"Whew, you're so sexy," he murmured before he could stop the words.

Logan had slipped his underpants off with his shorts and stood naked, the clothing bunched around his ankles. His long legs gave way to an erection that took Alex's breath and a pair of balls that made him drool. He wanted a taste. He wanted to nip and tug at the soft halo of hair covering the hefty looking sac.

"You did this to me." Logan thrust out his hips, shoving his erection against Alex's thigh.

Alex took only a second to slip out of his shoes and socks. Kicking them off to the side, he tugged off his shorts and boxers, tossing them after the shoes. Naked, he straightened and reached for Logan. His eagerness made his hands tremble, but he couldn't bear to wait a moment longer. The promise of the younger man's flesh against his own was much more than he could deny himself.

"Come here," he growled more forcefully than he'd meant to.

The young man swivelled his hips a moment longer, tormenting Alex unbearably. "Want this, stud?"

Alex, his heart beating like he'd run a race, reached for the long, fat rod. The smooth, soft skin slid across his fingers then he grasped the shaft. The warm length in his fist pulsed, and he pumped it slowly from its rubbery tip to the thicker base.

"Oh yeah, that's it. Stroke me. I love it, just like that," Logan crooned and thrust his hips even further ahead.

Alex winked up at Logan but didn't look at him long enough to see if he responded. Instead, he sank to his knees and focused on the man's enormous erection. The large, plum-shaped dome drew him, a tiny pearl of moisture glistening at its tip. Alex inhaled, taking in the heady scent of the man. With his hand still firmly wrapped around the thick shaft, Alex rubbed the thumb over the crown.

He glanced up then, and smiled at the expression of lust on Logan's face. Slack-jawed, the cook peered down at him. Keeping eye contact, Alex stuck his tongue out and carefully lapped at the slick head of Logan's cock.

"Fuck yeah," the blond man gasped. His hips twitched.

"Mmm, you taste fantastic," Alex murmured and ran his tongue over the dome again. Using just the tip, he flicked it along the slit. The shaft pulsed, as if going into a fit of excitement. Alex simply tightened his grip and continued tonguing the man, swiping up each new droplet of clear nectar as it emerged. When he tired of that, he opened his mouth wide and took in the entire head, allowing his teeth to grip the ridge and gently tug on the rubbery flange.

"Oh my god, oh my god," Logan crooned, his fingers going through Alex's hair. He wound the digits into the thick mass and tugged at it, mirroring the careful suction on his dick.

Alex was in heaven. A mouthful of delicious cock was the last thing he'd expected on this trip.

"Suck it, babe." Logan eased his fingers back, pulling Alex's mouth almost completely off the tasty glans. Then, just before Alex rebelled, he pushed him down, slowly sinking the full length of his shaft into Alex's mouth. The crown nudged the back of Alex's throat, and he eagerly swallowed it, fighting back the gag reflex.

He held onto Logan's thighs and let the man feed him the cock he so desperately wanted. The shaft throbbed against his lips, and he revelled in the feel of it. The sparse blond curls surrounding the base tickled his nose when he buried his face against it, and he adored every moment of the sensation. The smell of the man, the feel of sleek muscles in his hands, clenching when he thrust forward, were all Alex could have imagined.

"Yeah, more, harder, suck harder," Logan growled, his fingers tightening in Alex's hair.

Alex did the best he could, applying suction on the down stroke then holding it when he slid up the man's cock. By the time he held only the head in his mouth, the suction was at its greatest.

Alex released one of Logan's thighs and reached up between the man's legs. The firm roundness of his balls filled the hand. Nearly naked of hair, they were more like warm soft eggs than the testicles of a full grown man. Yet, he knew they were, and the concept of taking them into his mouth excited him tremendously. He cradled them, rolling them carefully around in his palm.

He pulled his mouth off the man's cock and moved in lower, wanting a taste of the soft round treats below.

Hands tugged on his shoulders, clawing at him to pull away.

He sat back on his heels, his own forgotten erection jutting out rampantly from his middle. It brushed his thigh, reminding him of its presence and its frustrated neglect. The sudden realised tension drew his hand down, his fingers around his shaft, and he stroked its length—a long languid caress that took his breath and blurred his vision.

When his thought process returned to something resembling normal, Alex looked up and smiled at the wicked look Logan sent him. He didn't however slow the delicious stroking of his own cock.

"You know, standing in the entryway isn't horrible, but getting into bed sounds like a much better idea," the young man quipped.

Alex blinked then clambered to his feet, grumbling, "Smart ass kids, never happy with what they've got." Pushing past the man, he made it to the bed in record time and stripped the covers down. He crawled onto the mattress and was about to flop onto his side when a pair hands grabbed him by the hips.

"Yeah, ungrateful, too. Never content," Logan mumbled and climbed onto the bed behind Alex. "Greedy and we don't listen to our elders."

Alex spun his head around, just in time to see Logan lean down and bite the left cheek of his ass. The sharp pain shocked him, and he yelped. But then he realised it felt fantastic and thrust his ass back for more.

"More, yes," Alex hissed, rolling his back with pleasure.

"Ah, the man likes a little bite now and again, does he?" Logan gently nipped and bit his way from cheek to cheek, then down the backs of both of Alex's thighs.

For his part, all Alex wanted was for the sensations to go on and on. He laid his head on the bed, his arms crossed underneath. Arching his back, he presented his behind to the best of his ability.

Apparently not enough. After a few moments of biting, Logan straightened up, only long enough to kick Alex's knees wider apart.

Alex complied readily and pushed his knees even further across the sheets, opening himself for whatever the man wanted. His balls dangled, his cock thrust upwards.

"Don't move, you're perfect, right there." Logan's voice was gruff and more demanding than Alex had ever heard before.

"Wouldn't dream of it," he muttered and wriggled to get as comfortable as possible.

A large warm hand slid along Alex's back, caressing him in just the right manner. Alex sighed then smiled when the hand continued on its journey of exploration. Over his ass and down between his legs, the fingers toyed with his balls, tugging at each then cupping them both. The sensation made his cock twitch, the head tapping his belly in the excitement.

"You like that, don't you?" Logan slipped his hand further beneath Alex, allowing the balls to slide along his forearm as he gripped the pulsing shaft of Alex's cock.

"Oh yeah." He wanted to say more, but before he could, Logan had taken his next teasing bite. The soft flesh along the crease of his ass became the man's meal, ever so gently, delicately, he slid his teeth and tongue along the furrow, nipping at the flesh. Once or twice, he tugged at just the hair, and Alex had to bite his inner cheek to keep from crying out with surprise. And pleasure, he couldn't remember feeling such sheer bliss without spewing.

Logan flicked his tongue around the crinkled opening of Alex's anus, sending a shiver of ecstasy raced up his spine. A soft nip made him grunt his appreciation a moment later.

A smooth fingertip grazed Alex's anus, slowly pressing its way inside. Another joined it, and the two digits flexed and spread his anus until he groaned for more.

"Tell me what you want," Logan finally asked him.

Without a breath of hesitation, Alex gasped, "Fuck me. Slide your cock in me. I need it bad."

"Lube, rubbers, where?"

For a heart-stopping instant, Alex couldn't think of anything other than his own bottom. Finally, his heart threatening to burst through his chest and breathing like a freight train, he stammered, "Night table. Small tube of lube, a couple of condoms."

The bed shifted, and he struggled for balance as Logan retrieved the necessaries. A tearing sound followed by the rubber being pulled over the man's erection sent another shiver along his spine. He was about to get fucked by someone he hardly knew. The slick noise of lube being applied then the cool touch of Logan's fingers sliding over his anus brought his thoughts back to the present.

"Are you okay with this?" The cook's soft voice came from so close behind him, Alex felt his breath.

"Yeah, it's been a while. Go easy," he urged, suddenly a little unsure of himself.

Logan's strong hands on his back sent reassuring vibes through them. "No rush, babe, when you're aching for it."

The man's cock head nudged against his opening, and he involuntarily clenched, trapping it. He fought to relax his grip, but as soon as the lube-coated cock slipped free, he wanted it back. He spread his knees and leant back, seeking the escaped tease, only to bump into it against his right cheek.

Logan, his hands on Alex's hips, shifted his body, guiding his cock to the entrance. He didn't push, didn't move other than to stroke Alex. Softly, then more instantly, he massaged the large muscles of Alex's back then his ass — opening him, soothing any discomfort or anxiety.

"You're good, Logan," Alex murmured then pushed back.

Logan inhaled, noisily, his cock trapped at the entrance to Alex's hole. If he moved, he'd either pull free or enter further.

"More," Alex growled, hungry for his own fucking.

"Yes," Logan hissed and shoved forward. The head popped in, and he held there for a moment while Alex became accustomed to his girth. When Alex pushed back, Logan suddenly felt as if he'd been waiting all evening for the signal. He thrust forward, burying his cock to the hilt in one long smooth stroke.

Alex reached under himself and took hold of his shaft, squeezing it. He was close. It had been too long since he'd climaxed. Too many nights of being alone, too many thoughts of the sexy young stud in the kitchen had left him with an ache that wouldn't be denied.

"Yeah, oh yeah!" His litany of pleasure could barely have reached his lover's ears, but it didn't matter. The careful in and out motion of the man's cock, filling him and dragging out, sent him soaring in a matter of moments.

Logan seemed to sense it. His movements quickened; the pace of his fucking eased into high gear without so much as a single rough stroke. His hands were firm, sure, and his thrusts carried Alex into a world of heart stopping bliss he hadn't visited in much too long.

"Yes, now, god, yes," Alex cried as his universe shattered. His grip tightened around his shaft, a pulse of pleasure sent a stream of cum towards the bedding, and he soared. Another spasm struck, and he clung to the sheets, sure he was about to fly.

Logan's fingers tightened, not painfully, but close to it, when he grunted and joined Alex's ride to nirvana.

A healthy throb in Alex's ass dragged him back to his senses. Logan's body slammed against his bottom, driving his knees forward. He pushed back, craving the few thrusts of the man's cock buried so deep he couldn't feel the coolness of his spasms.

When Logan fell forward, his sweat slick chest against Alex's back, euphoria clung for several moments longer. Alex turned his head and kissed Logan's damp brow, feeling the beginnings of something he hadn't thought he'd feel again. Not ever.

He whispered, "Thank you," and kissed the man again.

A flicker of movement caught his eye, and he turned towards where he knew the mirror was. Bliss turned to horror when Russ's face appeared, watching them from the reflected glass.

"Fuck!" Alex swore and struggled to get up.

"Hang on." Logan patted his back, pressing a kiss to Alex's shoulder blade. "I was just getting ready to thank *you*, and you're hopping up like you're outta here."

"The mirror." Alex gasped for the breath that had whooshed out of him when he'd seen Russ. "Oh, god."

Logan shifted in that direction. "Son of a bitch." The younger man eased his cock from Alex's anus and stood. "There he is, again. That same face."

"Russ." Alex tore the sheet from the bed and wrapped it around him as he went to the mirror.

Dark eyes stared back at him.

He reached out and touched the mirror. It felt normal, smooth and cool, but that was all. He could see Russ's image but couldn't feel the man he would have given anything to hold in his arms just one more time. The vision baffled him. "Why are you here?"

Logan came from the bathroom, pulling on his boxers. He stood next to Alex and studied the mirror. "So this is Russ."

"Yes." Alex didn't look away, just kept watching his late partner's face.

Russ stared in their direction, his lips moving as if he were speaking, but there was no sound.

"Is he trying to say something?" Logan asked.

"I have no idea." Alex placed his palm flat against the mirror, but the image didn't change.

"He doesn't seem upset."

"No, I'm sure he's thrilled to find me here fucking you." The words came out sharper than Alex intended, but he felt as if he was being unfaithful.

Logan put his hands on Alex's shoulders and spoke directly into his ear. "Technically, I was fucking you. And you need to remember something. *Russ is dead*. This inn plays weird tricks on the mind, sometimes. I think you and I should go back to my place. Hasn't been a ghost sighting there yet."

Alex continued to caress the glass. "You're suggesting I ignore this? Run away from it?"

"For now. But I don't think there's any need to run. He doesn't seem like he means us any harm."

"Are you serious?" Alex turned to face Logan. "This doesn't bother you?"

Logan shrugged. "Sure it does. I guess I've gotten used to weird stuff happening since I've worked here, but yeah, it still bugs me. That's why I'd like to…" He nodded sideways towards the door.

"I can't leave with him here like this." Alex faced the mirror and saw nothing but his own reflection. "Oh."

"He's gone," Logan confirmed. "Now, let's go. Get dressed. Throw some stuff in a bag. I'll tell Ethan we're going to my place for the night." The younger man slipped into his clothes.

"I don't know." Alex looked back and forth between Logan and the mirror. The previous night, he couldn't wait to get out of the room with the ghost in it. Now, he felt strange leaving.

"Look. You're tired and vulnerable right now. You need a good night's sleep. We can talk about whatever the hell this means tomorrow."

Alex's shoulders sagged. *He's right.* The best thing to do was put some distance between him and the inn. He'd be able to evaluate the situation more clearly in the morning. "I'll get dressed."

"Good. I'll go tell Ethan. Meet me in the parking lot. I've got a yellow Jeep. You can't miss it."

He nodded and watched Logan open the door to the hall. Somewhere in the distance, a door slammed and another immediately after it.

"Oh for Christ's sake." Logan muttered, glancing back at him. "There's Angry Annie, making her presence known. Hurry up, let's get the hell out of here."

Chapter Four

Mind racing, Alex dressed and tossed some clean things in his overnight bag. He wondered how Ethan stayed in business with so much excitement every night. Adrenaline buzzed through his system, and he realised he wasn't afraid, more excited and intrigued by the events. Maybe the other guests felt that way, too. It was hard to believe that no one had ever gone screaming into the night, though.

He locked his room and passed through the empty lobby on his way to the car park. From the front, the inn looked homey and peaceful. He chuckled to himself at the anomaly, and when the cool evening air hit him, had to admit he was glad to be out of there.

There were a dozen cars in the lot, but only one Jeep, painted the brightest shade Alex had ever seen on an automobile. He climbed into the passenger seat and tossed his bag in the back. "When you said yellow, you meant *yellow*."

Logan grinned and manoeuvred the Jeep onto the street. "I don't do anything halfway. It's all or nothing for me, man." He turned onto an unpaved side road and the ride grew bumpy.

"I can see that," Alex called over the noise of the vehicle. Before he had the chance to suggest Logan slow down, they stopped.

"Here we go. Home sweet home." Logan shoved the Jeep's long slender stick shift into first gear and killed the lights.

"That was fast." Alex gathered his bearings then reached for his bag. He glanced out the window at the house in front of them. He couldn't see much, but the wooden home appeared well-kept. "This is a nice little place."

"Yeah. I told you I lived just up the road. Some days, I walk it, unless I know I'll need the Jeep. This morning I was lazy."

"You, lazy? I doubt that." As he climbed out, he thought about the cook working late into the night and being there early for the breakfast crowd. He might have lazy moments, but the man had one hell of a work ethic.

He followed Logan to the front door of the small log building with the shake roof. Logan had called it a cottage and that's definitely what it was. Larger than the cabin Alex had discovered earlier in the day, but nothing like the houses in the city where he came from.

Logan unlocked the door and went in, flipping on a lamp. "Make yourself comfortable. It's not much, but it's all I need right now." He tossed his keys on a table at the end of a brown sofa.

Alex set down his bag and looked around. The place wasn't fancy but nicely furnished. The front room, which also sported one comfortable-looking easy chair, was divided from the compact kitchen by a bar with two stools. "Big enough for one, that's for sure. I can see why you'd prefer to cook or bake at the inn."

Logan chuckled. "Yeah, I don't keep much food here at all. Just a few snacks and leftovers. If you're hungry, I think I might have some cookies."

"No, thanks, I'm good." Alex wandered through the place, surprised by how comfortable and homey it felt. Two doors to the right, led to what he surmised were the bedroom and bathroom. There didn't seem to be room for much else.

His place back home had three bedrooms and two offices, his and Russ's. Both contained tall shelving units, stacked high with law books. The advent of the internet made a lot of the books unnecessary. If he were to move, perhaps the books he wanted to keep could go to his judge's chambers. His next home could be a little less stuffy. He'd make it more of a sanctuary, less of a workplace. The simple lifestyle Logan led appealed to him tremendously.

Judge's chambers? Where had that thought come from? More unsure than ever about accepting the job, Alex wondered if Russ had appeared to influence his decision.

He paused, placing one hand on the back of a barstool. "Do you think Russ could be trying to tell me something?"

Logan raised his eyebrows. "You think so? Really?"

Alex smiled at the surprised expression on Logan's face. "You're the one who lives here amongst the ghosts. I figured you'd know more about it than me."

The handsome younger man shrugged. "I steer clear of paranormal stuff as much as possible. Frankly, I pegged you for a no-nonsense, legal-headed type who'd look for the explanation behind the sightings before you believed them."

"I saw myself in that way, too. But this is different, more personal." He allowed Logan to put both hands on his shoulders and steer him into the bedroom. Neat and tidy, the room's uncluttered simplicity appealed to Alex as much as the rest of the place had. "This is nice."

"It works for me." Logan yawned. "I want to hear all about you and Russ. I really do. But I'm beat. Can we talk about this tomorrow?" He tugged his clothes off until only his boxers remained.

Alex's mind went in several different directions watching the sexy stud disrobe. He eyed Logan's package and murmured absently, "Talk, tomorrow. Yes."

Logan grinned and tossed back the covers. "Of course, that's just one of the things I plan to do tomorrow."

Stripped to his briefs, Alex climbed in next to Logan. When his lover curled around him and spooned, Alex was surprised but not unhappy. He settled back against the warm body and relished how good it felt. "I'm tired, too," he said softly.

"Sleep." Logan kissed his earlobe. "I'll wake you before I go to work in the morning."

"Sounds good." Alex closed his eyes and relaxed.

* * * *

Alex was disappointed to discover Logan gone in the morning, but a note on the nightstand explained the absence. He'd left for work early and hadn't wanted to disturb Alex. He suggested Alex go to the inn whenever he was ready, and they'd have breakfast or lunch together.

Alex sighed and stretched. *Ten a.m.* He'd never slept as late as he had the past couple of mornings. It felt decadent but good. He wouldn't have minded waking up to another round of sex like they'd experienced last night. It'd been ages since Russ had felt well enough for such strenuous activity. He closed his eyes. *It's been a long time since Russ died.* Was the man's spirit there to give him a message?

Go on without me.
Don't go on without me.
Take the job offer, and sell the house.
Don't sell our house!

Alex had no idea what kind of message Russ was sending him, if any. Maybe he just needed more time.

He climbed out of bed and headed for the shower. A glimpse of Logan's jeans tossed over the back of a chair had his cock rising to attention. *Idiot.* He was in Logan's house. It was no wonder everything he saw reminded him of the handsome man. His erection throbbed as he lathered it, a bit more thoroughly than the rest of his body, but he didn't linger. His last climax, at Logan's hand, had been perfect. The next one was sure to be just as good.

Bathed and dressed, he gathered his things and strolled down the rocky lane leading back to the main road and the inn. It was a nice distance to walk. If he'd been going in the opposite direction yesterday, he would have stumbled over the place.

He headed for the main entrance and reconsidered, deciding to drop off his bag first. The outside entrance to his room used the same key card, and Alex got in with no problem. The room looked neat and tidy. Housekeeping had apparently made up the bed, and nothing seemed amiss.

Alex stepped in front of the mirror, staring at his own reflection. "What are you trying to tell me, Russ? I wish I understood."

Nothing happened. He hadn't really expected anything, but in this inn, one never knew. With a heavy-hearted sigh, he moved to the window and looked out at the beautiful view of the ocean.

Cade passed by on the sidewalk, a pair of garden trimmers in his hands.

Alex tapped on the window.

Cade jumped, smiled then walked to the door.

Alex let him in. "Good morning."

"Yes, it is. How are you doing? I heard you had another rough night."

Alex shrugged. "I guess it's commonplace around here. I just wasn't expecting it." He sat on one chair and motioned for Cade to the other. "I did wonder what your other guests thought. Surely not everyone is comfortable sleeping with ghosts. Has anybody ever freaked out?"

"Not for a long time. It's funny, most people who pass through here never encounter any of the local spirits. Hell, we had a paranormal investigator here a while back and *nada*. He was disappointed as all get out. Had to go all the way down to the lighthouse before he found a ghost."

"Remind me to stay away from the lighthouse." He smiled, but his stomach muscles tightened.

"The keeper, Hunter, has posted plenty of signs and chained off driveways to do just that. You won't stumble on it by accident."

Alex remembered the signs. "I guess I did see that yesterday. I just can't believe I'm the only one around here seeing ghosts."

"If you asked our guests, and I'm sure Ethan would prefer you didn't, the majority of them would say they haven't seen anything out of the ordinary."

"Are you serious? Then why me?"

"Logan said you two saw a special ghost. One that wasn't here before you arrived. I'd say that's 'why you'."

"I'm not buying it. Russ could have haunted me at home for all these months, but I haven't heard a peep out of him. Why wait until I'm here? Why follow me?"

"Maybe it is something to do with the inn. Perhaps the curtain between life and death is thinner here and it's easier for spirits to pass through, or some shit like that." Cade scratched his head and looked bemused. "I know Ethan never had any supernatural encounters before he came here. Then he met Angry Annie. Shocked the hell out of him."

"Logan said she was here last night, slamming doors."

Cade nodded. "It's what she does best. If one door slams, we chalk it up to a guest or a draft of wind. But when there are two slams in a row, it's usually Annie."

"I'll remember that," Alex said wryly. "I was just sitting here, wondering if Russ was trying to send me a message."

"Sometimes the spirits want something. Sometimes they just want us to leave them the hell alone. Tell you what, Delia Nelson is an old woman who lives here year round. She seems to have a pretty good understanding about the ghosts and spirits. You might talk to her. Tell her I sent you." Cade smiled. "She likes me."

Alex chuckled. "Who wouldn't? You're a damned likeable guy, Mr. Wyatt."

A thoughtful expression crossed Cade's face. "Maybe you could help me with something. You know Ethan and I have been together a year, now. I was thinking about celebrating that milestone by asking him to marry me."

"Oh my god!" Alex grinned and reached over, pumping Cade's hand up and down. "Now I wish I was a judge, just so I could do the honours."

"Thanks." Cade's wide smile nearly split his face. "There's a really great minister in town—Quinn Stevens—

but before I even think of that, I have to pop the question. I want to surprise Ethan, do it up right. He deserves something big, something special."

"Like what?" Alex wasn't sure how he could help.

"Damned if I know. I've been thinking about it for a while. You've known Ethan longer than I have. I thought you might have a suggestion."

"Tell you what, I'll give it some thought." Alex's stomach rumbled, and he stood up. "It'll be a nice distraction from all my worries. I should get to the dining room before Logan thinks a bear dragged me off."

"Oh, sure." Cade got to his feet. "I'll just get back to work. Let me know if you come up with any ideas. And think about talking to Delia. If anyone knows what's going on around here, she's the one."

"I will. Thanks, Cade." Alex saw him out and locked the door behind him. He double checked for his key card and left the room by the inner door.

In the dining room, Logan worked by himself clearing tables. Alex snuck up behind him and said, "Guess I've missed breakfast, *again*."

For an instant, Logan was obviously startled, then he turned around with a smile on his face. "Yes, you did. But seeing as you have an 'in' with the cook, I'll see if he can rustle you up something."

Alex took a step closer and said quietly, "I'd hoped to be wrestling the cook himself this morning. You said you'd wake me before you came to work."

"I know." Logan looked apologetic. "But you were sleeping so soundly. After last night, I figured you could use the rest. Actually, I came up with another plan. I've already told Ethan I'll be gone for a while this afternoon."

"Oh yeah?" Alex raised his brows.

"Absolutely." Logan nodded confidently. "I'll get you something to eat, and see to the noon crowd. Then you and I can take a nice long walk and talk or whatever we want to do."

"Talking sounds good," Alex agreed. "*'Whatever'* sounds better."

* * * *

The lunch crowd had been boisterous but not large. A family with two young children ate noisily and untidily, leaving just before Alex's temper had time to flare. Several couples followed, dining then departing as if urgent business called.

After serving Alex a meal fit for the proverbial king, Logan approached the table holding out a small bundle wrapped in paper. "Cookies," he said with a wink and a smile. "Just in case you need a little added energy after *'whatever'*."

"Smart ass," Alex chuckled and reached for the packet. "Is it all right if you leave for a couple of hours?"

"Sure is. I won't have to get back until mid-afternoon. Just let me get the dishwasher going, and we'll get out of here." Logan gathered up the dishes from Alex's meal then spun on his heel and headed for the kitchen. Even with his arms full, he managed to pull his apron off before he cleared the doorway.

Alex finished off the last gulp of coffee and had just returned the mug to the table when Logan reappeared.

"Here, let me just wipe that down while you ditch the cup in the sink, then we're off." He flicked a dishrag out and quickly washed down the table, while Alex went into the kitchen. The place was spotless, which impressed him.

"You ready?"

Alex looked over his shoulder and smiled at the eager-faced blond. "Yeah, more than ready." The packet of cookies clutched in hand, he followed the man out of the dining room and through the door leading to the beach side of the inn.

"A walk on the beach okay with you?" Logan held out his hand.

Alex looked around self-consciously. The beach was busy, kids played, parents lazed beneath multicoloured umbrellas or paddled in the chill waters. It didn't seem to matter to Logan, who simply stood with his arm outstretched.

Logan strode towards him, and unceremoniously grabbed his hand. "We're okay here, Alex. The locals don't care about the gay guys who own the inn or that some of their guests might hold hands."

"Reputation means a lot in the city. Gay, straight, people take notice," he countered but hated that he was such an uptight jerk.

"Means a lot here, too, but maybe in a different way." Logan tugged on his hand, and they walked. The surf to their right crashed on the sand not a metre from them and seemed such a calming sound.

"Yeah, maybe so. I got used to showing the world my straight face; it became second nature."

"You mean not everyone wants a queer lawyer?" Logan turned towards Alex as he said it and smiled. "I'd have thought it would make for some interesting cases."

"That might be, but neither Russ or I were after just one particular brand of client."

Logan released Alex's hand and stopped walking. For a moment, Alex wondered what was going on, until the man leant forward and removed his rugged work boots. He tore his socks off, stuffing each into a boot. Once he'd tied the laces together, he slung the footwear over his shoulder, sighed and reached for Alex's hand again.

"Wait a sec," Alex said, as he too slipped out of his footwear and socks. "Much better."

They walked, hand in hand, for a good half hour, leaving the inn and its guests in the distance.

"Cade mentioned a woman, Delia Nelson. Said she lived at the inn and knew more about the ghosts and spirits than anyone else." Alex veered towards the water, letting the frigid liquid cool his hot feet.

"Yeah, she's apparently been at the inn for years."

"You think she'd know anything about why Russ would be here?"

"I doubt it, but you never know until you ask her. She's a weird duck. Sometimes she comes down for her meals, but mostly she keeps to herself and Cade takes 'em up to her. Doesn't like storms at all."

Alex stopped walking and dropped his shoes in the sand. He pulled Logan towards him and, after flicking the man's boots to the ground, drew the long lean body into his arms. Looking deeply into Logan's beautiful blue eyes, the words came before he had time to think about them. "You know about Russ, or a little bit, right?"

"I know he was your lover, and he died. That's all." Logan's face showed concern, yet there was something more there, too. Passion, lust, emotions Alex hadn't experienced for a while.

"Yes, he died. We had a good many years together, before the end. Pancreatic cancer. By the time we figured out something was wrong, it was too late to do anything. The only good thing was he went fast." The stab of pain knifed through Alex's gut but seemed somehow less with the blond cook there.

Logan leant forward and pressed his lips to Alex's forehead, whispering, "I'm so sorry."

He didn't offer anything or say he wished he could change what had happened. The man just held him and let the feelings of sorrow be what they were. When Alex felt able, he went on. "I am, too, Logan. He was an amazing man." He raised his chin, bringing his eyes in line with his young lover's. "But, I'm also glad I found you."

"I think it was me who found you." Logan smiled. After a moment's thoughtful silence, he asked, "Did Russ die at home? Did you at least have time to say goodbye?"

"Yes, he died at home in our bed. It's what we both wanted. As for having time to say goodbye. That's a difficult question. Is there ever enough time for that?"

"I don't know. Maybe not. I can't imagine what you've gone through, Alex."

"It happened eight months ago, so the pain isn't as sharp."

"Is that why you're at the inn? To get away from the memories, perhaps the house? It must be hard to stay in the same place." Logan ran his hands down Alex's back, gently cupping his ass and pulled him closer. The sexuality was there, but there was no pressure or insistence.

"No—well, not entirely." How much to tell? Alex wasn't sure the man would even be interested in his worries.

"You can't stop there." Again, Logan leant forward and kissed Alex ever so lightly on one cheek then the other. "I want to know all about you." He sealed the demand with one more kiss, directly onto Alex's mouth. A soft thing that promised more than it actually delivered, their tongues barely touched, yet when Logan pulled back, they were both breathing heavily.

"You're a pushy young man, that's for sure." Alex looked at the ocean, watched the waves crest, their white froth swirling towards shore.

"I did mention I don't do things halfway. I want it all, all the time." Logan released his hold on Alex and, with their hands still entwined, walked to one of the bleached white logs crisscrossing the sand a few feet away. "Come here, sit with me." He parked his butt on the largest of them and patted the wood beside him.

"Okay, but stop me if you get bored." Alex sat down and cringed when he felt something crumble. He quickly rose and dug into his pocket, rescuing the cookies he'd stuffed in there. "Well, crap. I was looking forward to these."

"There's more where they came from." Logan took the packet and dropped them on the sand at his feet.

Alex resumed his position and slung an arm around Logan's waist. It felt comfortable yet sexy, too. "When Russ passed away, I thought I'd never be able to get over it. He was an enormous part of my life. We not only lived together, we worked together, too.

"Anyway, once things settled down after the funeral and I got back to work, I took on as many cases as I could. I guess I tried to lose myself or bury the memories. Who knows?"

"It had to be horrible for you." Logan snuggled closer and laid his head on Alex's shoulder for a moment.

"It was, but it also helped me pass the time. I needed to heal, and work seemed the best option, at the time. I managed to put a lot of cases to rest during that time."

"Prosecuted a lot of bad people, I bet." He kissed Alex's shoulder and slipped his free hand under the front of the loose fitting shirt he'd worn.

Warm fingers slid across his belly, and Alex sucked in his breath. "Yeah, my share and maybe a few more." The shorts he'd worn suddenly felt much too tight as his cock thickened.

"Keep talking. Why did you come to the inn? Vacation?" Logan moved the hand slowly upwards.

"I've been offered a judgeship. It'd mean moving, and I'm not sure I'm ready." His mind suddenly reeled. Logan had found a nipple and was industriously tormenting it, alternately pinching and pulling on the tiny nub. When Alex thought he'd go insane, Logan slid his palm across the fur covered chest to the other neglected nipple.

"You've stopped talking," Logan whispered into Alex's ear then nipped at the lobe. "A judgeship. That's pretty impressive. Should I call you 'sir' or something?"

Alex grabbed the younger man's wrist through his shirt, trying to stop the teasing torment, if only for a moment while he caught his breath. It didn't work. No matter how hard Alex pulled, Logan simply continued his ministrations. Alex writhed, and only then did the young upstart relent, releasing the tortured nubbin.

"Damn, you're..." The words trailed away as Alex realised Logan had simply moved the torment south. His cock, eagerly thrust against the too tight shorts, was now trapped in Logan's grasp. A quick look down confirmed it, and he tried to keep from smiling his approval. It'd been a heck of a long time since he'd felt so lusty.

"I'm eager to hear more about you, sir," teased Logan, while gently stroking the length of Alex's shaft.

"Yeah, and eager to drive me crazy." He reached down and laid his hand over Logan's, not trying to stop him this time but enjoying the sensation of another hand on himself.

"Nah, I just can't get enough of you."

"So it would seem." Alex shifted and spread his legs, offering easier access to the hungry cook.

"Keep talking, please. Seriously, I want to know more about you." Logan slowed his stroking and looked up into Alex's eyes.

"Okay, but you're making it difficult to concentrate." An understatement if there ever was one, he thought. "I'm not sure I'm ready to take on a judgeship." He shook his head, focusing on what he was saying. "No, that's a lie. I know I'm ready. I've worked all my life towards it. It's moving I'm not sure about. How can I leave the home Russ and I shared? All the memories we have there. Every nook and cranny has a special place in my thoughts. I can feel him there still, even after all this time."

"But, have you been able to move on? I mean, have you dated anyone else yet?"

Logan's question caught Alex off guard and he stammered, "Well...uh, no. I haven't so much as looked at anyone since he passed away. Not until you, that is."

"Why not? Jeez, man, you're still young and in great shape. I'm pretty sure your Russ wouldn't want you to live celibate. Am I right?" He slid his open palm down until he'd cupped Alex's sac. Giving it a squeeze, he couldn't have been surprised when Alex groaned.

"You bring a lot of guys to the beach like this?" Alex asked impetuously, ignoring the question Logan had asked.

"Hell, no. Don't have time."

"Why don't I believe you? You answered way too fast. I bet this is one of your favourite make out spots."

The blond man chuckled. "Yeah, well maybe. Not this spot exactly, but if we had more time, I could show you a great place just a little further along."

It was Alex's turn to chuckle. "Ah, youth and energy."

"Which you still have in abundance," finished Logan. "I think it's time you thought about selling your house. Moving on. That might be why Russ is here."

Alex let that thought sink in. Could Russ be taking care of him, even now? The memory of his lover lying so quietly in their bed was daunting. The thought of the man sticking around to make sure he moved on...well, that was even more overwhelming.

"Russ is dead, that's all there is to it," he said in tone of voice that was more stern than necessary. A tone he regretted immediately. He looked into Logan's face and added, "I'm sorry. It's just a lot to think about."

"I can only imagine," whispered his lusty young cook.

"Are you going to finish me off out here, or would you rather wait until later?" Alex reached for Logan's crotch. The man's shorts were pulled tight emphasising the swollen girth of his erection. "This is a hell of a way to take an afternoon break."

Logan checked his watch and grumbled, "Unless you want a real quickie, we better start back." It was his turn to grit his teeth; his turn to grunt with pleasure as Alex slowly massaged and caressed the full length of his cock. When the ball of Alex's hand pressed down against the bulky sac, he didn't slow down or even think about it. He simply cupped them and pulled gently downward.

"Oh yeah, that's what I like to see," Alex murmured. He ran a thumb along the length of Logan's shaft, smiling when he noticed it pulse when he reached the head. "But, you're probably right. We'll save this for later." He looked up into Logan's eyes and winked. "Think you can hold off?"

Logan gave Alex's shaft a sensual stroke and in a gruff voice asked, "Think you can?" With one last caress, he let go of Alex and got to his feet. Extending a hand, he pulled a lust shaken Alex up and reached down for their footwear.

"Yes, I'm sure I can. Not too happy about it right now, though." Alex retrieved his shoes and slung them over his shoulder. Readjusting his aching cock into a less annoying position, he held his hand out, more than willing now, to hold Logan's.

"I really do think Russ is watching over you." Hand in hand, they started back towards the inn.

"But, why now? Why not appear at home, where I'd at least expect him, sort of." *Like I'd expect him anywhere!*

"No idea, I don't know much about ghosts, spirits, whatever. I'm just the cook, remember?"

"Oh yeah, *just* the cook." Alex smirked. "What does that make me?"

Logan answered in a much quieter voice, "The guy who's stealing my heart."

Alex heard but chose not to let on. They walked in silence for a while, until they came around a rock strewn point and saw the inn in the distance. He decided to change the subject.

"Hey, did you know Cade is thinking of asking Ethan to marry him?" Alex immediately wondered if he should have kept that bit of information to himself. Cade hadn't said anything, but he wasn't sure.

Logan's eyes grew wide and an enormous smile made his face shine. "Seriously?"

"Yeah, but keep it under your hat, will you?" he urged. "I don't know if I was supposed to say anything. Ethan doesn't know about it."

"That's great news. Those two were meant to be together."

"I have to agree with you there. Ethan and I had some good times in college, but it was just innocent fun. Neither of us was ready for anything serious. We parted the best of friends. I guess Cade knows all about that. He wondered if I had any idea about how to ask Ethan, something romantic."

"Cade's a cool guy. His wanting to surprise Ethan is amazing. I'm sure they'll want a wedding by the ocean. Those two spend all their spare time at that cabin on the beach."

"It's where they met, too, so you're probably on to something." They were nearly back to the inn. "You just keep your mouth shut." Alex wanted to give Logan a final kiss and maybe a caress before they were too close to 'civilisation'. He stopped beside one of the ocean twisted cedars and pulled Logan into his arms. "Or let me shut it for you."

Logan's breath against his face sent a shiver down his spine. Their lips touched softly then their tongues met and battled wetly. Alex wanted more, much more, but knew they were nearly out of time. He slid his arms around the sleek young man and pulled their bodies closer together. Chest to chest, belly against belly and their crotches thrust with abandon for much too short a time.

Both were hard when they parted, yet neither seemed to care as they hurried towards the back door of the kitchen.

Standing on the steps, Alex below his sexy young man, he looked up and blinked into the glaring sun. "I'm going to see if Delia Nelson is around. Maybe she's got an opinion about Russ and why he's here."

Logan traced the tip of his index finger along Alex's jaw as he replied, "She'll be in her room most likely. She's in room twelve, but be careful. She's a little nuts."

Alex trapped Logan's finger and suckled on it for several moments, thinking about what else he'd like to be sucking on. Finally, he released it. "Seems to be quite a few nuts in the place. Some more appetising than others." He reached forward and slid his hand between Logan's legs.

Logan jerked away and chuckled. "Yeah, well, we'll get to those nuts later. I better get to work, or dinner is going to be late, then we'll never get together."

Alex grinned and followed Logan into the kitchen. "Don't work too hard."

"See you later. I'll reserve your special table." Logan smiled at him.

The expression on the younger man's face caused Alex to stop in his tracks. Logan was gorgeous, his eyes a sparkling, clear blue colour. The lusty desire in his gaze was enough to take Alex's breath away. But there was something else reflected in those shining eyes that surprised him even more. *Adoration?*

Logan seemed to be falling for him, hard. While Alex was enjoying the distraction, he knew, deep inside, nothing permanent could come from their relationship. He and Logan were from two different worlds. The cook, though no doubt hardworking, was used to a much more laid back lifestyle than he was.

Alex thought the inn and the ocean were nice for a short getaway, but he'd go insane if expected to stay much longer. His work was his life force, the thing that had kept him going for years, with Russ and after. Whether he took the judgeship or went back to his legal practice, he wanted to work. *Had to work.*

With one last smile at the younger man, Alex went through the kitchen and out into the dining room. Ethan was talking with a customer at the front desk so Alex kept walking. Down the hall past his room, and up the stairs in back, he paused for a moment to remember the last time he'd been upstairs, with Russ. He expected to feel melancholy, but the business with Russ' spirit was all he could think about just then. He continued walking down the hall to the last room on the top floor.

He glanced around, wondering for a moment about the other ghosts that supposedly inhabited the inn. *Do they come out in the daylight? I hope not.* One otherworldly being at a time was all Alex could deal with. He inhaled and rapped on Delia's door.

"Hang on, hang on," a cranky-toned woman's voice called from inside. "Let me get my pocketbook. I'll be right there."

Alex blinked. Why does she need her purse?

The door opened, and a petite, grey-haired woman peered up at him. "You from the pharmacy? I've been waiting for this delivery all the live-long day."

"No, I'm sorry, I'm not. I'm Alex Brookfield. I'm a lawyer…a friend of Ethan's…a guest here at the inn." Alex never remembered stammering in his life. Something about the look in the woman's steely eyes made him feel as tentative as a law school graduate trying his first case.

"Oh, yes." Delia pushed her glasses up on her nose and examined him head to toe. "You are a bit long in the tooth for a delivery boy."

Alex chuckled. "Thanks. You certainly know how to cheer a guy up."

"Isn't that young cook cheering you up? You and he have been sneaking off at all hours of the day and night."

He cleared his throat. "Logan and I are just friends, ma'am."

"Friends, right." Delia snorted. "Is that what the man in the mirror is telling himself?"

Alex blinked. *She knows about Russ?* He struggled for an answer, again. "The man, he's, uh, someone from my past. I've never seen him reflected anywhere before I came here."

"Maybe that's because you weren't diddling anybody before you came here."

Diddling? He tried to keep a straight face as he replied. "Actually, I came up here to ask if *you* have any idea why Russ was appearing to me. Cade says you know everything that goes on around the inn."

"Oh he does, does he?" She squinted up at him.

Alex couldn't tell if she looked pleased or irritated by the statement, but he watched her tap one finger against her chin.

"So you and Chef *Boy*-ardee don't see any connection between your relationship and the sudden appearance of the ghost?"

He ignored the dig and replied, "Not really. I saw Russ' image the first night I was here. Before I ever..." The word 'diddled' was stuck in his head, but he couldn't bring himself to use it.

"Maybe Russell isn't trying to tell you what *you think* he's trying to tell you. Have you ever thought of that?"

Alex shook his head. He'd never spoken with anyone more cryptic, and it was getting to him. His lawyer instincts kicked in and he frowned. "I find the straightforward approach works best in most matters. Could you just say whatever it is you're hinting at?"

It was Delia's turn to frown.

"No." She stepped back into her room and closed the door between them.

Alex blinked.

"Well, fuck." He couldn't believe what had just happened. He'd apparently alienated the one person who might have been able to shed some light on the situation.

"Stop that cursing!" She hollered from inside the room. "And search your heart for your own answers. If Russell was a mean and spiteful person in life, he'd be of the same nature in the spirit world. A leopard doesn't change its spots." Shuffling noises indicated that Delia had walked away.

Frustrated, Alex descended the stairs. When he reached the bottom, but before he rounded the corner to return to his room, he smelled the foul odour of rotting fish. He covered his nose and mouth with one hand, at the same time he spotted a trail of water on the floor. Hesitantly, he looked around the corner, not sure what he expected to see.

There were four wet boot prints but nothing else. Besides the lingering odour, he spotted nothing out of the ordinary. Alex dodged the wet spots as he entered the hall. He paused in front of the door to his room. Dinner wouldn't be for at least a couple of hours. He had time to catch a quick nap, just in case he didn't sleep much that night. Key card in the lock, he opened the door and walked in, smiling at the prospect of a long night ahead.

He glanced warily at the mirror but saw only his own reflection. At that moment, something Delia said popped into his mind. When he'd mentioned he and Logan were just friends, she'd replied, 'Is that what the man in the mirror is telling himself?'

Alex swallowed uncomfortably. *Is she talking about Russ or me?*

Chapter Five

That evening after dinner, Alex stared through the large window in the lobby. "This place certainly has its charms."

Ethan straightened some magazines on an end table and grinned. "I'm not sure you're saying that like it's a good thing."

Alex sighed. The last thing he wanted to do was insult his old friend, but he couldn't imagine living in a place that was inhabited by ghosts. "The inn is great, Ethan. I'm just on edge, is all."

The innkeeper nodded sympathetically. "Logan mentioned you'd seen Russ again. I was trying to remember, when you and Russ stayed here before. Was there any paranormal activity that time?"

"Yes, and not so much as a door slam. I was geared up for it, too. We'd heard all your stories, and back then, well, I guess we figured we could face anything together. Little did we know what was ahead of us."

Ethan winced. "You didn't know about the cancer?"

Alex shook his head. "We found out about it when we got home. He died a few short months later."

"That really sucks, my friend."

"Yes, it does." Alex smiled. "Time is helping. Or at least, I thought it was. I'm still trying to figure out why Russ is appearing to me here, of all places."

"Cade will tell you that it's the inn. Some line about the curtain between life and death being thinner here, or some shit like that."

Alex nodded. "That's exactly what he told me, complete with the 'some shit like that' part."

A grin crossed Ethan's face. "I don't know anything for sure. I do know the paranormal encounters I've experienced have been shocking at times, but never sinister. What goes on here is relatively mild. I've heard stories that the spirit at the lighthouse pushes people down stairs."

"Oh my God!" Alex couldn't imagine facing an angry ghost. He recalled something Delia had told him and scratched his head thoughtfully. "I talked to Delia Nelson this afternoon. She said something about Russ that I don't understand."

"Not surprising. Delia is a character, for sure. She knows stuff, but she likes to string people along. You may have noticed."

"Are you serious? Of course, I did. And when I asked her to get to the point, she shut the door in my face. She told me if Russ was a mean and spiteful person in life, he'd be the same way in the spirit world. But that's the thing. Russ didn't have a spiteful bone in his body. He trusted everybody. Didn't always believe them, mind you, but that's what made him a brilliant attorney. People sought him out, and admired him for the work he did. No one ever would have described him as 'mean'."

"That's a puzzler." The phone at the reception desk rang and Ethan looked in that direction. "Excuse me," he told Alex, and went to answer it.

"Of course." Alex stared through the window again. The sun had started to set and the colours reflecting off the ocean were breathtaking. At times like that, he thought he might enjoy living at the inn. Then he recalled the rotten fish stink in the hallway earlier and quickly reconsidered.

"Nice evening." Cade appeared next to him.

"Hi, Cade. It sure is. Ethan and I were discussing your non-paying guests when duty called." He nodded to the man with the phone in one hand and guest register in the other.

Cade nodded. "Between the paying and the non-paying types, it's a hopping place. Ethan makes it all look easy, though."

Alex enjoyed hearing Cade speak about his partner with such obvious admiration and love. He felt slightly guilty when he realised he hadn't given Cade's upcoming marriage proposal any thought. They deserved something special. *Both of them.*

As if he'd been reading Alex's mind, Cade asked, "Did you come up with anything for me? I mean, I could do the down-on-one-knee straight proposal. But Ethan is so great. He deserves the best."

Alex put one hand on Cade's shoulder. "I think he's got the best. I know he wouldn't argue that fact. I haven't come up with anything, yet. Let me sleep on it. I'll try to think of some suggestions for you real soon."

"Thanks, Alex." Cade beamed, nodding.

"Speaking of the best, I should go and see if Logan has any more of that peach cobbler from dinner. That kid can cook, can't he?"

"Yeah, the guy's amazing." Cade agreed. "Go on in. I'm sure he'll fix you right up. I'm going to grab my sweetie, sit on the veranda and watch the sun set."

Interesting suggestion.

"Have a nice night." Alex waved and headed for the kitchen.

Logan was wiping off a counter when he walked in.

"I wish you'd have let me help you with these dishes," Alex told him.

"All done." Logan spread the rag over the edge of the sink. "Just coming to find you. Ready to get you alone and naked."

Alex pressed his body up against Logan's. "Both of us were thinking along the same lines. Ethan and Cade are going to watch the sun go down. I'm more interested in a different kind of 'going down'." He ground his burgeoning erection into Logan's groin.

Logan nibbled Alex's lower lip between kisses and groans. "Sounds good to me. Where we headed? Your room's closer, but we could go to my place."

Alex hesitated, not sure he was ready to get intimate in his room again after everything that had happened there. The uncertainty bugged the hell out of him. He prided himself on his decisiveness.

Before he could speak, Logan planted a soul-searing kiss on him then slowly backed away. "Let's move this party to my place. It'll only take a minute. I think I can keep my pants on for that long."

"Hope I can." Alex nodded, relieved the choice had been made for him. They left through the back door. When they spotted Cade and Ethan necking in an Adirondack lounger in the garden, Logan doubled back and guided them around the inn, to avoid interrupting the couple.

Both were quiet on the short Jeep ride to Logan's cottage. Once they got there, neither needed words. Logan let them in and locked up behind them.

Alex went straight to the bedroom and began peeling out of his clothes.

Logan joined him, smiling with approval. He shucked his clothing and tossed back the bed covers then stretched out, on his back.

Alex admired the man's physique as he walked slowly around the bed, bobbing erection leading the way. He eyed Logan's full, thick shaft and licked his lips. The very thing he'd been fantasising about was right in front of him.

When he reached the opposite side of the bed, he crawled onto it. He crept forward, coming to a stop only when his head came level with his lover's toes. Satisfied, Alex lay down and rubbed his fingers lightly over the man's muscular calves, following the caresses with kisses.

Logan writhed under him. When he mimicked the light touch on Alex's legs, Alex understood why. The whispery, feathery soft touch of his fingers felt amazing and highly arousing. Alex was hard as granite. He could see Logan was, too. A drop of pre-cum glistened from the tip of the younger man's bulbous cock head. It took all the strength Alex could muster not to zero in and give the shaft the attention it deserved. He restrained himself. They had all night. *Sometimes slow and torturous is more fun.*

He kneaded the flesh of Logan's tanned thighs, occasionally brushing against the waving cock or low-hanging balls. Each time he did, Logan squirmed and bucked his hips, obviously desiring more. Alex smiled and proceeded with the erotic massage of Logan's legs.

His lover continued to mimic his actions until, apparently, he couldn't take the delightful torture any more. Logan muttered, "Fuck it," and suddenly, a wet, warm mouth closed on Alex's erection.

Alex's breath caught. Logan's tantalising sucking and licking couldn't be ignored, and he didn't want to try. With a hand on a firm thigh, Alex drew his lover's delectable cock into his mouth.

The heady scent of masculinity, combined with the salty taste of pre-cum, sent thrills of desire down Alex's spine. He suckled the pulsing rod, tracing his tongue along a ridged vein running down the side.

Logan thrust his hips forward to the same rhythm he sucked Alex's cock.

Overwhelming sensations battled for dominance. The intense pleasure his lover gave, strong, wet suction and languorous licks, was enough to make Alex come by itself. Coupled with a mouthful of Logan's tasty treat, Alex knew he wouldn't last long. His balls drew tight against his body, the need to come his foremost thought.

Logan groaned but didn't slow his pace.

Alex's heart lurched when it dawned on him Logan obviously loved the act as much as he was. *What's not to love?* Simultaneous blowjobs. *Double the pleasure, double the fun.*

Before he could think anything else, Alex's orgasm exploded. Streams of warm cum jetted from his body. Ripples of the most exquisite pleasure imaginable flowed through Alex. He tensed, wanting to hold on to the feelings for as long as possible, then decided to let go and relax. Incredible sensations rocked him, making him extremely happy to be where he was at that moment. He sighed as the orgasm crested and peaked.

Just as his shuddering subsided, Logan's body jerked and his cock pulsed, sending the first stream of cum into Alex's mouth. Alex swallowed mouthfuls of creamy nectar, not wanting to miss a drop. He clutched his partner's thighs and took as much cum into his mouth as he could. When Logan stopped twitching, Alex licked him clean with slow, methodical strokes.

He sighed, realising Logan was doing the same to him. *Perfect.* He couldn't imagine a better way to end a day.

Drained and exhausted, Alex released his grip on Logan and flopped onto the mattress. "Oh. My. God."

Logan chuckled and lay back similarly. "Ditto. That was amazing."

Alex yawned and scratched his chest. "And exhausting for an old guy."

Logan rolled onto his side and spun around, facing Alex and slid a hand along his belly. "I don't do, 'old guys'. But, I'll agree with you, exhausting. Been a long day, sexy. Time for both of us to get some shuteye." He leant forward and brushed his lips against Alex's.

Before Alex's cock could stiffen, Logan flopped back and whispered, "I'll make you a nice breakfast."

* * * *

Alex looked up and groaned. "What time is it?" He rolled over onto his belly and tucked his arms under the pillow.

Logan, standing in the doorway, naked and gorgeous, smiled. "It's early, just past six."

"Six. Oh my lord. I'm on vacation. Why would I wake up at such an ungodly hour?"

"Well, I was going to cook you breakfast, as promised. Then I checked the cupboard and found it damned bare.

Food will have to wait until we get to the inn." Logan approached the bed and sat on the edge. "Sorry if I woke you."

Alex smiled into the pillow. Turning his face to the side, he looked at the sexy man perched on the bed beside him. "I'm not."

Logan leant down and kissed the back of Alex's neck. "I was going to make you bacon and eggs." Another soft kiss, against the back of his neck. "And anything else you'd like."

Alex clenched his ass cheeks, fighting to control the burgeoning erection pushing into the mattress. His hips thrust forward, and the head of his cock pulsed.

Logan slid his hand under the blanket and down Alex's back, until the palm rested on the curve of his ass. "You all right?"

"Bugger," Alex said then gasped when Logan squeezed his ass. "Yes, I'm all right. But, I'm not interested in breakfast." He rolled over and drew the covers aside. By then, he was fully erect and eager for some action. He reached up and curled his hand around the back of Logan's neck, drawing him forward. When the man was inches from his face, Alex stopped pulling and said, "Last night was amazing. I want more." The final few inches vanished when Logan leaned in and pressed his lips to Alex's. Tongues flicked out, battling for some imaginary superiority.

When Alex needed a breath, he pushed Logan away and sat up. "Get lube and a rubber."

"Pushy, pushy," Logan teased, but was on his feet reaching for them even as he said it. "Just the way I like my men." With a foil packet in one hand and lube in the other, Logan eyed him seductively.

Alex worked his cock, ensuring it was as hard as it could be. "Yeah, pushy, pushy, that's me. Climb onto my pole, and we'll play pushy, pushy for as long as you like."

Chuckling, Logan shifted, sitting cross-legged beside Alex's hip. "Move over, big boy. And get your hands out of there. My turn." He reached out and after pushing Alex's hand away, took hold of the pulsing cock. With a firm grip, he eased the skin up and down the shaft.

"I'm greedy, too," Logan murmured and reached for the condom packet. He tore into it with his teeth, never slowing his tormenting stroke of Alex's dick. Before he slid the condom on, he leant forward and sucked the head in. As Logan swirled his tongue around the head, Alex couldn't hold his hips still and began a gentle fucking motion.

"That's it, babe. Suck it first. Make it good and slick, nice and hard." Alex thrust upwards, each stroke of Logan's fist increasing his lust a little more. He wanted to bury himself in the man's mouth but was denied until it seemed his young lover either took pity on him or grew as hungry for it as he was. Suddenly, instead of just the head feeling the sweet sucking sensation of a lusty mouth, his shaft slowly sank in as well. Deeper and deeper his staff went, until Logan's nose touched the curls at the base. The gagging reflex struck, clenching the man's throat around him. Though quickly controlled, it gave Alex an extra thrill to know he was big enough to cause it.

"Easy, don't hurt yourself. Just suck as much as you can." Alex eased back, pushing his ass into the mattress, trying to pull a little of his cock out. Even that control slipped from him as Logan pushed his face down, again taking it all.

Stars flashed behind Alex's eyes as excitement soared. He gripped the sides of Logan's face, straining to keep from fucking his mouth ruthlessly in search of just his own pleasure. The man seemed to understand and, within seconds, was ramming his face up and down. Alex knew it couldn't go on for long. No matter how much Logan wanted to please him, his throat couldn't take the battering.

When Alex was on the brink of losing it, Logan slipped his tightened lips up the shaft of Alex's cock, then after swirling his tongue rapidly around the head, he pulled free. Struck dumb by both the words and the lust rising within him, Alex simply stared up at the blond hunk. Logan knelt beside him, lips puffy from the abuse. Breathing deeply and smiling like a maniac, he said, "Better than eggs and bacon, that's for sure."

"Huh?" muttered Alex, before he could gather his thoughts enough to reply properly. When the meaning of the man's remark came to him, he smiled. "Glad you think so. But, I really want to fuck that tight ass of yours. I've been dreaming about it all night."

"Is that why you've been jabbing me in the ass?"

Chuckling, Alex nodded. "Yeah, I guess so. I hope I didn't leave any bruises."

Logan pushed off the bed and turned his back, bending forward. Ass presented not a foot from him, all Alex could do was admire the taught muscular globes.

"Any bruises?" Logan asked and wiggled his bottom.

"Uh, not that I can see. Maybe you should get up here so I have a better view." He patted the bed, one hand on either side of his hips.

Logan chuckled and faced the bed again. "Before I do, give me that dick." He held up the condom he'd been holding and reached for Alex's pole. "Time to sheath this monster." He placed the nippled end over the tip of Alex's cock head, and with practiced ease, rolled the latex glove down the shaft.

The snugness of the condom made Alex groan. The special treatment he was getting added to his pleasure. He wanted more and knew he'd get it as soon as the blond tease finished. Once the rubber was on, Logan stroked his cock a couple of times before releasing him. He hopped up on the bed and, turning his back, straddled Alex's thighs.

Peering back over his shoulder, Logan asked, "See any bruising?" He reached back and stroked his thighs. Bent forward, he slid his hands from the back of each knee up to his buttocks. Still looking Alex in the eye, he smiled and slowly pried his ass cheeks apart.

Alex couldn't stop the groan that escaped then. The man was driving him crazy and knew it. With his gaze glued to the cleft between the muscular buttocks, he reached for his own cock and gave it a couple of hearty tugs. His balls tightened, and he knew he'd better stop, or risk coming before he even entered the crinkled dark hole.

He sat up, bringing his face to within an inch of touching Logan's bum.

"Let me check," he said in a voice so rough it was barely recognisable. He licked his lips then leant forward. Slipping his tongue out, he slid it along the cleft, until the crinkled flesh of the man's anus clenched, trapping it. He wiggled the tip, tasting the bitter musk of the man on his tongue. His mind reeled.

"Yeah, fuck yeah," Logan whispered breathlessly.

Alex heard but refused to stop his tongue action to reply. Instead, he stabbed in and out, fucking the tight hole as deep and fast as he could. The slick walls clenched on his tongue. The more Alex worked the inner muscle, the softer and looser the man's anus became.

Satisfied he'd relaxed him all he could with just his tongue, Alex backed away. "Don't move."

"Wouldn't dream of it, stud." Logan shifted his feet, apparently determined to stay as long as Alex wished.

"Lube, where is it?" Alex looked around but couldn't see it anywhere.

"Here," Logan offered, and the tube dropped from his left hand onto the bed.

Alex retrieved it and unscrewed the cap. The large dollop he squeezed into his palm would be enough, he knew. He slathered both hands. One went to his own latex covered erection, while the other went to Logan's anus.

His index finger slipped in easily, and he immediately began to stretch the hole sideways. Gently pulling and probing, Alex was soon able to slip another finger inside. A short while later, he slid a third finger inside and worked all three in and out, then side to side. Logan moaned—a soft raspy sound that went on and on, until Alex pulled his fingers free.

"Squat, sit on my dick, babe," Alex said in a gruff voice.

Logan looked back and nodded. He lowered himself, slowly, while Alex guided him with a hand on one hip. His other gripped the shaft of his cock, aiming its shiny crown at the dark crinkled opened descending towards it.

The soft outer membrane touched the tip of his cock, and Alex fought hard to hold still. He didn't want to lunge upwards, unwilling to hurt the man and desperate to make the experience as good for Logan as it was assuredly going to be for him. The man's anus flowered open, the anal ring slid over the head of Alex's cock, gripping tight when the crown popped in.

"*Yes*, babe, do it. Sink down on my cock. Fill that ass of yours," he crooned as he leant back. He released the shaft of his own cock and took firm hold of Logan's hips. Not so much to guide the man as to help him slide down.

"Oh my god, this feels amazing," Logan murmured as his ass devoured Alex. Faced away, the angle of his penetration was slightly different than it had been, the pressure of Alex's cock touching spots perhaps untouched before.

Holding as still as he could, Alex simply enjoyed the sensation until the man was fully seated upon him. When he was sure Logan was settled, Alex lay back on the bed and thrust his hips up. "When you're ready, raise up a little then let yourself sink back down."

"Can't move, for a sec. Gimme a minute. This feels so damn different."

Alex smiled. He remembered the first time he'd been fucked like this and knew how his cock would be dragging over Logan's prostate. The angle was just right to stimulate that tiny organ to perfection. And, Logan had all the control. Or he would until he got too excited then Alex would take over again.

Logan rose up, nearly pulling completely off Alex's cock. When his asshole pulled at the rim of Alex's cock head, he stopped and let himself down again. "Fuck, that feels awesome."

"Yeah, it does. Want me to hold your hips or are you okay?"

"No, hold my hips. I'm scared I'm going to lift right off you. Don't let me."

Alex took hold and churned his hips around, stirring his cock inside Logan's ass. "Now, lift up."

Logan rose, but Alex controlled how fast and how far. When the man's anus seemed to be about ready to pop over his cock head, he tightened his hold, stopping Logan from moving away. Then Alex churned his hips again, slowly pulling Logan back down on him.

"Oh fuck," Logan groaned, and Alex felt the man's balls press more firmly against his own.

Alex shifted his legs, spreading his knees wider which forced Logan to move his feet apart. "I can't reach your cock, but you can reach my balls, babe. Masturbate, but don't forget me."

A moment later, Logan's fingers slid over Alex's sac and pulled on his balls. He closed his eyes, revelling in the sensation of Logan toying with his testicles then easing down to nestle a finger against his anus. An easy target, it took only a moment for Logan to worm his way inside.

"Keep that up and neither of us will last long." Alex clenched his ass, clamping down on the invading digit.

"Then fuck me. I need it." Logan rose and slammed himself down hard, while continuing to work his finger in Alex's hole.

Alex lifted Logan then released him, allowing the man to drop. It didn't take long for them to get into a rhythm. Each helped the other rise towards a mind-blowing climax. Thrusting upwards, Logan let his weight drop, driving Alex's pulsing cock deep. The gentle cupping of Alex's balls just before Logan tugged the shifting sac sent him soaring.

"Yes, fuck me, yes, more," Logan chanted while slamming his body down, harder and harder.

Sweat trickled from his lover onto Alex's chest. His cock throbbed, the imminent a stroke nearer.

"Now, fuck hard, now!" he growled and lunged upwards. His body taut, his cock swelled then sent its first volley of cum high. The latex contained it, but the sensation was as if he'd filled his lover's ass. Heat shot from him, and he groaned.

"Fuck yeah, fuck," crooned Logan, just before his body tensed, and his ass clamped hard on Alex.

The pressure sucked at Alex's cock, drawing still more cum out of him. Blinded by the flashing lights and breathless from the climax, it took several long moments for him to come down from the high. He pulled Logan's ass tight to his crotch, felt the man's balls jerk and another volley of cum splattered his inner thigh.

Alex held Logan's hips tight and waited for the younger man to finish. It didn't take long before Logan's breathing calmed and he looked back over his shoulder, a huge smile on his face.

"Awesome," Logan said, in a breathless voice.

Alex slid his hand up the blond man's back, gently massaging the muscles. "Yeah, it was. Very awesome."

Logan shifted then carefully climbed off Alex.

For his part, Alex held the condom in place and as soon as Logan was clear, he scooted out from under the man.

"Back in a sec," he mumbled over his shoulder as he headed for the bathroom. Once inside the small bathroom, he tossed the rubber and washed up. He snatched up the washcloth and after rinsing it out, returned to the bedroom.

"Here, lay on your belly," he told Logan and waited for the sexy blond to comply. He washed the man carefully. Done, he leant down and pressed his lips to the back of Logan's neck, whispering, "That was one hell of a way to wake up."

Logan turned back over and reached up, wrapping his arms around Alex's neck. "Sure was, and one we'll have to do often."

"For as long as I'm here, anyway."

A smile brightened Logan's face. "Longer than that. Much, much longer, I hope. I'm falling for you, Alex, hard."

Panic gripped Alex's belly. *What the hell?* He eased himself up and sat on the edge of the bed, trying not to frown. Gathering his thoughts, he said, "You haven't known me long enough to fall for me."

Logan sat up, crossed his legs Indian style and grinned. "Long enough, it seems. I think I'm falling in love with you, Alex. I'd like to share more than just a week with you." He reached out.

Before Logan's hands could wrap around him, Alex got to his feet. The panic rose, and he looked around for his clothes. *There, on the chair.* He grabbed his underpants and slipped into them, feeling much more in control once he had them on. Facing Logan, he again tried to be as diplomatic as he could. "A few days. You're so young it must feel like more, but—"

"But nothing. I know how I feel. I can't wait to see you in the morning. When I'm at work, I'm looking for you all the time. When someone enters the dining room, I check to see if it's you. That's got to mean something."

"Sure it does. It means you're infatuated with an old fart." When he'd finished talking, he noticed Logan bristle.

"How many times have I told you, you're not old? At least, I don't think you are, and isn't that what's important?" He fumbled his way out of bed and reached towards Alex. "I care for you. I want more. This job, I can do it anywhere. I can—"

"Logan, stop, please," Alex interrupted. He pulled on his shorts and the shirt he'd worn the night before, making sure he was out of the young man's reach. "You've got a great job here, and honestly, I'm just not sure I'm ready for a relationship yet. It's certainly not what I'd planned when I booked a room here."

Looking crushed, Logan lowered his hand. "Let's go to the inn. I'll make breakfast. We can talk."

Alex knew he couldn't let it go on. A clean break would be best. "I'd better go. You'll have to be at work soon, and I should just get back. The walk will do me good."

Logan got to his feet and, naked, followed Alex out of the room. "You don't have to do this."

At the door, Alex slipped into his shoes and faced his young lover. For an instant, his heart felt as if it was about to burst from a sudden ache.

"I know," he said softly. He reached out and slipped his fingertips under Logan's chin. "I'll see you around." A quick peck on the cheek before he turned and walked out the door was the hardest thing he'd done since he'd buried Russ.

He trudged back to the inn, feeling no better after the hike. Yet, he knew what he'd done was right. He wasn't ready for a new relationship. The pain he felt must be from losing Russ. *It has nothing to do with Logan. It couldn't.*

Alex stopped just outside his room and stood gazing at the door to his empty room. He swiped his key card walked in. The air was stale, and he went straight to the door across the room and opened it. He stood on the threshold and inhaled the cool morning air. There weren't any guests about yet, not even Cade working in the garden.

"A walk, maybe that'll clear my head," Alex mumbled and stepped into the morning sun. "At least, I'll be away from the damn spirits." He thought of Russ for a moment, but pushed the memory of his last appearance aside. He heard the surf and headed towards the ocean.

When he reached the water's edge, he looked left then right and decided to head away from the lighthouse. A good walk would give him time to think. Maybe he should leave the inn. He'd planned for a week, but no rules said he had to stay. He'd pretty much decided to take the judgeship, and that's why he'd come.

But, what about Cade and his proposal? The beach and that cabin he and Ethan slipped away to when they had a chance, those were important places to both of them. Alex felt both places should be part of their wedding and the proposal. A plan formed and even though the morning had been anything but rosy for him, he had an idea to share with Cade when he saw him next.

Further along the beach, the logs crisscrossed and he clambered over them. The sand dragged at his feet, slowing him down but not stopping him. Hunger gnawed at his belly, but he was determined not to see Logan again if he could help it. Not until he was ready to leave. He needed to make a swift, clean break. He truly didn't want to hurt Logan any more than he already had.

Damn, who would have imagined the boy would fall for me?

Chapter Six

Alex was relieved to see Cade outside when he returned to the inn later that day. Dapper as always, the long-haired groundskeeper was sweeping the patio. Cade paused and leaned on his broom. "How's it going?"

Alex forced a smile and shrugged. The last thing he wanted to do was talk about him and Logan, but he did need to speak with Cade. "Not too bad, I guess. Hey, I had an idea for your proposal."

"Great!" Cade rubbed his hands together. "Let's hear it."

"Seems to me, the cabin would be an ideal place for you to pop the question. You could sneak in before Ethan and set the table with the inn's fanciest china. Get a nice bottle of wine, have lots of candles and maybe spread some rose petals around. Sweet talk the cook into preparing you a really fine meal. Maybe finish that off with some strawberries and whipped cream. You could tuck the ring into the plate of strawberries. I'd recommend leaving it in the box. I've heard too many horror stories about people eating rings."

Cade laughed, but his eyes were shining. "Hey, that's a great idea. We could take the strawberries into the other room with us, start feeding them to each other, and he'd eventually find his surprise."

Alex waved a hand. "Yeah, yeah, you got the idea. I don't need to picture what comes next. I'm sure you can take it from there."

"I like it!" Cade pumped Alex's hand up and down. "Thanks a lot, man. You really came through for me."

"Happy to help out." Alex smiled. "Perhaps you wouldn't mind doing one small thing for me? Could you get me a sandwich and bring it to my room? I haven't eaten all day and I'm half-starved."

A confused expression crossed Cade's face. "Why haven't you eaten? Logan's been working all day."

Alex didn't answer, just set his jaw.

"Uh oh. Trouble in paradise?"

"Not really paradise, Cade. It's been a nice, relaxing stay, but nothing more. I didn't come here expecting anything else. And if you ask me, a few days just isn't long enough to..." He stopped talking when he realised he was spilling his guts, exactly what he *hadn't* wanted to do.

Cade smiled, seeming to understand. "It only took me a few days to fall in love with Ethan. Sometimes it happens fast, Alex."

"And sometimes, young people confuse love and lust. I've seen it hundreds of times in divorce court. You know what they say about fools rushing in."

"Yeah, and I know a few more expressions about 'fools' if you'd like to hear them."

"I'll pass, thanks. But, I would appreciate that sandwich."

"If you were just a friend, I'd tell you to go ask Logan yourself. But, you're a guest, so I'll get you something and bring it to your room. A half hour, okay?"

"Fine." Alex nodded. "Thanks." He entered his room through the outside door and, before he could shut it, heard Cade speak one more time.

"Any message for Logan?"

Alex paused without turning around. "No. But you can tell Ethan I'll be checking out tomorrow."

Regret tinged Cade's voice. "We'll be sorry to see you go."

Alex closed the door and didn't look back.

* * * *

The 'sandwich' he'd ordered turned out to be a full meal of roasted chicken, potatoes and vegetables. Alex was hungry enough not to complain and cleaned his plate with little difficulty. He set the tray outside his door and, once back in his room, glanced through the window at the view. The sky had darkened considerably in the time it had taken him to eat. A noisy wind blew, and fat raindrops splattered against his window.

"Great, a storm." He hoped the weather wouldn't hamper his leaving now that he'd made the decision to go.

Alex decided to stop procrastinating and start packing. He retrieved his suitcase from the closet, but before he'd taken two steps with it, the leather bag flew back to where it had been and the sliding door slammed.

"What the fuck?"

Hesitantly, he opened the closet a second time and reached for the suitcase. It was as if the bag had been glued to the floor. It wouldn't budge.

"Oh, come on, now."

He tugged the handle again, to no avail.

"What stupid trick is this?" He glanced around the room, not sure what he expected to see but braced for anything. Nothing happened.

A loud clap of thunder outside startled him, and he jumped. Jagged bolts of lightning crackled through the sky. It hadn't stormed since he'd been at the inn, but this one promised to be a whopper.

Alex returned his attention to the closet determined to show the suitcase—or whoever—exactly who was in charge. Before he could get there, the lights went out, thrusting him into pitch blackness. "Oh, for fuck's sake!"

He froze in his tracks until the next flash of lightning illuminated the room enough to see. Alex checked the mirror and spun around in a circle. "Russ, you wouldn't have anything to do with this, would you?"

The sounds of the storm were all he heard. He tried to remember if there were any candles or battery operated torches in the room, but couldn't recall seeing any. As much as he *didn't* want to visit the lobby, it was the only place he knew to go for a light.

He opened the door to his room and paused to acclimate himself to the dark hallway. He took one step out and ran smack into a petite figure, a full head shorter than him. He grabbed an arm to steady whoever he'd nearly tackled and recognised the feel of an old, worn sweater. "Delia? Is that you? I'm sorry. I can't see a thing out here. Are you okay?"

The old woman didn't reply. She raised her hands and Alex caught a glimpse of a torch.

"Oh, you have a light! Great. Do the batteries work?" He fumbled his fingers over hers and flicked the switch back and forth several times. "Apparently not. Is that why you're down here? Come on, we'll see if we can make our way to the lobby together. I'm sure Cade's got fresh batteries."

She raised the torch until it was just below her chin. Suddenly, it illuminated, and Russ' face was superimposed over Delia's.

"Don't go," he said.

Alex staggered backward and practically fell into his room. He caught himself, but continued to back up as Delia-slash-Russ followed him in.

"Why are you leaving?" The voice was raspy, a mixture of Delia and Russ' and barely sounded human.

"I was going to get a light." Alex's calves brushed the bed, and he stopped.

"Your objective here is not complete." Delia paused in front of him. Russ' face was translucent and looked frightening co-mingled with the face of the wrinkled old woman.

"Objective? What are you talking about? I didn't come here for a specific reason."

"If you believe that, you're more naïve than I thought. I brought you this far. Do I have to push you every step of the way?"

Alex's thoughts reeled. With the furious storm raging behind him and the not-much-friendlier ghostly visage in front, he felt trapped and incredibly confused. "Russ, what are you talking about? Are you trying to tell me something?"

"You have to let me go," the spirit implored. "It's time to move on."

"Move on. Okay, I'm doing that." Alex nodded. "I'm going to take the job and sell the house. Is that what you wanted?"

"Search your heart." Russ' face ballooned and soared near Alex then backed away.

"My heart," Alex repeated, barely able to think with the barrage assaulting him from all directions.

"*Your heart!*" Delia screeched, and her frail body convulsed. Russ' spirit whooshed out of her, and she crumpled to the floor.

Before Alex could catch her, a gust of wind sent a branch crashing through the window. Shards of glass and debris flew everywhere. The violent gale knocked him forward, and he cracked his head on the dresser. His last thought, before passing out, was to search his heart. He only found one thing there. *Logan.*

* * * *

"Alex! Wake up, man!" a frantic male voice called as if from some distance.

He opened his eyes but could barely see. Smoke filled the room and burned his eyes. "What the—?"

"Fire!" Ethan's face appeared before him. "Lightning struck the inn. We've got to get you out of here." He helped Alex to his feet and, with the aid of a torch, lit the way to the lobby.

"The others?" Alex's head throbbed, and his brain was fuzzy, but he remembered the inn was filled to capacity.

"Cade and Logan are getting them. Come on." Ethan guided him to the lobby, which was less smoky but waterlogged and laced with fire fighting hoses. "The cops are transporting guests to a lodge in town. You'll be allowed back tomorrow to get your things." They stood in the doorway under the small overhang.

Torrential rains and wind buffeted them, nearly flooding the car park. Once they left the lobby, there was nowhere dry to go. It made sense to move the guests to another location. Alex shouted over the din, "I'm not leaving. I can help."

"You've been injured," Ethan shouted back. "We need to get you checked out."

"I'm fine! I want to help you." He swallowed and admitted, "I can't leave Logan."

Ethan gave him a quick smile. He cupped Alex's neck and pulled his head down to examine it. "There's no blood. I guess you'll live. Okay then, let's go." He darted back in to the lobby.

"Here!" Logan called and ushered a family still in their pyjamas towards them. He carried a toddler, whom he thrust into Alex's arms without making eye contact. Logan panted and coughed a few times. He looked at Ethan. "The main floor is clear. Cade's starting on the upstairs. I'll go help him."

Ethan guided his guests by the shoulders and led them to the door.

"Good!" he called to Logan.

Alex watched his young lover head back into the fray and his heart ached. "I'll come with you," he yelled.

"No!" Logan glanced back at him. "Get these people out." He disappeared into the smoke.

Squirming toddler in his arms, Alex knew it was the right thing to do, but he hated watching Logan go back inside.

"Where are the fire fighters?" he asked Ethan on the way out.

"It's a small, volunteer force. More should be here, soon. The guys that got here first are upstairs, battling the blaze. The rain will help. The wind, not so much."

A woman in a police slicker met them with a couple of umbrellas. "This way, folks. We've got a van over here to take you someplace warm and dry. Come here, little guy." She scooped the child from Alex's arms.

Ethan said, "Thanks Ruthie. Make sure everyone knows we'll provide transportation back here tomorrow so they can get their things and their cars."

"Will do. Joe's on his way with another van for the next load."

"Great." He dashed back to the inn, Alex on his heels.

Cade and Logan reappeared with another group of people. "Upstairs is clear," Cade shouted.

Ethan scanned faces and turned to Cade, frowning. "Where's Delia?"

Coughing, breathing heavily, Cade shook his head. "Wasn't in her room. I figured she was already out."

"She's not!" Ethan exploded. "I've counted every head that left this place. She has to be in her room still! Did you feel around on the floor?"

"Ethan," Cade grabbed his shoulders. "The lightning struck her room. The fire fighters are there now. It's a hell of a mess, but I promise you, *Delia is not there.*"

A burst of memory floored Alex. "Oh my God! I know where she is!" He took off in the direction of his room.

"Alex, no!" Logan yelled.

"I've got him," Cade said.

Alex could sense the long-haired man running just behind him. He hadn't thought to grab a torch and was grateful for the light Cade's shed. "She was in my room before any of this happened."

"Your room?" Cade repeated with a tone of disbelief.

"It was her, but it wasn't exactly. It was Russ, too." He reached his room and shoved the door open. It was breezy, and Alex remembered the broken window. Yet smoke billowed, thick and black, making it difficult to see or breathe.

Alex dropped to all fours and crawled to the last place he'd seen Delia. Eyes burning, he felt around on the floor, but there was nothing. "She was here!" he insisted.

"Keep looking!" Cade called from across the room in the opposite corner.

Alex crawled, hands extended like feelers. He reached the closet and felt the leather suitcase that had given him problems earlier in the evening. He shoved it and it rolled out of the way. "Sure, now you move," he muttered.

He heard a weak moan.

Alex fumbled around the inside of the closet until he touched a gangly arm in a wool sweater. "Delia!" he breathed with relief. In a louder voice, he shouted, "Found her!"

He reached into the closet and lifted out the woman who couldn't have weighed ninety pounds.

Cade crouched over him and aimed the light at Delia's face. "She's breathing! Thank God. Come on." He touched Alex's shoulder and both men stood, Cade lighting the way for the retreat.

Alex held his breath as long as possible but began coughing once he hit the lobby.

"Oh lord!" Ethan met him halfway. "Is she—?"

"She's breathing." He nodded between fits of coughing.

"Here, let me take her." Ethan grabbed Delia and carried her to the sofa in the far corner of the lobby where the smoke hadn't reached.

Alex and Cade stood coughing, hands on their knees, trying to expel the last of the black air from their lungs.

"Mr. Roberts." A fresh, clean pair of fire fighters strode into the lobby.

"Yes." Ethan stood to meet them.

"We've got oxygen masks. We're going to search the building now. Keep your people out of there."

Ethan glanced at Cade and Alex and rolled his eyes slightly. "'My people' are out, and they got everybody else out, too. But please, search the building. Never hurts to be safe." He glanced at Delia and the men standing around the lobby. "We could use some oxygen in here, too. And I'd like a status report on the structure as soon as you can get me one."

"Will do." One of the fire fighters radioed for a medic.

Alex could hardly tell she was a woman under all her gear.

"Med tech will be right in. We'll get started, now." She donned an oxygen mask and moved towards the hallway with her partner at her side.

"Whew!" A woman in the yellow slicker stepped into the lobby and shucked it off. "How we doing in here?" She had a medical case and a small oxygen tank under her poncho.

Ethan stepped forward. "Ruthie, great. Please look at Delia. She inhaled a lot of smoke."

Ruthie sat on the edge of the sofa. She fastened an oxygen mask on Delia and began checking vital signs. "Everything looks good. How are you feeling?" she asked the older woman.

Delia nodded.

"If you're up for travel, we'll take you to the lodge in town."

"No!" Delia shook her head vehemently and pulled the mask off. "I'm not going anywhere."

"You can't stay here, honey," Ruthie repositioned the mask.

Delia looked up at Ethan. "You staying?"

Ethan exchanged glances with Cade and replied, "Well, yes, but I don't think our quarters sustained any damage. Plus, we've always got the cabin."

"Then you can find a room for me." She closed her eyes, effectively ending the discussion.

Ruthie stood up and faced Ethan. "Stubborn woman."

He smiled. "You have no idea. It's fine if she wants to stay. Hey, would you check out the rest of my friends? They all took a lot of smoke."

"Let me look." Ruthie took vitals from Cade, whose blond-pony tail was askew, and coated with black ash. His face and clothes were smudged, but he seemed in good health. "You'll be fine. Just take it easy for the rest of the night."

"I intend to." He smiled and stepped aside so she could look at Logan.

"Hey, blondie." She ran a hand through his short hair and black smudged fingers came out. She wiped a streak off his face, and smiled. "You're one cute mess."

Alex cleared his throat. "How are his vitals?"

"Oh." Ruthie got back to the job at hand. "He's fine. Just needs a nice hot shower and someone to soap his back."

"Thanks." Logan stepped aside before she could say anything else. From the expression on his face, he was concerned she might invite herself over to do the job. Ethan and Cade seemed to be trying not to chuckle.

Alex scowled, a bit harsher than he'd intended.

"Let's look at you, grumpy." Ruthie took Alex's pulse and blood pressure then checked his oxygen saturation level. "You're fine." She turned away quickly, obviously not as interested in him as she had been her previous patient. Ruthie looked around, but Logan had vanished. "Where'd he go?"

"He had someplace to be." Ethan told her. "Thank you so much for checking everyone out."

She shrugged and gathered her things. With one last look at Delia, she said, "*That* one really should be checked out by a doctor. I'll leave the oxygen here. Have her wear it as long as she can."

"I will," Ethan shook Ruthie's hand. "We really appreciate all your help."

She glanced towards the back of the inn. "I'm just happy it wasn't worse. You did a good job here tonight, Ethan. I'll be back, early tomorrow to check in and pick up that tank."

"See you then." Ethan stood in the doorway for a moment then turned to the others. "It's stopped raining."

"Good," Cade said, "Although the rain may have been a godsend tonight. It helped contain the fire."

Delia pulled her oxygen mask forward and sneered to where Ruthie had just walked out. *"That* one is a snippy little minx. Scared poor Logan half to death."

Alex couldn't resist smiling. "Where *did* Logan take off to?"

Ethan moved next to Delia. "He went in the kitchen to make coffee. The gas stove still works, so it'll be perked rather than drip, but coffee is coffee, and I could use a cup."

He reached down and snapped Delia's oxygen mask back into place. She started to protest, but Ethan cut her off. "Keep this on at least until the coffee comes. Then we've got some decisions to make." He glanced at Cade. "I wonder how long we'll have to close the inn?"

Cade stepped behind and wrapped his arms around his man. "It won't take that long. A few weeks, a month. We'll be back in business in no time."

Ethan leaned back into Cade's strong chest and sighed. "This is all so surreal."

"It's going to be fine." Cade nuzzled his ear.

Alex turned away. The owners obviously needed some time together. *And I need to find Logan.* He headed towards the kitchen. "I'll just go see if I can lend a hand."

"I'm sure you can," Ethan's voice echoed after him.

Alex heard and kept walking.

He found Logan by the stove, staring at an old campfire coffeepot as if he were daring it to percolate.

"You okay?" Alex asked.

Logan didn't look up. "What are you doing here? Shouldn't you be packing or something?"

"Logan, look," he began, but the man cut him off.

"I can't believe you were just going to leave without saying anything. That's the shittiest thing I've heard in a long time. I didn't expect that from a man who's mature, responsible, and what did you tell me? *Old enough to know better?*"

"I would never have done that to you. I intended to say goodbye. I just wasn't sure I could face you before I did."

"*Goodbye.* Great." Logan nudged the coffeepot as if that might hurry it up.

"I told you this was happening too fast for us. I care about you, Logan, I truly do. But you're so young. I'm not sure you realise what you're getting into."

"Fuck you!" Logan stormed and stomped around the kitchen, knocking off pots and pans as he went. "I'm almost thirty years old. I've been in love a few times. Once with an abusive asshole who got his jollies tossing me around. Back then, I took it, because I thought that's what love was."

Alex cringed at the man's admission. He started to speak, but Logan wasn't finished.

"I've seen a lot in my years, I can tell you that. And I understand now what love's supposed to look like. *Or so I thought.* See, I always imagined it looked a lot like you and me, at my place, last night. Being so close to someone, staring into his eyes until the intensity forced me to look away—holding him while we're joined in the most intimate way possible."

"Logan, you're right." Alex placed a hand on his lover's forearm. "That did feel like love's supposed to. I was being overly cautious. Not for me; I'm a big boy. But for you. I can't have you making life changing decisions based on a few days of really hot sex. You deserve better than that."

Logan turned to face him. "I'm not sure what I deserve, but I know what I want. *You.* Don't tell me you're too old, because you're not. And don't tell me we haven't been together long enough for me to know what I want. Because I do. *I really do.* I want you, Alex Brookfield. I love you."

Alex used his thumbs to wipe away two tears streaking Logan's soot smudged face. "I love you, too, Logan Emerson. And not because Russ told me I should. He told me to search my heart. I did that, and the only thing I could find there was you."

Logan shuddered a sigh of relief, and they came together in a sooty, musky kiss. "I love you, Alex," he repeated, as if he needed to keep saying the words.

"Love you too, babe." Alex understood the need for reassurance after everything they'd been through that night. He held his partner tight and murmured the words over and over again.

"Promise me something," Alex said when they separated. "Don't make any rash decisions. Ethan said the inn will be closed for a while. Come home with me. See if you like the city. We'll get to know each other better and see how this thing plays out."

Logan smiled. "If that's they way you want it, sure. But I know how this is going to play out. You'll absolutely love waking up with me every morning and will never want to let me go."

The first real laughter of the evening bubbled from Alex. "You're probably right, sexy. I'm not too anxious to let you go right now."

The coffeepot gurgled and overflowed. Logan pulled away and grabbed it. "Let's take coffee out to everyone. Then we can pack your things and move them to my place until we're ready to leave. I should probably stay and help get the clean-up started, at least."

Alex piled cups and the makings on a tray then followed Logan who carried the coffeepot out to the dining room. "I'll help too," he offered. "Especially since it seems like this whole thing was my fault."

"Your fault?" Logan looked at him with disbelief. "How do you figure?"

"What's your fault?" Cade met them and took the tray from Alex. He set it on a table and they all began fixing their drinks.

"This business with Russ. I don't know if he started the fire. God, I hope not."

Ethan led Delia to the table and helped her sit. "Of course, it wasn't Russ," he said. "The fireman said lightning struck a corner of the inn. Delia's room is a mess, but the other upstairs rooms just have smoke and water damage. The downstairs rooms have minimal water damage except for Alex's, which only got smoke, plus the broken window. The rest of the inn is fine. We were really lucky."

"Thank God," Alex murmured. "But Russ—he did something to Delia. I can't exactly describe it."

"Yeah," Ethan said softly. "He saved her life. Imagine if she'd been in her room when that fire started. She might not have made it out."

"Oh!" Alex glanced at the woman, who sipped from the cup Logan handed her. "I hadn't thought of that."

She looked up at him. "Russ wasn't a bad man," she said and smiled. "He knew what he wanted and went after it. I believe he was trying to get you to do the same thing."

Alex nodded. "I figured that out. At least, it only took one conk on the head to get it through my thick skull."

Logan touched the back of Alex's head lovingly. "You're lucky to be alive, too. It's been quite a night." He looked at the others sipping their drinks. "After we finish our coffee, Alex and I will put his things in my Jeep. He'll be staying with me for a few days, until we can get the clean-up started."

Ethan smiled and exchanged glances with Cade. "Sounds good. Cade's going to board up the window first thing, and we'll clean that room for Delia. It looks like we'll be closed a few weeks while we get things back to normal."

"If you can spare me, I plan to go home with Alex during that time. Spend a couple of weeks in the city, see how it goes."

"Really?" Cade's eyes lit up. "Well, congratulations you two."

Alex felt his face redden, something that never used to happen to him. Since he'd met Logan, he'd found it happening more and more. "No need for congratulations just yet. We're going to take things slow and watch what develops."

"He loves me." Logan beamed. "I just have to help him see that change doesn't always mean baby steps. Sometimes, you just have to take a leap."

"Lord." Alex closed his eyes. "Now there's actual leaping involved."

They all chuckled, and Logan added, "Don't worry, Ethan. I'll come back and help you find someone to take my place. And of course, we wouldn't miss the wedding for anything."

"Wedding?" Ethan blinked.

It was Cade's turn to blush. "Shh! I haven't said anything yet."

Logan's eyes bulged. "Oh, shit. Sorry. Hey, the cat's out of the bag now. Just do it."

Cade stammered, "But I had this whole big thing planned. Alex helped me come up with the perfect arrangements."

Alex grinned and shook his head. "Just do it."

"What the devil are you talking about?" Ethan's glanced from one man to the other, his eyes narrowed.

Cade sighed. "I wanted to make it perfect for you. I was going to have wine, and rose petals, and dinner, and strawberries—"

"Sounds wonderful," Ethan interrupted. "But what the fuck are you talking about?"

"Just do it!" Delia demanded.

Everyone laughed, and Cade shrugged. He dropped to one knee and clasped Ethan's hand. "Ethan Roberts, I've loved you since the minute I laid eyes on you, a year ago, at this very inn. Would you make me the happiest man in the world and marry me?"

Ethan's face turned three shades of red before he blubbered, "Absolutely! Yes. I love you, too."

Cade stood up and swept Ethan into his arms. They kissed, and Alex turned to Logan.

"That was perfect," he whispered.

"Oh, yeah." Logan placed a hand over his heart.

"Sappy, sappy, sappy." Delia got to her feet and walked around the table to Alex. "Come on, you two. Let's go get to work on your room—I mean, my room. I want to take a nap."

They set their cups on the table and followed her into the hall. Alex tossed one arm over Logan's shoulder and waggled his eyebrows. "A nap sounds good to me."

Logan pinched Alex's butt then left his hand resting on the hip. "I might argue with Cade about that 'happiest man in the world' business, because I do believe that's me. But I'd hate to interrupt him right now."

Alex glanced over his shoulder and saw Ethan and Cade, still lip-locked in an embrace. "Nah, let's not disturb them. But I promise you, as happy as you are now, you'll be even happier later." He winked and hugged Logan close to him.

"Counting on that." Logan rested his head on Alex's shoulder, and they strolled from the room together.

QUINN'S BLESSING

Dedication

To all those spirits of loved ones who can't gather the courage to leave, not quite yet.

Chapter One

Jack Donner's heart skipped a beat when he saw the sign, 'Whiskers' Seaside Inn, next left.' The place was well known in the area. When he'd seen the job notice in the paper, he couldn't wait to apply. His last job, working on a fishing boat, had paid the bills, but it definitely wasn't what he wanted to do with his life.

When he pulled into the car park, his hopes soared. The inn was as beautiful as he remembered. Not too big, but with a view that never failed to take his breath. He'd always admired the place. He parked and turned off the ignition.

A gust of cool ocean air curled around him the moment he opened the door of his beat-up old sedan. He got out and stretched the kinks out of his back, looking towards the front doors. He spotted two men embracing, and wondered about it, and them. He'd heard rumours about the owners of Whiskers' being gay.

The couple parted, spoke a few words and one of them, a very handsome man who looked to be in his late thirties or early forties, got into the waiting car. The younger man stood quietly for a moment, his face a study in thoughtfulness. The T-shirt he wore with the Whiskers' logo made Jack suspect the guy worked at the inn. The car pulled away, and they both watched it go.

He ran a hand through his unruly brown hair and tugged the corners of his collar straight. "Ready or not, here I come," he mumbled and retrieved the manila folder from the passenger's seat. Plastering on a smile, he headed towards the door.

"Howdy," Jack said to the younger man who'd turned and opened the door just as he got there.

"Hi there, welcome to Whiskers'."

"Thanks." Jack walked into the lobby and stopped for a moment to get his bearings.

"Can I help you?"

Jack turned and smiled. "Jack Donner. I'm here to apply for the chef job."

The blond man smiled and offered his hand. "Then you're in luck, Mr. Donner. I'm Logan Emerson, the chef you'd be replacing."

The two shook hands, and Jack returned the man's smile. "Call me Jack, please. Can I ask why you're leaving, or is that too personal a question?"

Logan nodded. "It's personal, but a fair question. What the hell." He turned and headed deeper into the inn, saying over his shoulder, "Come on, we'll get coffee and talk."

Jack followed the handsome cook, eyeing the way his ass moved inside his cut-off jeans. They went through a nice-sized dining room, the tables empty for the moment, but already set for the evening meal. The fireplace drew his attention and he wondered how often they used it. He had visions of cold winter nights, a storm raging and the firelight flickering off a masculine face. Jack shuddered and dragged his attention back to the present. "This is a really great place."

"Yeah," Logan agreed. "You could probably never tell there was a fire here a few weeks ago."

"A fire?" Jack looked around again, surprised.

"Caused by a lightning strike. Not a whole lot of damage, mostly smoke and water. We had to close for a while, though. Thankfully, we're up and running again."

"That's good." Jack shuddered again. Fire was not his favourite element.

The chef opened a door, and motioned him to follow. "If you get the job, this'll be your domain." He waved his hand expansively around the room, which wasn't all that big, but looked well-stocked. Logan filled two large mugs with coffee and continued farther into the room. A small bistro-style table and two chairs filled most of the area making a cosy place to sit and chat.

Logan sat on the far side and nodded towards the other seat. "Take a load off."

Taking the proffered seat, Jack set his elbows on the table and sipped his coffee. "Looks like a solid kitchen. So you don't mind if I ask why you're leaving?" He let his gaze rest on the cook's face, trying to focus on that rather than the way his shirt pulled tight across his chest. The man was a hunk, but he'd also seen him show feelings for someone else.

"You saw the guy I was saying goodbye to, outside?"

"Yeah, a nice-looking fellow," Jack replied.

"He's my guy. We're moving in together. He's going to be a judge. I'll go with him, and find work where he's posted."

"Makes sense."

"Before I go, I'll need help with a wedding we're having here."

Jack nodded. The place would be popular for weddings. "A big affair?"

"Not sure yet. It's the owner and his lover."

"I heard a gay couple ran the place."

Logan chuckled and nodded. "You heard right. Ethan and Cade are finally going to tie the knot."

"Very cool." Jack drank his coffee. "I'm, uh, gay, too." He blushed, not sure why he felt the need to mention it. But if the owners were gay, and the chef, too, it seemed as if it might help his chances of getting the job. Suddenly uncomfortable, he glanced around the room. "The kitchen seems to have all the necessities. Looks to be in good shape, too."

"It is. Cade takes care of all the upkeep. He's not just the live-in boyfriend, he's the handyman, too." Logan downed the last of his coffee. "You have any references?"

"Right here." Jack handed over the folder he'd been holding.

Logan took it and opened it, laying it on the table.

While the man went over his work history, Jack studied the room. He got up and put the two cups into the sink, quickly washing them and setting them into the rack. A large mixer sat on its stand in the corner, a couple of torches on the windowsill. The stove looked scrubbed, the counters spotless. He wandered over to the large fridge and peered inside.

"This looks good," Logan's voice interrupted his perusal.

Jack closed the cooler door and returned to the corner where Logan sat looking at the folded papers. "Good enough to get the job?" He smiled hopefully.

Logan looked serious and handed back Jack's resumé. "Might be. I'm not the boss, though. I just check over your qualifications. Ethan does the hiring and firing."

"I figured as much."

"From what I can see, you've got the experience. We like to hire local as often as we can, and that two-year stint you did at *Echoes* didn't hurt. Why'd you leave?"

Jack looked down and grimaced. "The owner was a little too friendly for my liking. She's a great gal, but not my type. It got uncomfortable, so I asked to be let go."

"Aw, I see. Did she know you…"

"Prefer men? She knew it, but thought it didn't apply to her. I left on good terms." *It hadn't been easy*, he added, but only to himself. The woman, Adrienne Loft, was used to getting what she wanted.

Logan nodded and got to his feet. "I've got to get busy. I'll take you to meet Ethan. He's a good guy. I'm sure you'll get along."

"That'd be great."

Logan ushered him out of the kitchen and into the dining room.

Jack glanced outside and got his first glimpse of the ocean from inside the inn. A magnificent view of sandy beach and rippling waves through the trees greeted him. Off to the side, he spotted a shirtless man chopping wood.

Logan must have been looking in that direction as well, because he said, "That's Cade. Ethan won't be far away. Those two are inseparable since Cade proposed."

"What do you mean inseparable?" came a loud voice from across the room.

Jack turned, immediately spotting the tall, extraordinarily good-looking man heading towards them. Dressed in a pair of black slacks and the same crisp polo shirt Logan sported, the guy was a walking wet dream.

Shaggy brown hair, perfect for grabbing, added just the right amount of sex appeal to make Jack drool.

"Hey, Ethan," Logan said and headed for the owner. "I was just going to ask Cade where you were."

"You were, why's that?" He eyed Jack up and down, but smiled when he got to his face.

"This is Jack Donner. He's after my job." He chuckled then added, "The resumé he showed me is pretty impressive. He worked for *Echoes* for two years and they're damn particular about their kitchen staff."

The handsome hunk held out his hand. "Sounds like you're someone I should take a closer look at."

Jack shook Ethan's hand. "Thank you, sir. I've heard nothing but good things about Whiskers'."

Cocking his head, Ethan grinned. "Have you heard the stories about our spirits?"

"Some." Jack felt a little uncomfortable discussing the one aspect of the inn that unsettled him. Ghosts were for kids to scare each other in the night, not for reasonable adults. "I never paid too much attention to them."

The smile on Ethan's face got bigger, but he didn't comment further on the ghostly inhabitants, or on Jack's take on the subject. "Why don't you come and meet Cade? He's the other half in the decision-making team when it comes to hiring." He turned and walked towards the door leading to the back of the inn.

Jack followed.

Logan simply said, "I'll see you later. The dinner crowd will be showing up in a while."

"Thanks for the welcome, and your time." Jack hurried after Ethan.

Once outside, the owner headed straight for the shirtless stud cutting firewood. The garden was beautifully maintained, and the smell of ocean air mixed with a variety of flowers was heady.

"Cade," Ethan called before they got too near the man. "Hey, sexy, I need to talk to you for a minute."

Jack watched the big man swing the axe to his side and turn to face Ethan. Even if he hadn't known the two were a couple, the way Cade's face brightened would have been a dead give-away. The smile clinched it, and Jack instantly knew these two had something very special.

"I'm trying to get enough wood split to carry us for a couple of months." Cade joined them and turned his attention towards Jack. "And this would be?"

Ethan rested his hand on Jack's shoulder. "Jack Donner, our new cook, if he passes muster."

"Ah, the man not to piss off." Cade beamed and offered his hand. "Nice to meet you."

Jack shook it and marvelled at the strength in the man's grip. "Same."

"Logan's talked to Jack and seen his resumé. From the report I got, he has the right qualifications for the job." Ethan strode over and stood closer to Cade. "What you think, babe, give the guy a try?"

Cade looked over Ethan's shoulder, eyeing Jack up and down. Jack fought the urge to squirm. The jeans and blue cotton, button-down shirt suddenly didn't feel quite right for the interview. At least he'd cut his crazy mop of hair. He smiled, but his stomach did flip-flops.

"Yeah, I have a good feeling about him." Cade winked. "Let's give him a shot. Put him to work in the kitchen. I'm sure Logan will be able to tell pretty quickly if he's right for the job."

Relief washed over Jack and he let out the breath he hadn't realised he'd been holding. He needed this job.

Unemployment paid the rent and bought groceries, but other expenses came out of his nearly depleted savings.

"Great," he said, his tone maybe a little too eager, but he didn't care. "That's all I need, just a shot."

"Did Logan mention we're getting married?" Cade slipped his arm around Ethan.

"Yes. He said you were inseparable since the proposal."

Chuckling, Ethan replied, "The man follows me everywhere."

Cade laughed loudly. "All this time, I thought you were following me. Whatever, as long as we're together."

Ethan grinned. "Jack, why don't you go and see what Logan needs? I'm afraid the wedding has stressed the poor man out, and after he's just had to say goodbye to his lover for a few days."

"Yeah, he told me. Nice-looking guy I saw him with at the door."

"Yes, Alex Brookfield, soon to be Judge Brookfield."

"How cool is that?" Jack felt a pang of jealousy. It seemed everyone around him was either in love, or in a relationship. He'd broken up with his last boyfriend some months ago and hadn't found anyone since. A date or two, but nothing promising.

"Logan agreed to stick around and do our wedding reception this coming weekend, but then he and Alex will be moving on." He looked up into Cade's eyes then turned back. "I'm afraid we haven't given him much time to get organised."

"*This weekend?* My lord, poor Logan. He must be run ragged with this place, and the wedding on top of it." Jack was surprised Logan had given him the few minutes he had.

Cade looked confused, as if he couldn't see what all the fuss was about. "We don't want anything fancy. Just a simple ceremony and a big party afterwards."

Jack smiled. "And a cake, and decorations, invitations, hors d'oeuvres and booze, right?" He knew the answer before either man spoke. Of course they wanted all the bells and whistles. They just didn't know how much planning it entailed.

"Yes, you got it." Ethan gave Cade a kiss on the neck.

Jack shook his head. Logan was going to need all the help he could get. He couldn't wait to see the man.

"Well, congratulations." Jack backed away from the pair. They certainly did look happy.

He retraced his steps to the inn, and into the kitchen. Standing at the door, he looked in and spotted Logan standing in front of the flat top, flipping burgers. "Ethan's given me the green light to get started. Said you could evaluate as we went along. I think he feels guilty with the wedding coming so soon."

Logan looked over his shoulder and grinned. "Yeah, this weekend. I'm only under a tiny bit of pressure."

Jack chuckled. "Sounds like it. So when and where do you want me to start? Cade said it was up to you."

"Tomorrow's good enough." Logan shook his head and seemed to reconsider. "Hell, why not right now? Those two are so lost in each other, they really don't have a clue how much work this 'simple little wedding' is turning out to be."

"Yeah, I gathered." Jack entered the kitchen and saw the variety of salads Logan had already laid out ready for the dinner crowd sitting along the sideboard. "You're the only cook?"

"Yup, I'm it." He grinned at Jack and added, "Until you walked in the door."

"Timing is everything."

Logan flipped six large burger patties, added strips of bacon to three and cheese to the others. "There are perks to the job. There's a room available here, if you want it. Or, I live in a small cabin close by. After the wedding, it'll be up for subletting."

"This is sounding better, all the time. I wondered about keeping my place in town until my first paycheck. If I could move in here, that'd sure help." Jack was so relieved he could have kissed the man. Just thinking about that made him smile.

"Tell you what, give me a hand to get the dinner out, then take off and pick up your stuff. I'll make sure you get a decent room."

"Excellent." Jack rolled up his sleeves. He cleared dirty dishes off the counter and loaded them into the massive dishwasher.

"I'll also grab you three or four uniform shirts. Mine should fit you, unless you prefer new."

Jack looked at the polo shirt with the Whiskers' logo. All the men wore them, in various colours. The shirts looked casual with Cade's jean cut-offs, and dressier with Ethan's slacks. "Used works for me, thanks. What do we do about pants?"

"Shorts, jeans, or slacks, whatever you prefer. Ethan doesn't care about pants as long as they're clean and decent looking. Cade gets away with ratty cut-offs because he works outside, and, well, because he's Cade." Logan smiled. "Besides that one bit of flagrant nepotism, Ethan's a stand-up guy to work for. You couldn't ask for a better boss."

"I like the sounds of that."

Logan plated the burgers and side dishes, and loaded up a tray. "This order is ready to go. I'll be right back." He hefted the tray onto his shoulder and carried it to the dining room.

Jack rested against the counter and inhaled, enjoying the few minutes alone to let his thoughts settle. The job was going to work out fine. He knew it. Tomorrow, he'd cook something spectacular and let the rest of the staff at Whiskers' know it, too.

He picked up a menu and perused it. They offered a buffet most mornings. *Perfect.* Breakfast was one of his favourite meals to cook.

Logan returned to the kitchen and set his tray on the counter. "Keep that and look over it. Tomorrow I'll show you how I make the house specialities. Eventually, Ethan'll let you add some of your own dishes, but for now, we'll go with what we have."

Jack nodded his agreement. "Looks like a fine selection. I'd really like to jump in and cook breakfast tomorrow morning. What time can I get started?"

A slow smile spread over Logan's face. "Dining room is open from seven to ten. I usually get here a little before six."

I'll be here by five-thirty. Jack had a lot to prove in the next few days, mainly, how indispensable he was. "I'll be here with bells on."

Logan raised his eyebrows. "Bells? Cool. Anything else?"

"A fresh, clean, Whiskers' polo shirt. If you can find me one." He gave the guy a cheesy grin.

"You got it." Logan glanced around the kitchen. "Wow, you finished the dishes. Thanks. I forgot how nice it is to have help." He piled a plate high with chocolate chip cookies and handed it to Jack. "You can shove off to get your stuff. Stick this on the dessert cart on your way out, will you?"

"Sure. I won't be long. I'll pack a bag for a few days."

"I'll be here. We've got more guests scheduled for dinner. The inn's only about half full right now. We'll be at capacity by the weekend, with all the wedding guests."

Jack took a step towards the door then paused. "If you need any help with those plans, just ask. I'd be happy to anything I can."

"I might do that, thanks. For now, knowing you can take some of the responsibility of the meal shifts is a huge help."

"Glad to do it. See you later."

"You betcha." Logan turned to the stove and fired up a burner.

Jack slipped into the dining room and spotted the dessert cart against one wall. He lifted a silver dome and set the plate of cookies on top of the empty tray. His stomach rumbled, and he tried to remember the last time he'd eaten. With a quick glance around the room, he snatched a couple of cookies and replaced the lid.

He munched on them while walking to his car. The cookies were delicious and probably a big hit with the guests. Jack polished off the last bite and climbed into his sedan. *My recipe will be an even bigger hit.* He baked one hell of a chocolate chip cookie.

Watch out, Whiskers'. Jack Donner's on board, now. He eyed the inn in his rear-view mirror as he drove off, and smiled.

* * * *

Jack burrowed under the covers but jerked wide awake when a pair of warm hands slid up his thighs. He'd gone to sleep alone, in the comfortable bed at the inn. *Did my solitary status changed at some point in the night?* He lifted the blankets to see who was pressing heated kisses in the hollow behind his knee. It was too dark to see properly, but Jack thought he caught a glimpse of red hair.

Terry! Jack didn't know whether to be irritated that his old boyfriend had followed him, or grateful for the attention he'd been sorely lacking. He hadn't seen Terry for months—had no idea why the man would show up now—but he couldn't argue with the lips making their way towards his aching balls. "What the devil are you doing here?" he murmured.

"Shh," came a muffled voice from under the covers. "Relax and let me love you."

Jack's slumbering cock roused to its full size when a warm breath of air wafted over it. He squirmed for a moment, trying to resist the seduction. A laundry list of reasons why Terry *shouldn't* be there flitted through his mind. They'd been through it all months ago, when his lover admitted he didn't want the same things Jack did. Terry was a playboy, plain and simple. He loved men, lots of them, and couldn't resist a new conquest whenever the opportunity presented itself.

Jack had been heartbroken. They'd been lovers for four years, living together the last two. Yet, he had no idea what his partner was really like. The man's curly red hair, black framed glasses and pale, freckled complexion belied his inner self—his true personality. No one had taken Terry for such a lothario. Jack wasn't the only one surprised by the truth. He'd been hurt the most, though.

He opened his mouth to object, until Terry sucked his erection between agile lips. Jack groaned, wanting to push the violator away. Deep in his heart, he wanted to tell Terry to take a hike. Instead, he thrust his hips forward, encouraging the man to swallow his length. "Damn it." Integrity lost out to horny almost every time.

Terry just sucked harder and massaged the heavy ball sac nudging his chin when Jack drove deep.

The touch sent shivers of pleasure through Jack's system. He gave up any attempt to resist the sultry enticement. He'd definitely have to talk with Terry later. Right now, more important things beckoned, like an orgasm so sweet he could almost taste it. It'd be the first non-solo climax in so long. Jack hoped he wouldn't choke Terry with the flood preparing to burst.

He bucked his hips wildly, their old signal that he was close. Terry's nod of encouragement proved the only thing he needed to really let go. The tension in Jack's body shattered, and a wave of cum let loose.

Jack gasped for breath. He shuddered, revelling in the glorious feeling he'd missed for too long. A second spasm followed the first, and another, until he lay empty, sagging against the mattress. Pure pleasure flowed through him and he sighed, never wanting the moment to end.

Terry groaned and climbed up Jack's torso. Before his head emerged from the covers, he grasped Jack's waist and flipped him onto his stomach. Without a word, Terry grabbed a couple of pillows and shoved them beneath Jack's belly.

"Wha—?" Jack muttered, but didn't have the strength, or desire, to complain. His head and arms fell limp to the bed, his ass protruding in the air. "Oh, god."

The ripping of a foil packet prepared him for what was about to happen. Jack closed his eyes when a slick finger circled the rim of his anus, then probed inside. *He's using a rubber. Everything's fine.* He feigned reassuring himself, but secretly he was thrilled beyond belief. He could wank his own willy, had done it often enough, but nothing could replace a skilled ass-reaming.

"Yes." He sighed when more fingers joined the first. He bucked his ass back and forth, pressed it against the digits invading him, practically begging for more.

Terry leant forward, his stomach bent around Jack's back. "I don't think you're quite ready for this."

"Fuck yeah, I'm ready. Come on, man. Let me have it." Jack arched backwards and discovered not only were the fingers gone, Terry had moved away. He shoved the pillows aside, flopped over and sat up, looking around.

The man kneeling at the bottom of the bed wasn't Terry. This fellow had shiny, light brown hair, and a killer smile. He flashed a glimpse of teeth at Jack before he vanished.

Jack blinked. He dropped down on the bed and closed his eyes. When he opened them again, he found the blankets covering him neatly, as they apparently had been all night. Astonished, he looked beneath and spotted a pool of cum on his belly, next to his sticky hand.

It's all been a dream? He sat up and kept going when the cum ran down his body. He stumbled to the bathroom and found a towel to wipe his stomach and fingers. He pounded the wall for the switch and grimaced when the bright lights popped on.

Once his vision adjusted, he stared at himself in the mirror. *A dream.* A fucking sexy one to be sure, but of course, it hadn't been real. He hadn't seen Terry for months and couldn't fathom why the man would even enter his mind. *Or had he?* Jack had assumed the dream was about having sex with Terry, but it definitely wasn't Terry's face he'd seen at the end of the fantasy. *No one I've ever seen before. A pity.* He was a sight to behold.

Jack glanced at the clock on the nightstand. *Four-thirty.* Too early to get up, yet his nerves were jazzed about the new job and he wasn't sure he could get back to sleep. Just as he'd decided to try, something caught his eye in the corner of the main room. He stepped out of the bathroom and followed the movement.

White, cottony *something* floated like a cloud until it settled in the shape of a person. A woman stood in the corner, wearing a long alabaster wedding dress with matching veil.

Jack remembered the man he'd *thought* had been in his room, just moments ago. He blinked, but this visitor didn't disappear.

She stared at him from behind her veil, her eyes filled with sadness.

He studied her. The ornate dress, covered with tiny pearls and fabric flowers, looked old. Its wearer, however, did not. "Who are you?" he asked softly.

She held out both hands, reaching for him. "Charles?" The word sounded like a question rather than an answer.

To his continued amazement, when she moved, the woman and her fancy get-up became transparent. Jack saw the wall right through her.

A Whiskers' ghost! He couldn't believe how calm he felt, but the entity seemed unthreatening. He took a step closer and said slowly, "Well, obviously you're not Charles, so you must be looking for someone. I'm not him, either. I'm afraid I can't help you."

Her expression of sorrow morphed into a scowl. She tossed back the veil, planted her hands on her hips, and took a step towards him.

Jack gasped at his first glimpse of her without the lace barrier. Her young, delicate face had been bruised and bloodied to the point he doubted even her family or friends could recognise her.

"What the devil happened to you?"

Her dark eyes shot sparks of anger. "*He* said he'd never let anything happen to me! *He* told me no one would ever hurt me!"

Jack raised his palms in self-defence. "Someone hurt you. I get that. I'm so sorry, but if you could just—"

"Where is Charles?" she screeched, and flew towards Jack with a rush of wind.

The force knocked him against the bathroom door. He crumpled to the floor in a heap. He tried to stand but thought better of it when the ghost tore through the room, knocking over furniture and shattering glass.

As quickly as the whirlwind began, it stopped. Jack clutched the wall and looked around, but the woman was gone. He got to his feet and hurried to the door. Opening it, he glanced both ways down the hall. *Not a soul in sight.*

He closed and locked the door, then rested his back against it. Jack took a moment to catch his breath, then chuckled when he realised he was stark naked. *Good thing no one was there.* He gazed around the messy room, deciding it could wait until later. He'd planned to get to work at five-thirty, and it was nearly five.

Gingerly stepping around broken glass, Jack headed for the shower. He was ready to hit the kitchen and start work. Getting as far away as possible from this room didn't sound like a bad idea, either. He entered the shower and turned on the water.

Chapter Two

Half an hour later, Jack entered the dark, quiet kitchen. He found the lights and proceeded to pull out the pots, pans and utensils he expected to use. A notebook with Logan's recipes lay on the counter, and when Jack had completed all the initial prep, he leafed through it.

Muffins. Several different kinds. He guessed they'd offer at least three choices daily, so he whipped out the mixing bowls and began.

The kitchen aroma was wonderful when Logan arrived just before six. "Good morning!" He inhaled the scent of fresh baking. "Banana nut muffins?"

"Hey." Jack nodded. "Yep, and blueberry. With your approval, I was going to make some chocolate chip, too."

Logan washed his hands and joined Jack at the counter. He pinched off a bite of a cooling banana muffin and tasted it. His eyes rolled back in his head, and he quickly reached for another bite. "Oh my god. I'm in love."

Jack grinned. "Can I take that as a yes?"

"Absolutely. Cade loves chocolate chip muffins. Go for it. I need you to make one batch of regular bran, too. Delia will raise hell if she doesn't get a bran muffin with her breakfast."

"Bran, sure." Jack found the recipe in the notebook and marked the page. "Who's Delia?"

Logan shoved the last of the muffin into his mouth, and washed his hands again. "Delia Nelson is the inn's only permanent guest. She lives in the last room upstairs. She's a tiny little thing, but don't let her stature fool you. Delia's cranky as hell on a good day."

"Great." Jack's gut churned. After everything that'd taken place that morning, he was beginning to wonder exactly what he'd gotten himself into.

"Don't worry about her." Logan nudged his elbow against Jack's. "She'll warm up once she gets to know you. If you ever have a problem with her, just go through Cade. He's got Delia wrapped around his little finger."

Jack thought of the handsome man with the long, blond ponytail. "I can see why." He cleared his throat. "I, uh, I'll remember that."

Logan laughed. He removed food from the refrigerator as he talked. "So, how was your first night at Whiskers'? Sleep well?"

Jack hesitated and wondered how much he should share with the other cook. "Yes, at first. Then I had this really weird dream. And when I woke up…" He paused. The story was too weird to say out loud, even to him. He shook his head. "I saw something. I dunno."

"A ghost?" Logan's eyes lit up. "Was it Ben, the fisherman? You can't miss ol' Ben. He leaves a fish stench that's unbelievable."

"No, it wasn't a fisherman. I'm not sure exactly what I saw." The more Jack thought about it, the more he realised none of it could be believed. He'd surely been imagining things.

"Was it Laura? Little girl, wears a flannel nightgown, with long, black hair. You can usually hear a music box playing when she's around."

"Shit." Jack shoved the next batch of muffins into the oven. "No, it wasn't a little girl. It was a bride, okay? A woman in a fancy wedding dress. Only when she lifted her veil…"

The kitchen door swung open and Ethan joined them. "Good morning, gentlemen. Smells like someone got an early start today."

Jack's description of the ghost trailed off, and he floundered for something to say.

"It's all Jack," Logan spoke up. "He makes one hell of a muffin. I'm getting ready to check his omelette skills."

"Wonderful!" Ethan grabbed a napkin and looked over the muffins. "Logan, the reverend is stopping by around eight to talk about the ceremony. If you think Jack can handle it in here, I'd like you to sit in on the meeting." He chose a blueberry and smelled it, a wide smile spreading over his face.

"I'm pretty sure Jack can handle things." Logan covered the rest of the muffins protectively, as if he hadn't been the first one to sample the wares.

Ethan winked at Jack and headed back into the dining room. "I think so, too. See you all later."

"Yeah, you bet." Jack finally found his voice and turned to Logan. "Where's your omelette pan?"

"On top of the fridge. Don't ever let me see you using it for something else."

Jack nodded and went to retrieve the large, slope-sided skillet. "Any particular kind you want?"

"Surprise me," Logan said as he loaded muffins onto a tray and headed into the dining room. "I've got to fill the buffet tables." He exited the room and Jack reached for a metal bowl to break eggs into. In another skillet, he fried sliced mushrooms and ham. He finished and slid the fluffy mass onto a warmed plate, sprinkling it with parsley.

Logan poked his head in and asked, "When did you get the coffee going?"

Jack looked up from the stove. "Maybe twenty minutes ago."

"Excellent, the breakfast herd is just beginning to arrive."

Jack handed the freshly made omelette to Logan and watched while the blond-haired man took a large bite. A second forkful followed and finally a nod of approval. "Nice, I like the way you fried the ham with the mushrooms."

"Thanks."

Logan dropped his dishes into the dishwasher and nodded towards the dining room. "There's still a little to do out there."

Between the two of them, they quickly brought a variety of cereal, packets of instant oatmeal and a selection of fruit to the buffet tables. Logan filled containers while Jack watched and soaked up information. The next time he looked at the clock, it was almost eight.

"I'm going to clean up," Logan said, slapping Jack's back in a friendly manner as he headed into the kitchen.

Jack followed, but one of the guests called him back. After taking care of the man's request, he glanced around. The room was filling fast. Two couples sat at small tables along the wall, a family of four occupied a table in the centre of the room. A small group of people stood in front of the buffet table, talking and picking up their morning fare.

He checked the coffee urn and after deciding it was still at least half full, returned to stand by the kitchen door.

An older woman strode into the room, fluffy white hair like a halo around her stern face. She wore a blue-flowered dress that reminded him of a tablecloth. An oversized, tan-coloured handbag hung from her arm and fuzzy pink slippers finished her ensemble.

From over his shoulder Logan said, "Ah, there's our Mrs. Nelson."

Jack looked back. "The permanent resident you mentioned?"

Logan smoothed the clean shirt over his chest and down over his torso. "Yes, that's the one, Delia Nelson. Nice lady, but a little batty sometimes."

Jack smiled. "I guess, at her age, she's got a right to be exactly how she wants."

"Probably."

Delia went directly to the corner table and sat down. Her eyes moved around the room as if expecting *something*. She placed her handbag on the table and rested her hands on top.

"Seems she'd like service today," Logan said in a hushed voice. "Come on, I'll introduce you." He eased passed Jack and walked across the room.

Jack followed, and they both stopped when they reached Delia's side.

"Good morning, Mrs. Nelson." Logan bowed ever so slightly and shuffled to the side, apparently wanting Jack to be clearly visible. "I hope you slept well."

"Humph, I always sleep well. Unless those dratted spirits act up." She turned her attention on Jack and asked, "And who are you?"

Taken aback, it took a second for Jack to reply. "I'm Jack, ma'am. Jack Donner. I'm here to take over the cook's position when Logan moves on."

The old woman eyed him from tip to toe, then peered into his eyes. "You're another one, aren't you?"

Still unsure of her place at the inn, Jack answered as kindly as he knew how. "Another what, ma'am? I'm a chef. That's all."

"Do you believe in the spirits, boy?" Delia snapped impatiently.

"Uh, I'm not sure," he replied uncertainly. *What the hell is she after?*

"Humph, yup, another doubter. I knew it." The old woman glanced through the window, then back to him. "I'll have my usual. You do know what that is, don't you?"

Jack glanced at Logan who smiled. When he looked back at the woman, she hadn't shifted her gaze away from him.

"A bran muffin and tea," he ventured, knowing he was at least right on the muffin.

"Yes, and be quick. I'd like the muffin warm, with lots of butter on the side."

"Yes, ma'am." Jack hurried to the kitchen, where he knew there were still a couple of dozen bran muffins ready to be put out. He microwaved the muffin and plated it, adding three pats of butter and a pot of tea on the side for the snippety woman.

On the way out, he saw Logan chatting with someone just inside the entrance to the inn and stopped dead in his tracks. The guy was gorgeous. Slim built and wearing a pair of jeans and a dark shirt. The man's light-brown hair lay in waves around his head. He wasn't really tall, just a nice height. But when he looked up and Jack saw his eyes, it was as if the world centred on him.

Logan took a few steps towards him.

Across the dining room, Delia called, "Is that my tea getting cold?"

Jack gave himself a shake and looked over at the woman. She sat with her hands still clasped and a stern look aimed his way.

"Oh, she's going to be a treat," he mumbled under his breath, but quickly approached the woman.

"Is the tea hot?" she snapped and took the pot from the tray. Without waiting for him to reply, she lifted the lid and peered inside, giving an aggravated *humph*. "It'll do, I suppose."

Sitting back, she waited while he placed her plated muffin on the table in front of her, the cup and saucer to her right.

"Will that be all, Mrs. Nelson?" Jack stepped back and stood quietly. Inside he wanted to strangler the obnoxious old twit. Instead, he smiled.

"That's all. Thank you."

Jack turned away, but before he could take a step, a hand grasped his wrist. He looked down and saw it was hers. "Yes?"

"Be careful, young man. Strange things can happen here. Don't let your stubbornness blind you." She released his arm and went about buttering her muffin as if he'd vanished from her presence.

Confused, but satisfied Delia wasn't going to stop him again, Jack gazed around the room until he spotted Logan and the man he'd been talking to. Logan saw him and motioned him to them.

"Jack, this is Quinn Stevens, the reverend Ethan mentioned." He stepped back, giving Jack an excuse to move closer to the handsome newcomer. "Quinn, this is Jack Donner, the cook who's going to take over for me."

Quinn's Blessing

Hand extended, Jack shook hands with Quinn and said, "Nice to meet you." *A reverend, well that takes care of any lusty thoughts I might have had.*

"Nice to meet you too, Mr. Donner."

The handshake was firm. The tingling sensation going up his arm came close to making Jack swoon. The man definitely got his motor running, and he'd have to watch what he let out of his mouth for sure.

"Jack, think you can handle this crowd while Quinn and I go talk to Ethan and Cade?"

"Sure can. If I can't find something, where will you be?" He glanced around but didn't see anything that looked like a conference room.

"Here," Logan grabbed him by the arm and guided him into the lobby. Facing the reception desk, he pointed to a door behind it and said, "That's Ethan's office. Yell if you need anything."

"Got it." Jack stepped back and bumped into someone behind him. He whirled then gulped. Quinn stood there, a smile on his face.

"Oh, sorry!" The handsome reverend moved away but not far.

"My fault. I should look before I walk into people." His face grew warm and he knew it had to be a nice rosy shade of red. The feel of the man's firm body pressing against his, even if only for a second, had Jack's thoughts diving below the belt.

He looked into Quinn's eyes and a flash of recognition made him falter. The reverend reminded him of someone, but for the life of him, he couldn't put his finger on who. The waves in his hair begged touching, and he clenched his fists to keep from reaching up and smoothing a wayward curl lying across the man's forehead.

"Might be better, if you didn't walk into them at all." Quinn's smile widened.

Jack's face grew even warmer. He opened his mouth to apologise again, but the words wouldn't come out. He nodded, and trying to hang onto the last shred of dignity, he turned back towards the kitchen. After a few steps, he glanced over his shoulder. Quinn stood looking at him, that enigmatic smile still plastered on his face.

Where have I seen that face before? "I'll try that. It might be a better idea after all," Jack managed to say.

Logan took Quinn by the arm, and after a final look towards Jack, the two men entered Ethan's office. Once the door closed, Jack took a much-needed breath.

"Wow!" he mouthed as a shudder went through him. He hadn't felt such a rush from a man in a very long time. It was a great feeling, but knowing the guy was a reverend definitely put the brakes on anything more than just looking, and dreaming.

The breakfast crowd never got a lot bigger, but calls for more muffins came steadily for the next hour. Jack was glad he'd made so many. He prepared several orders of the breakfast platter and talked to Delia a little more. She seemed an odd duck, but nice enough in her own snippety way. He refilled the fruit bowl once and added more coffee to the urn twice before things slacked off.

While clearing away the refuse from where a family had sat, he looked up and saw Ethan, Cade and Quinn standing outside the office. Logan was just returning to the kitchen.

Again, Jack's interest centred on the reverend. To his surprise, his cock pulsed against his jeans and thickened. With a tray full of dirty dishing in his hands, he couldn't do much about it. He took a step and bowled into Logan.

Both of them scrambled for the dishes skittering off his tray.

"Damn!" Jack backed up and reached for a cup heading for the edge of the tray. Capturing it, he sighed. "Sorry. This is getting to be a habit. Falling over people, I mean. A habit I better break or you're going to think I'm a complete klutz."

Logan placed a plate he'd caught back on Jack's tray. "You were fine until...hey wait, until Quinn showed up."

Jack would have given anything if he could have come up with a smart retort to Logan's comment. But, he couldn't. "Yeah, well, he's pretty hot. You have to admit that."

"He sure is. And he's available, as far as I know."

Not ready to get cornered into talking relationships or personal trivia, Jack changed the subject. "How'd the meeting go? The plans should be nailed down by this time."

"They are, mostly. If they'd just stop adding to the menu, I'd be one happy camper."

Jack walked over to the dishwasher and loaded the contents of the tray into it. The guests had left the dining room in a shambles, so he headed back out immediately. Across the room, Quinn stood looking down at the buffet table.

Forcing himself to take a deep breath, Jack approached the man. When he stopped within arm's reach, he asked, "See anything you like?"

Quinn turned and faced him. "Yeah, I do."

Jack's mouth went dry. He fumbled with the cloth in his hands, suddenly feeling like a school kid caught with his fingers in something they shouldn't be in. The man had a way of befuddling him that was for sure. He looked passed Quinn and saw most of the trays were next to empty. "Can I get you some breakfast, Reverend?"

"Quinn," the man said and smiled. "The name's Quinn."

Jack's stomach did flip-flops. The smile—he knew where he'd seen it. He was sure. *The face in the night.* The man in his bed. But, how could that be? *I must be crazy!*

"And yes, I'd love some breakfast, if it's not too much trouble. I left home early and didn't get the chance to have any." Quinn strode to one of the cleared tables by the window.

He followed, eagerly. When Quinn sat down, Jack asked, "Coffee or tea?"

"Coffee, please. And whatever's left from the breakfast rush. I'm not a picky eater."

Jack couldn't get past the realisation that he'd seen the man in his dreams. Felt his mouth and hands on him. Fuzzy headed, he struggled to make sense of the man's words. He finally managed a weak, "I'll see what's in the kitchen."

"Good enough."

Jack headed for the kitchen, his mind in a jumble of lusty memories from the night before. By the time he got there, his cock was ready to burst through his jeans.

Logan looked at him and tilted his head. "What's up? You look like you're in la-la land."

"The Reverend, Quinn, he…" He let the words trail off, not sure he should go any further. He didn't know Logan all that well and wasn't sure what the cook would say about his dream.

"Quinn's a good guy. From what I've been able to gather, he's been a friend of Cade's for a while."

Jack's thoughts raced. "He wants breakfast. Does he eat here often? Do you know what he likes? How well do you know him?" He clamped his mouth shut, stopping the barrage of inane questions before they became uncontrollable.

Logan grabbed the skillet off the stove and rinsed it. The counters were cleared, most of the breakfast turmoil cleared up already. "No, he doesn't eat here often, but I'm sure he'll be around more, at least until the wedding. I've no idea what he likes to eat." Using the dishcloth, he wiped down one of the long counters. Over his shoulder, he said, "I'd take him a couple of those muffins you made this morning, if there's any left."

"Good idea," Jack grabbed three muffins and set them in the microwave. Once they were warm, he plated them and added a small pile of butter pats. On the way to Quinn's table, he filled a mug of coffee.

"Here you go." He set the plate and cup in front of the reverend. "Fresh baked this morning. I'll be happy to whip you up some eggs or bacon or something."

Quinn waved a hand. "No, thanks. This is fine." He inhaled the aroma of the warm muffins and nodded, a look of satisfaction on his face. He cocked an eyebrow at Jack. "Can you join me for a few minutes?"

Jack's heart leapt, but sank just as quickly when he glanced around the messy dining room. "I'd love to, but I've got to finish cleaning up in here."

As Jack spoke, Logan came through the swinging door with a tray in hand.

"Sit, I'll get this. You did an amazing job with breakfast. Take a load off and I'll finish the dishes."

"I couldn't let you—"

"Listen, I won't be around much longer, so take advantage while you can. Grab a break, and report back to the kitchen in an hour or so. We'll start prepping the noon meal."

"Okay, thanks." Jack nodded appreciatively at Logan and slid into the chair across from Quinn. "That was nice," he said when Logan had returned to the other room. "I feel kind of guilty, though."

"You know what they say about gift horses. Sit back, relax and enjoy." Quinn bit into a muffin and, a moment later, closed his eyes, apparently savouring the first bite. He swallowed and looked at Jack. "This is incredible. Are you this talented at everything you do?"

Jack felt the warmth of yet another blush and fumbled for the appropriate answer. Before he could come up with anything, Quinn let him off the hook.

"Cooking, I mean."

"Oh, Jesus." He exhaled, trying to focus. "Shit, I shouldn't have said that! God, I'm sorry." He dropped his head to his hands and clamped his mouth shut, to keep from compounding one more wrong phrase after the others he'd blurted.

"I'm just saying, I do okay in the kitchen, but this...I'm impressed you're such a good cook. And really, really easy to fluster. I think that's cute."

Jack glanced up at him and detected an ornery gleam in the light-brown eyes. "Are you really a reverend? Because I think you're kind of mischievous to be a man of the cloth."

Quinn shrugged. "Hey, no one ever said God doesn't have a sense of humour. My mother would tell you that allowing me to be a reverend is the perfect example of his irony. I gave her more than my share of trouble growing up. She's forgiven me, but she doesn't let me forget it."

Jack grinned and leant back, studying the handsome hunk. "She sounds like a special woman."

"She is. I'm not embarrassed to say that I love my mom. My father died in a car accident when I was seventeen. It was a huge blow to the whole family. I have a younger sister and brother, and we all tried to help out. But, Mom stepped up and took care of whatever needed to be done. She saw the three of us through college, and supported me when I told her I was gay. Never batted an eyelash. I've always been grateful for that. Some kids don't have it so easy."

Gay, and not afraid to say so. The longer they talked, the more Jack liked the reverend. "You're right about that. I didn't have major problems with my parents, although I'm not sure my dad was thrilled when he first found out. He got used to it." Jack hesitated. "I'm sorry about your dad. Think he would have accepted your being gay, too?"

Quinn looked thoughtful for a moment, then smiled slyly. "Oh, sure. After he bitched and moaned up one side of me and down the other. Once he finally realised there was nothing he could do to change me, he'd have been fine."

Jack laughed. "That sounds about right."

"So what about you?" Quinn asked. "Parents still around? Any brothers or sisters?"

"Oh, yeah. One of each, both in college. Folks still kicking around in the same house I grew up in, a couple of hours away from here. They're good people."

"Nice." Quinn finished his breakfast and pushed the plate back from the edge of the table. He emptied his coffee cup and set it down. "So, you're the new cook here at Whiskers'." It was a statement rather than a question. "I like Ethan and Cade, but I'm not sure I'd want to work here."

Jack looked at him thoughtfully. The reverend had apparently heard about the spirits. He had the urge to tell the man about his encounter that morning. "I haven't officially been hired, yet. I'm still in trial mode. But, yeah,

I'm wondering about this place, myself. I hadn't given it much thought, but when I woke up, something fuc—" He caught himself, "*freaking* weird happened."

He paused as Logan returned to clear the last of the tables.

Quinn looked at Logan, then at Jack. "Would you like to get out of here for a while? We could take a short walk. You'll be back in plenty of time."

"Yes, I would." Jack exhaled with relief. He stood and told the other cook, "Back soon."

"Have fun," Logan called without looking their way.

"Not sure we have *that* much time." Quinn opened the door leading to the beach and held it so Jack could pass in front of him.

The words sent a tingle of excitement through him as he brushed past the reverend. Quinn had made a couple of flirty comments, and Jack wondered if it was something more than casual banter. His cock twitched at the idea. He wondered about being forthright, and bringing up the subject. He thought about it as they strolled towards the beach, walking comfortably side by side.

Quinn spoke first. "I got the feeling you'd be more comfortable talking outside the inn. Did something happen? You see something?"

"Yeah." Jack kicked a small rock as he walked. "This morning, I had a really strange dream. It was—" He remembered seeing Quinn's face and suddenly felt too embarrassed to talk about it. "Never mind, it's not important. But when I got up, there was someone standing in my room. A woman, in a fancy wedding gown. It was frilly, but it looked like it was really old."

"No kidding?" Quinn looked at him with obvious interest. "What did she look like?"

Relief swept through Jack. *Quinn believes me.* He'd wondered if anyone would. "At first she seemed transparent. I could look right through her. But when she lifted her veil, I saw her plain as day. She was a frigging mess, battered and bloody. I don't know if she'd been in an accident, or if someone beat the shit out of her. Damn, I'm sorry."

Quinn stopped and turned to face him. "Look, Jack. I'm a man, not just a man of the cloth. Whatever words slip out of your mouth, I've heard them all before. So could you stop apologising every time you swear? You're making me self-conscious, like I need to watch what I say, too."

"Sorry," Jack said sincerely, then realised he'd just apologised again. "Well, fuck."

Quinn batted his lashes. "I'm still not sure we have that much time. I'll take a rain check, though."

"You are bad!" Jack poked his finger into Quinn's chest. He was sure his face was beet red, but he no longer cared. This guy was obviously coming on to him, and it was the best thing he'd heard in ages.

"Oh, yeah." Quinn clutched Jack's hand and lowered it so he could press their bodies together. "I could be very bad with you. But I don't just fall into bed with every hunky stud I meet. I have a reputation to uphold, you know."

Jack stared into Quinn's eyes. "Now you're toying with me. I'm more of an 'average Joe' than a 'hunky stud,' and I'd do nothing for your reputation."

"I'll be the judge of that, on all counts. Maybe we could have a late dinner after your shift tonight? If you're not too tired."

"I won't be tired." Jack had trouble getting his breath. He wondered if it conveyed his extreme horniness as his cock thickened and grew hard in his slacks. "A late dinner sounds good."

Quinn pressed his groin against Jack's, proving there were two erections in play. "I can call you later, see how your day is going, and we can firm up the time."

Jack groaned. "Firm up. Yeah."

The reverend gazed into his eyes for a moment, and Jack steeled himself for a kiss. Instead, Quinn pulled back and released his hold on Jack's hand. "Tell me more about your visitor this morning. A bloody bride?"

Jack frantically tried to shift gears. He cleared his throat and willed his erection to fade. "Yeah. She was in rough shape. Angry, too. Asking for somebody named Charles. She said he'd promised he'd never hurt her. The more she spoke, the more she worked herself up. Ended up flying around the room, breaking things and trashing the place. Knocked me into the wall. It was incredible."

Quinn's expression changed to concern. "Were you hurt?"

It felt good to have someone care enough to ask. "No. Just a little freaked out. I cleaned up and got the hell out of there."

"Did you tell Ethan?"

He shook his head. "Once I got to work, I guess I forgot to mention it."

"You should tell him. Seriously, he needs to know stuff like that. I've heard about some of the spirits at the inn, but never anything about a bride."

"Lucky me." Jack smiled wryly.

Quinn glanced down Jack's body and back up again. "I don't know. I think I might be the lucky one." He kissed Jack lightly on the lips and backed away just as quickly. "I need to leave now, before I don't want to go."

Jack feigned a frown. "What am I supposed to do?"

Quinn smiled. "Go tell Ethan about the ghost, then cook up a storm for Logan, so you'll land this job. I think I'd like you to stick around awhile."

"I can do that."

Quinn winked, then turned and headed for the parking lot. "Talk to you later," he called over his shoulder.

"Planning on it!" Jack stood there a moment, gathering his bearings. His day had definitely taken a turn for the better. He went inside, mulling things around in his mind. He'd done well at breakfast—Logan had confirmed that. If he could pull off a smooth noon meal, he'd have the job sewed up, which seemed more important now than ever.

After only three strides into the dining room, Ethan's stern voice rang out and he halted.

"Jack! Spare a minute, please?"

It doesn't sound like a request. Jack turned and followed the voice to the check-in desk. "Hey, Ethan. I was just on a short break. Logan said I could take a few minutes—"

"Yeah, no problem." He waved a hand. "What *is* a problem was the condition housekeeping found your room in this morning. Broken glass, the linens shredded to shit. Have a rough night?"

Housekeeping. Fuck! Not used to staying in a hotel, he'd forgotten the cleaning staff entirely. "Damn, I'm sorry about that. I had a little trouble this morning. I was in kind of a hurry to get out. Once I started working, I guess I forgot to say anything."

"Or didn't want to mention it." Ethan folded his arms across his chest. "Look, I know there's a lot going on here right now with the wedding and all. But I'm still running this place, and if anyone has a problem, be it a guest or a *potential* staff member, I want to know."

"I'm sorry." Jack plastered an appropriately repentant expression on his face. He briefly retold the story of the bride ghost, and how she seemed determined to get even with someone named Charles.

"Hmm." Ethan scratched his head. "Angry Annie is the only adult female spirit I've seen around here. I've never seen her in a wedding dress, because she never made it to the altar. She can screw her face up to look like an ugly thing, but she's otherwise very pretty. I don't believe she was ever battered in any way."

"Doesn't sound like the same woman."

"That's curious. Where the blazes did she come from?" Ethan looked at him as if he expected an answer.

"I don't know. I'm sorry."

Ethan waved a hand. "Stop apologising. I don't expect you to know. It's just rotten timing on her part, with the wedding and all." His eyes lit up and a thoughtful expression crossed his face. "Unless, that's exactly why she's here."

Chapter Three

For the rest of the day, Jack's mind wandered from the success of the meal prep, back to the events of the previous night. The ease with which Ethan had accepted his explanation surprised him, but not a great deal when he thought about the inn's history. Even so, the idea of her being a 'new' ghost intrigued him, as much as he hated to admit it.

People came, ate, then left quietly for the most part. Jack managed to grab a bite just before the evening meal and was ready for anything when the diners trickled in. The occasional squeal of a child punctuated the passing of time, until the dining room finally emptied but for the dirty dishes and slightly littered floor.

"You get the dishes, I'll do the floors," Logan said on his way through the door.

"Yup." Jack followed with a tray and began clearing the tables while the cook ran a sweeper. Glancing outside, he saw the sun on the horizon and sighed with relief. The workday was nearly done. He knew he'd done well and hoped Logan agreed.

They loaded the dishwasher and stored the remains of the meal in the large fridge. Logan sank his hands into the sink and scrubbed the few pots they'd used. Jack dried and learnt where everything went in the nearby cupboards.

"You did a good job today," Logan said quietly.

Jack smiled at the man. "Thanks. It felt good. This place grows on you."

"Yeah, I think you're right."

About to say something else, Jack was surprised into silence when a voice called from the doorway.

"Looks like I got here right on time."

Jack turned and smiled at the handsome reverend peering through the open door. "Yeah, we're just finishing up. Five minutes earlier and we'd have put you to work."

Quinn took a few steps into the room and crossed his arms over his chest. "You'd do that too, wouldn't you?"

Grinning, Jack replied, "You bet."

Quinn's smile widened and he nodded. "Good. Now, are you ready to take off for a while, or do you have more to do?"

Jack looked at Logan and tilted his head to the side. "Do I?"

"Nope, you're done for today. Be here at six in the morning and prep for breakfast."

"Hey, I did have great timing," Quinn laughed and reached for Jack's arm. "Come on, let's go for a walk on the beach."

Ready to say yes, Jack remembered Ethan's comments about his room and changed courses mid-thought. "I want to check my room before I go anywhere else. Do you mind?"

"Heck, no." Quinn grabbed him by the upper arm and pulled. "I've been looking forward to spending more time with you since we talked this morning."

Jack's face heated up and he hurried out of the kitchen before Logan had a chance to say anything, or hopefully see how red he got when he blushed. With Quinn still holding onto his arm, the two of them walked across the dining room and into the lobby before Jack slowed down.

"You don't mince words," he halfway chided Quinn.

"I've been told that before, a time or two." He chuckled and dragged Jack back until they were walking side by side. "I guess I like to catch people off guard. Makes for some very honest responses."

"I bet, and some very red faces. Jeeze!" He stopped and faced the reverend, and again wanted to sink into the man's beautiful eyes. "If you want to wait here, I'll be back in a flash. Just want to make sure everything's okay in my room." He didn't want to get into details about the ghostly bride again. He had other things on his mind.

"Sure, I'll be outside. I feel like I've been cooped up in here way too much lately." Quinn gave Jack's arm a squeeze, then turned towards the door.

Jack made his way down the hall and stopped in front of the room he'd been assigned. Apprehension gripped him. Would the battered bride be there? Was the room going to be trashed again?

"Oh for fuck's sake, just open the door," he muttered to himself and turned the knob.

The room was clean, the bed made and no sign of the apparition. He stepped inside and peered around— nothing, and no one. He even went into the bathroom, just in case, but nothing seemed out of the ordinary. He quickly changed into a clean T-shirt and tossed the soiled one on the floor at the foot of the bed. He reached into the bedside table and fisted several foil packets, which he thrust into the pocket of his jeans.

With a last look around, he hurried to the exit, anxious to be with the handsome reverend. A chill went down his spine as he opened the inn's front door.

Outside, Quinn turned and faced him. "Everything okay?"

Pushing thoughts of the bride from his mind, Jack approached Quinn. "Sure is. Just wanted to put on a fresh T-shirt."

Quinn eyed him up and down then trapped him with his gaze. "You look good enough to eat."

The remark caught Jack off guard and he again felt his face grow warm. The reverend definitely enjoyed teasing. Rather than shy away from it this time, he knew he had to dive in and get as good as he got. "You haven't even seen the meal yet."

He smiled when the man's jaw dropped.

It took Quinn a moment, but his comeback made Jack shiver.

"I'm hoping to get a peek soon." The reverend winked.

Raising his hands in surrender, Jack said, "Okay, I give up. You win. Can we go for that walk before I embarrass myself further?"

Quinn laughed and reached for Jack's arm. "Come on, let's hit the beach. We'll walk and…" He winked at Jack again, this time with more meaning, "maybe I'll get that peek I mentioned."

"You're definitely pulling my leg."

Jack allowed Quinn to grip his upper arm and guide him towards the end of the building. A walkway appeared and they wandered down it to a large lawn and garden. Cade poked his head out from behind the hedge and waved, but didn't call him over or say anything.

"It's really cool to see Cade and Ethan getting married. Gay men don't usually have that pleasure." Jack's thoughts went to his last relationship, but he quickly thrust it aside and smiled at Quinn. "I don't think I've ever met a gay man of the cloth, either."

"It happens, probably more than you'd think. Like I said before, we're human."

"I guess. But when I think of religion, I think celibate. Most people do, I assume."

"Depends on the religion, but yeah, I think you're right. For many of us, celibacy went the way of the dinosaur. We can get married, have kids, and being gay isn't an issue, thankfully. Of course, I'm still expected to be respectful, and public displays of lust are frowned on." He stopped and looked at Jack, a twinkle in his eyes.

"So screwing in broad daylight outside city hall is out, I take it?" Jack was determined to be just as brazen as Quinn.

"Yes, but if it should happen, I'm to blame it on celestial intervention, or some such weirdness."

They continued walking, and when Jack managed to tear his eyes off the luscious man who seemed determined to get his goat, he realised they were on the beach. He paused and looked first one way, then the other. In the distance, he spotted a lighthouse on the end of a finger of rocks.

"This way." Quinn's voice cut into Jack's musing.

Jack remembered hearing about the lighthouse and the sexy keeper there. Turning back to his own hunky partner, he nodded. "Hang on, I want to get out of these first." He sat down in the sand and unlaced the heavy work boots he'd been wearing all day. He stuffed a sweaty sock into each boot, laced them up and slung them over his shoulder before climbing to his feet. Quinn had also slipped out of his shoes and socks, but held them in his left hand.

Taking a chance, Jack reached for Quinn's free hand and took hold. He held his breath for a moment, wondering if he'd pushed too far, too fast. A gentle squeeze reassured him and together they headed along the smooth sand.

Waves crashed a few feet away and every few paces a rush of water covered his feet and crept towards Quinn's. They talked very little, both seeming to enjoy the peaceful serenity of their surroundings. Half an hour later, they'd outdistanced anyone from the inn, or anywhere else it seemed. They had the beach to themselves. The occasional squawk of a seagull and the movement of the water across the sand were the only sounds.

Jack stopped and let his boots drop. "So, no screwing on Main Street. What about in the woods, or on the beach?" He pulled Quinn around and rested his forearms on the other man's shoulders.

The look on Quinn's face was priceless—mouth gaped, eyes wide and a rich red creeping up his face. Jack fought to keep from laughing, but lost the battle when the man closed his mouth, then tried to speak. Nothing came out, and Jack's laughter exploded.

A few moments later, Quinn managed to say, "Damn!" The two of them shared a good belly laugh.

Their merriment came to an end slowly. Jack took a chance and leaned in, brushing his lips against Quinn's. That first taste made Jack's head spin. Peppermint and man, and the soft breathiness of surprised pleasure, were more than he'd dared hope for.

Jack slid his hands down Quinn's sides to his waist. Gripping the belt, he had the perfect hold to draw the sexy man closer. His cock pulsed to thick hardness and he couldn't help but rub himself against the reverend's crotch. The responding bulge pressing against him encouraged him to continue. Parting his lips, Jack flicked his tongue out, truly tasting Quinn for the first time.

Hands caressed Jack's hips then his ass, pulling him tight against Quinn's firm body. Head spinning, Jack wanted more. Frantically, he fought the buttons holding Quinn's shirt closed. When each parted, he went to the next, until all were unfastened and it took nothing more than a gentle push to bare the man's upper body.

"Oh yeah," Jack murmured, their lips still touching. He struggled out of his T-shirt, tossing it over a nearby log. Pulling back, just enough to speak properly, he said, "I want you naked. I want..." The words trailed off when he realised he wasn't sure how to tell the man what he really wanted.

Quinn smiled at him and leant forward to steal a kiss. "Me naked? Bending you over to fuck your brains out?"

My thoughts exactly. "Yeah, that's it." He reached for the button and zipper holding his jeans up. Once unfastened, he pushed both them and his underpants down, eager to shed the last barrier. Eyes glued to Quinn, he inhaled sharply when the man's cock came into view. Long and thick, Jack instantly wanted to touch the hefty tube of flesh. As he watched, it bounced upward, its single eye weeping a pearl-like droplet of nectar.

When he'd tossed his jeans aside, Jack dropped to his knees in front of Quinn and reached around the man's thighs. Pulling him closer, Jack inhaled the musky man scent and swallowed the saliva suddenly filling his mouth. He pressed a kiss to the moist tip of Quinn's cock head then looked up into the man's eyes. "Fuck soon. Right now, I need to taste you."

Quinn slipped his fingers through Jack's hair and in a husky voice, replied, "You'll make me come if you're not careful."

"Wouldn't be such a bad thing." Excitement soaring, Jack leaned in and opened his mouth.

The tip of Quinn's cock touched his lips and Jack blew out a gust of air. The man's cock pulsed and pressed its smooth head against Jack's lips a moment before he sucked it in. The salty taste filled his mouth.

"Oh my..." Quinn stroked Jack's head and hunched his hips back and forth.

The gentle fucking motion sent a renewed thrill down Jack's spine. With his mouth full, he couldn't respond other than by sucking the reverend's dick in even deeper. The long shaft slowly sank in, until Quinn's balls pressed against Jack's chin. The curly black hair tickled his face as the smooth round sac shifted, the balls pulling in tight. Jack ran his tongue around the root of the man's cock, savouring the firmness and the way the head pulsed at the back of his mouth. The large dome seemed to be seeking entrance to his throat and there was nothing Jack wanted more. He relaxed the muscles keeping it out and groaned when the head slid in. He swallowed, which he knew squeezed the organ tight.

Before he gagged, Jack pulled back, licking the full length of Quinn's shaft until just the crown rested on his lips. He licked it then sucked the member in again, taking it all. For the next few minutes, Jack did everything in his less than extensive repertoire to excite Quinn as much as he could, without forcing the sexy man to climax. His own cock rubbed against his inner thigh, constantly reminding him of how much he needed to come himself. He refrained, by sheer will.

"Stop, for fuck's sakes. Stop or I'm going to lose it," Quinn gasped, his hands dragging at Jack's head.

Jack relented, but only after sampling another healthy trickle of pre-cum. He sat back on his heels and reached for his own cock with one hand, and Quinn's with the other. "I love the salty tang of you."

"And I love what you're doing to me, but I want more." Quinn gazed into Jack's eyes, a feverish glow showing his pleasure. He reached down and slid his hands under Jack's arms, pulling him to his feet. "I don't have anything…a condom," he stammered and looked guilty.

Jack released both cocks and bent to his jeans, digging into his pockets. He fumbled around, finally locating the foil packets he'd concealed there. "I do. Always prepared, for something like that."

He got to his feet and looked into Quinn's gorgeous eyes, "You said something about fucking my brains out. Still want that?" He gave the man a crooked grin.

"More than ever." Quinn reached for the packet and tore it open with his teeth while Jack stroked them both. His own cock felt like iron. Quinn's like silk covered steel.

"Turn around." Quinn's voice sounded harsh.

Without hesitation, Jack spun and leant forward, resting his hands on the log he'd slung his jeans over. The sand shifted and he tensed his legs and ass, realising the lewd display only after hearing Quinn groan.

Jack smiled wickedly and wiggled his ass a little more. His cheekiness came to a screeching halt when the warm wetness of a tongue slid between his ass cheeks. Hands spread his glutes, gently massaging them while Quinn went to work on his quivering anus.

"Oh my god," he mumbled and arched his back, straining to open himself even more to his lover.

The man's tongue wormed its way in, prodding and stabbing at him until he came close to snarling for more. He wanted more, the feel of Quinn's cock pressing against his hole, opening him, spearing him with its warm strength.

Just before he cried out his frustration, Quinn pulled back. It was as if he could read Jack's thoughts.

"You ready, stud?" Quinn asked in a breathless whisper. He eased a finger into the Jack's loosened hole, pushing past the softened sphincter until his digit lay deep inside.

It took all of Jack's willpower to keep from spewing as Quinn continued preparing his fluttering hole for the plundering he knew was coming. The man tugged and probed gently, then thrust another finger in to join the first. The snug fit thrilled him, and he knew he was as ready as he'd ever be.

"Fuck yeah," Jack growled. "More than ready. Fuck me before I explode."

Quinn chuckled, but moved ahead. His thighs touched the back of Jack's, the latex covered tip of the man's cock nudging his hole. Pushing out, he saw stars when Quinn's bulbous head entered him all in a single thrust.

Jack reached down, taking his own raging hard-on in hand and stroking it. As Quinn slowly filled him, Jack masturbated. Tension grew, his balls ached with a desire to come he hadn't felt in much too long. Quinn's pace quickened, again reading him as if they'd been lovers for months instead of minutes.

The seesawing motion grew more intense, insistent, even desperate. Quinn's breathing grew ragged and his hot breath washed over Jack's back as the man thrust harder into his ass. Jack swivelled his hips, grinding back into Quinn's body.

With a roar, Quinn slammed forward, his cock pulsing as it spewed its first volley of cum. A quick withdrawal followed by another hard shove sent Jack soaring, his own orgasm shattering his thoughts. He shuddered and moaned, each of the next few thrusts sending another brilliant flash of sensation into him. Cock pulsing, it didn't take long for his orgasm to fade. Quinn's cock in his ass throbbed, and made him shudder one last time.

"I think you've killed me," muttered Quinn, his cheek pressed against Jack's back.

Warm breath tickled his shoulder, but Jack didn't want to move.

"Nah, you'll live." He shifted his feet and released his cock. "Unless you've got some heart issues you forgot to tell me about."

"Nope, healthy as a horse."

"Built a bit like one, too."

Quinn chuckled and slowly eased himself out of Jack. "Not sure if that's flattery or just crazy."

Jack turned his head, just in time to see Quinn pull the condom off. He bent to his clothing and pulled out a tissue, wrapping the used prophylactic.

"Bit of both, I reckon." Jack straightened took Quinn into his arms. "That was amazing. I hope you're okay with it."

"I'm fine. Honest."

"Good. I want more of you. Not just this. I want to know you." Jack was momentarily flustered. "When I first saw you, I don't know, there was something about you. I felt as if we knew each other somehow."

"Let's go back to the inn." Quinn leaned in and kissed him. "I want to know more about you, too. I'm also curious about this ghostly bride you talked about earlier."

Jack slipped free of the man's arms and went about retrieving his clothing. When they'd both dressed, they slowly walked back towards the inn, hand in hand. "You can stick around awhile, if you'd like." He squeezed Quinn's fingers.

"Wish I could. Unfortunately, sneaking out in the morning might be considered, by some, as a public display." He grinned sideways at Jack. "You could come back to my place."

Jack sighed. As much as he'd like to spend more time with the hunky reverend, he had to wake up early in the morning. If he woke up at Quinn's place, chances are, he wouldn't want to crawl out of bed in order to make it back to the inn on time. The expression on his face must have conveyed his emotions. Before he could speak, Quinn beat him to it.

"Too much, too soon? I'm sorry, I didn't mean to push."

"Hey, I had the same idea. You know I'd enjoy spending more time with you. But as I mentioned earlier, I haven't technically landed this job, yet, and I really want it. *Need it.* Probably need to concentrate on that task, first."

Quinn wiggled Jack's hand affably. "Agreed. We'll have time. I'll walk you to your room and maybe we can neck a little bit before you shove me out."

Tingles of excitement raced down Jack's spine. 'Shoving him out' would take some strength. Even though they'd just made love, his cock twitched in his trousers, as if eager for round two. It'd be so much easier to flop on the bed and give in to the lusty cravings they were obviously both experiencing. But he didn't want to appear too needy. He'd be strong. Quinn was right. *There's plenty of time.*

The lobby was deserted when they passed through. Jack glanced around. Ethan wasn't in sight, but he'd most certainly be nearby. Jack knew that much about the man already. Ethan had an incredible attention to detail. He seemed to oversee every aspect of running the inn. *He loves Whiskers'. Probably second only to how much he loves Cade.*

Picturing the two men together made Jack smile. He looked forward to their wedding. As they entered the hallway to the rooms, he turned to Quinn. "Have you known Ethan long?"

The reverend shrugged. "He moved to Cape Harbour about a year ago. Nice. Quiet. He and Cade keep to themselves for the most part."

Jack inserted his key card into the lock on his room door and twisted the knob. "He seems to care a lot about the inn."

"Oh, I think so, too," Quinn agreed. "He takes this place seriously. I've heard he's gone on the defensive at times, when someone spoke badly about his otherworldly guests."

"That's the part I can't understand." Jack stepped inside and peered around the room. Everything seemed normal, as it had when he'd come to change his clothes. He dropped into one chair and motioned for Quinn to sit in the other. "I've never spent time in a place that was supposedly haunted."

"Ethan claims what they have here are 'spirits' rather than 'ghosts.' Are you familiar with the difference?"

Jack shook his head. He held his breath, waiting to hear the explanation.

"Well," Quinn smiled. "This is according to Ethan, mind you. He claims ghosts appear when they have unfinished business. If that gets taken care of, the ghost usually goes away. Spirits, on the other hand, don't have unfinished business. They just like to hang around places where they were comfortable in life. Spirits can supposedly cross over and back at will, showing up whenever they like."

"Really." Jack exhaled, noisily. He mulled over the comparison and scratched his chin. "I have to admit, I never gave it much thought." *Any thought.* "Like I said, this is all new to me."

"Fascinating stuff. As a religious man, of course I believe in the afterlife. I'd rather hoped it was someplace pleasant and cheery, rather than sticking around here, rehashing this life's events. But I'm open to possibilities."

Jack nodded thoughtfully. "So, have you ever seen any of the Whiskers' ghosts?"

"*Spirits,*" Quinn corrected gently.

"Ghosts, spirits, whatever they are. Have you seen anything? Because when I did, this morning, I have to admit it shocked the shit out of me."

Quinn chuckled. "I haven't. I've heard about Angry Annie, and how Ethan helped make her not so angry. I guess there's a child—"

"Laura." Jack offered what little he knew. "And a fisherman named Ben. Ethan says the bride is new to him. I find that interesting. Why did she show herself here, in my room? I get the connection about the wedding taking place this week, but I don't have anything to do with it, or any brides."

Quinn shrugged. "Maybe that's why. Maybe the major players in the wedding are too wrapped up in their own lives right now. If the bride is looking for help, perhaps she sees you as the guy to give it to her."

"She asked about a man. *'Where is Charles?'* she said, just before she knocked the wind out of my sails."

"You mentioned she looked as if she'd been beaten."

Jack studied the ceiling to remember the rest of her words. "Her words were something like, *'he said he'd never let anyone hurt me.'* Either he hadn't done a very good job of protecting her, or…"

"Charles hit her?"

Jack shook his head, clueless. "Why would she ask about him, then?"

"Could she have been wondering if he was still around?"

"Fear?" Jack blinked. "Worry that he might hurt her again?"

"Maybe she doesn't know she's dead." Quinn caught his eye. "She is dead, right?"

Jack recalled her transparency, and how she'd literally disappeared before his eyes. "She's dead." He nodded.

"Maybe we need to let her know that?" The reverend raised his brows.

Jack groaned and they both chuckled. "Enough ghost talk. I don't want to have to think that hard tonight."

Quinn stood and reached for Jack's hand. With one smooth move, the handsome hunk pulled him up and into strong, waiting arms. "Let's don't think about anything for a few minutes. Let's just feel." He pressed his mouth against Jack's.

Jack held off a whimper looming at the back of his throat. He parted his lips and sighed when Quinn's tongue accepted the silent invitation. The kiss deepened, and to show his approval, he leaned in and tilted his head.

There was no stopping the groan from slipping out as Jack sank into the pleasurable embrace. He didn't even try. It was obvious from Quinn's flushed expression, and the heated skin pressed against his own, that he was enjoying the exchange as much as Jack.

Several moments passed before Jack reluctantly pulled away.

Quinn panted. His clear eyes showed disappointment, before he nodded his understanding and agreement. He stepped back, but first captured Jack's lips in a last, quick kiss.

Jack smiled when they parted. He wanted to suggest Quinn stay, wanted to suggest many, many things, but knew the man's leaving tonight was for the best.

The reverend headed towards the door. "I promised Ethan I'd touch base with him tomorrow. Would you mind if I popped into the kitchen and said hello?"

"You'd better." Jack followed and gripped the door as Quinn left. "It might just be the highlight of my day."

That already familiar, ornery glint sparkled in Quinn's eyes. "Not if I have anything to say about it. Sleep well, Jack. Sweet dreams."

Jack winked. "You, too. Drive carefully. I'll see you tomorrow." He watched until Quinn exited the hallway, then realised he'd been grasping the door so tightly his fingertips had turned white. Jack released the door, closing and locking it.

He thought about Quinn while brushing his teeth. The man had a hold on him already. Jack rinsed then looked at his reflection. He jumped when he spotted a dark-haired man standing behind him, peering over his shoulder.

Jack spun around but no one was there.

"What the?" *Who was the man, and why had he appeared here?* He'd been frowning, and wearing a dark suit of some kind. Other than that, Jack couldn't recall much. The image had disappeared too fast.

Image. *Ghost.* Jack shivered and hurried to strip out of his clothes, wanting to put the vision behind him. He had someone much more pleasant to think about.

Quinn. They had a lot to learn about each other, no doubt about that. But there was time. He slipped between the sheets wearing nothing but boxers and a smile.

Chapter Four

Flowers blooming in the inn's garden provided the perfect backdrop for the large, festive wedding canopy. White pillars formed an aisle, lined on either side by a good number of folding chairs. Most of the seats were taken, Jack noticed with dismay, when he made his way down the aisle.

Am I late? He glanced at the guests as he hurried past. Something niggled at him, and he tried to put a finger on it. *What's wrong with this picture?*

Wedding attendees were dressed to the nines in immaculate, formal attire, but it looked like something from the previous century. Men sported high waistcoats and frilly ties. The women wore sweeping hoop skirts, elbow-length gloves and bonnets.

What's going on? Jack glanced down to check his own attire and discovered he was wearing nothing but his boxers. He gasped and dropped his hands in front of his groin before he realised it didn't matter. No one seemed to see him.

A dream? He breathed a sigh of relief, both for the fact he hadn't missed Ethan and Cade's wedding, and also that he hadn't showed up in his underwear. Before he could ponder the meaning of the dream, movement at the front of the crowd caught his attention.

"Where could he be?" The question rippled throughout the guests, spoken loudly by a woman — a woman wearing a long, white wedding dress and veil.

Jack blinked. *Is she the bride who came to my room?* He couldn't see her face, but the worry in her voice was clear.

"Now, now, my dear." An older man in a grey formal coat patted the bride's arm. "I'm sure there's a perfectly good explanation."

Jack studied the man's mutton-chop sideburns and handlebar moustache. They were obviously in the past, but he wasn't studied enough in history to place the styles with dates.

"I'm so worried." The woman turned towards the gentleman who tried to comfort her. "Father, something's happened. I know it has."

He drew his daughter to him and patted her back softly.

At that moment, Jack caught a glimpse of her face.

The ghost bride! It *was* the same woman, her pale complexion marred by worry. Her face was otherwise untouched, save a few tear streaks.

He scanned the crowd. *Where's the groom?*

The guests grew increasingly unsettled. Questions and murmurs became louder.

At the front, a man dressed in black approached the bride and her father, and spoke soothingly. "We can wait a few more minutes if you like, Mr. Montclair."

"Thank you, Reverend. I'm sure he'll be here any moment." The father rocked his daughter back and forth in his arms.

She'd begun to sob.

A lump formed in Jack's throat, the woman's misery almost palpable.

"Catherine!" Someone called from the back of the crowd. All eyes turned to focus on the dark-headed man in rumpled formalwear, hurrying down the aisle. A look of concern wrinkled his brow.

Yes! Jack cheered to himself. The groom had apparently encountered some problems, but he'd made it.

"Theodore?" The bride pulled away from her father, and met the newcomer in the aisle. "What's happened? Where is Charles?"

Jack bolted upright in bed and glanced around his room. Everything looked the same as it had the previous night, but nothing felt the same. The dream burned fresh in his mind. He hopped up and raced to the window to look out at the inn's gardens. Nothing unusual there, just the same trees, flowers and grass as always.

He turned away and pressed his back against the wall, needing its solid support. Recalling Catherine's last words, he repeated, "Theodore?" His thoughts raced and he blinked rapidly, recalling it all. *Who the devil is Theodore? And who appeared in my mirror last night?*

The alarm on his phone beeped, and Jack startled back to reality. He turned off the switch and climbed into the shower. He had twenty minutes until he had to report to the kitchen. He cleaned up quickly and donned a fresh uniform shirt and pants. Jack was at the counter, ready to bake, shortly before six.

"Morning." Logan slipped in the back door, tamping down a yawn. "Gotta admit, I won't miss these hours."

Jack gathered the ingredients for muffins and got to work. "What *are* you going to be doing once you move?"

"Not sure." Logan reached for pans and lined them up on the stovetop. "Not much for a while. Getting settled, mostly. We're moving into a new house and Alex will be starting his judgeship at the same time. I expect I'll handle a lot of the home stuff while he works." A goofy grin crossed Logan's face and it was obvious that sounded just fine.

"Cool." Jack nodded and paused to reflect. *Could I get into a relationship like that? Hooking up with a 'career' man?* Thoughts of Quinn drifted through his mind and he smiled. He'd always wanted to be a chef, the 'where' didn't matter so much. He could cook anywhere, as long as he had someone to be happy with. The reverend definitely had the potential to make him happy.

"You might want to stir that batter." Logan interrupted his thoughts good-naturedly. "Guests are going to show up in an hour or so."

Jack looked at him and decided to toss something out. "I work a lot faster when I'm getting paid."

Logan blinked, then grinned. "Well, hell. Of course you're getting paid. I expect Ethan to wander through at some point today and hire you. Remember, he's a tad sidetracked just now."

"I understand. It'll be nice to hear it officially, is all." Jack mixed bananas and nuts calmly into the muffin batter, but inside, his chest swelled with pride. *I got the job!* He suddenly felt as if he could walk on air.

"Tell you what. If Ethan doesn't mention it this morning, I'll give him a little nudge. I know your work impressed him yesterday. With only four days until the wedding, we wouldn't want to lose you. I'll work with you one more day, but by tomorrow, I'm going to need to focus on wedding stuff. Good thing is, the inn will be practically empty by then. The rooms are reserved for wedding guests. They'll start arriving in a couple of days."

"Fully booked?"

"Oh, yeah." Logan grinned. "Alex will be here Friday night. Course he'll stay with me. But the grooms have a bunch of friends coming in, and some family. I'm standing up with Ethan, but Cade's brother is going to be the best man."

Jack raised his brow. "Interesting. Ever met him?"

"Nope. Not sure Ethan has, either. That should be fun. Anyway, we'll have a lot to do. In my experience, weddings are always crazy, no matter how well planned you think everything is."

Jack recalled the wedding in his dream and was about to ask if Logan knew anything about the participants or what went on, when Ethan entered the kitchen.

"Good morning, gents," he said jovially, sniffing around the stove, where the aroma of baking muffins emanated. "How are things in the kitchen this fine day?"

"We're dandy," Logan answered. "But neither of *us* is hitching up to the old ball and chain in just a few days. How are *you*?"

Ethan grinned. "*I* am wonderful. The 'old ball and chain' is in fine form, as well. I'll tell him you called him that, by the way."

Logan's face reddened. "Hey, I didn't mean…uh, shit. Quick change of subject. Jack wondered if he's got the job or if we're just using him for slave labour until the wedding."

It was Jack's turn to blush. "I didn't say that! Damn it, man." He relaxed when he saw the smiles on both Logan and Ethan's faces.

"Slave labour sounds like fun, but I think we should probably hire him, don't you?" Ethan asked Logan.

The chef nodded. "I told him, I'd work with him one more day. Tomorrow, I've got to get busy with wedding stuff."

"Yes, you do." Ethan grabbed a napkin, and when the first batch of muffins came out of the oven, snatched one. "So do I. Quinn's stopping by after breakfast, and we're going to discuss the layout of the canopy and chairs in the garden. He's been through this more than we have and has some ideas to offer."

Once again, Jack's thoughts went to the wedding in his dream, set up in the garden. *I could probably tell you a few things myself.*

"In case anyone's interested," Ethan added.

Jack's mind bolted back to the present. "Hmm?"

Ethan took another bite of the muffin and grinned. "*I said*, Quinn is coming here today after breakfast, in case anyone is interested."

Logan piped up, "Oh, sure, boss. I'm interested. I can't wait to see the reverend."

Jack glanced from one man to the other and realised they seemed to know his secret. How much they knew was uncertain, but it didn't matter. He could tell by their expressive smiles and the wink Logan shot Ethan, they were pulling his leg. He felt sure no one here would have a problem with him and Quinn seeing each other.

"Shush, you," he told Logan.

Jack made a move towards Ethan, acting as if he was prepared to grab what was left of the muffin.

Ethan stepped back and shoved the last bite into his mouth. He waved his hands in a gesture of surrender.

"If you don't mind, I have work to do." Jack shooed his new boss out.

"I don't mind a bit. Save a couple of those muffins for Cade, will you? I know he'll love them."

"You got it." Jack returned to the counter with renewed enthusiasm. *Life is good.*

The scant breakfast crowd took little time to feed and he was nearly done cleaning when Quinn arrived. "Good morning." He greeted the handsome hunk who somehow managed to look sexier than he had the day before. Jack's thoughts immediately went to all things carnal, and wondered when he and Quinn might find time to be alone.

"Hey, good looking." The reverend smiled, his eyes shining. He tore his gaze away, long enough to glance around the dining room. "Slow day."

"Apparently most of the guests are on the way out. Making room for wedding attendees."

"Ah, gotcha." Quinn nodded.

Jack stepped closer. "You almost missed breakfast, but for you, I'd be willing to whip a little something out."

His lover chuckled. "Anything you could 'whip out' wouldn't be little. But perhaps we should save that for later. I've already eaten, thanks. Had an early meeting with some of the deacons of the church."

"Everything okay?" He asked nervously.

Quinn waved a hand. "Business as usual. Our monthly touch-base breakfast. No problems." He smiled. "Why do you look so worried? What could be wrong?"

"I dunno. I've never—dated—a reverend before." Jack lowered his voice. "Not that what we did yesterday could exactly be called *dating*."

"It was a perfect date. And I told you, I'm allowed to have a life like everyone else. Don't worry so much."

A sigh of relief whooshed from his chest. "It was a pretty perfect date, wasn't it?"

"The best." Quinn waggled his brows. "Any chance of a repeat performance tonight?"

"Every chance." Jack beamed. "Maybe even better, we could go to your place. We've got some celebrating to do. Ethan told me this morning I've got the job."

"Hey, that's great!" Quinn held up his hand and they high-fived. "Congratulations. A celebration is definitely in order. What do you say I fix you dinner, and we share a bottle of wine?"

"I say—can you cook?" Jack winced.

"Yes, I can cook." Quinn shoved Jack's shoulder lightly. "Sort of. Even if you don't like it, you're going to eat it and say you do, right?"

"Absolutely." Jack nodded, and smiled.

* * * *

He manoeuvred through the day as if his feet had wings. The thought of Quinn cooking for him surprised him a little. Of course, he wasn't the only one who could cook, but he'd rarely had anyone else offer.

The dinner crowd was even more scant than the lunch mob, so Jack was ready to go long before Quinn showed up at just shy of seven. The kitchen and dining room cleared, he checked in with Logan and asked, "It's pretty quiet, mind if I take off when Quinn gets here?"

The man looked at him and said, "Sure thing. It's so damn slow, I'll probably go find Cade or Ethan and let them know I'm shutting the kitchen down a little early."

"I'll be here at six." Jack rubbed his forearms, eager to be on his way.

"Did Mrs. Nelson come down for her dinner?"

"No, I took her a plate up a little earlier." Jack knew the old broad was special and had learnt quickly to treat her well. "She's a little odd, but she was really nice when I showed up."

"She must like you, for some weird reason," Logan teased.

"Maybe it's got something to do with the muffin I saved for her this morning." He chuckled and peered towards the door.

As if on queue, the sexy reverend walked in. He stopped just inside and looked around, spotted Jack and Logan, then made a beeline for them.

"Could be the muffins, could be a lot of things with her." Logan finished talking when Quinn joined them and extended his hand.

Taking it, Logan shook, then slapped the man on the shoulder and said to Jack, "Why don't you go get cleaned up and get out of here? I'll see Ethan." Releasing Quinn's hand, he added, "Make sure you're on time tomorrow, you'll be on your own in the kitchen. There won't be a lot to do. I think there's only Mrs. Nelson and one guest here. She'll be staying, of course, the guest will leave tomorrow sometime."

Jack looked at Quinn, and felt his face grow warm. "I won't be late, trust me."

Quinn, with a wicked smile on his face and an equally wicked leer, said, "I'll make sure he's not late."

Jack's face grew even warmer, yet, he loved the feeling of Quinn's easy acceptance of the two of them together. His feelings for the man deepened.

"Okay you two, get out of here before I change my mind. Quinn, I'll assume you got Cade and Ethan sorted out?"

"Yes, earlier. There's loads of room and Cade had a plan in mind already. I just had to tell him it'd work."

Jack went back into the kitchen, took off the apron he'd been wearing and hung it on its hook.

A moment later, Quinn's handsome face peered around the corner, smiling. "You ready to go?"

"You bet. Someone promised me a homemade dinner that I didn't have to cook." Jack couldn't remember the last time someone had fixed a meal for him.

"The roast is in the oven as we speak. The veggies are ready to go and the wine is chilling." He laid a hand on Jack's shoulder and steered him towards the front door.

Once they got out into the parking lot, Jack veered towards his car, saying, "I'll follow you. Save me getting you up in the morning…if I should spend the night, that is." He suddenly felt bashful, and lowered his head.

Quinn stepped closer and slipped the fingers of one hand beneath his chin, raising his face so he had to look him in the eye. "Good idea, although I really wouldn't mind getting up early with you." He leant forward and pressed a kiss to Jack's lips.

Before Jack could do much in the way of reacting, Quinn pulled away and walked over to a dark-blue sedan. "Follow me."

A short drive of ten minutes or so brought them to a modest little cabin on the beach. Lilacs in full flower lined the driveway and a welcoming light shone in the window.

"Nice!" Jack admired the place and wondered if it was big enough for two.

He looked around and thrust that thought aside. *We've only just begun seeing each other, for crying out loud.*

A tap on the car window jerked him back to the present and he looked up at Quinn. Getting out, he grinned and looked around. "This is really great. Beach front and all your own."

"Yes, I sometimes feel very spoilt." Quinn gazed at the expanse of brilliant blue water not fifty feet from where they stood. He got a faraway look on his face. "It's almost like I'm never alone here." He turned and smiled at Jack, then added, "Course, now I have you here, I won't have to be." He winked.

Jack slid his hand into Quinn's and squeezed. His stomach growled.

Quinn looked at him and chuckled. "I take it you're hungry."

"Pretty obvious, huh?" He rubbed his stomach and nodded.

"Come on then."

He pulled Jack towards the house and after unlocking the front door, guided him inside. The aroma of roasting beef and something else hit him and he sighed.

The house was small, but it had everything a man needed and was laid out beautifully. They'd entered into a small, but serviceable kitchen, and to the right was a living room set-up he'd be proud of, if it were his. A small fireplace in the far corner seemed like the icing on the cake.

"You go sit, relax, or get a beer from the fridge if you like," Quinn said, releasing Jack's hand and moving deeper into the kitchen. "I've got just a few things left to do before dinner's ready."

"Can I help?" Truthfully, Jack wanted to see what Quinn was doing. Whatever it was, it smelled amazing.

"No, you've been cooking all day." Quinn placed his hands on Jack's shoulders and marched him into the main room. He stopped once they'd reached the large picture window facing the beach. "Want that beer? Or would you rather wait for wine with dinner?"

"I'll wait. I'm good, thanks, Quinn." Sounds of the surf slapping the sand captivated him. The sun's rays made the crests of each wave glisten like diamonds against a satin background. Even the sand sparkled. The overhanging branches of the occasional pine tree gave enough shade to keep the place cool in the summer, he ventured.

He watched a gull ride the wind wave and another joined it. Out in the water, he saw a sailboat cutting through the waves at an incredible speed.

"Hey, you still here?" Quinn stood behind him, his arms suddenly wrapping him in a hug. He pulled Jack even closer and the obvious bulge in the front of his slacks pressed suggestively against Jack's ass.

"Wouldn't be anywhere else. This is such a perfect place."

"Glad you like it." He spun Jack around, and when they faced each other, pulled him close again. "I've wanted to do this all day." Quinn leaned in and pressed his lips to Jack's. This wasn't a fleeting, feather soft kiss. This was wet and hot, and full of passion.

Taken by surprise, Jack quickly caught up and slipped his tongue across Quinn's lips. Those lips parted and he entered the sweetest, most welcoming mouth he'd had the pleasure of tasting since their last encounter. Tongues batted at each other. Warm, strong hands moved down his back. When they cupped his ass cheeks, he couldn't stop a deep, needy groan from escaping his lips.

Quinn pulled his mouth from Jack's and smiled. "Like that?"

"Of course I do. I want more." Jack rocked his hips from side to side, rubbing his own erection against his lover's.

Quinn squeezed Jack's buttocks again, and asked, "Want to eat first?"

As if in answer, Jack's belly growled. Both men chuckled.

"I think we'll go ahead and eat. I don't want to rush anything because you're starving." Quinn lowered his hands and returned to the kitchen.

Jack took a moment to compose himself. He slipped a hand into the front of his jeans to ease his cock into a more comfortable position then followed Quinn. The man was just getting a large roaster out of the oven. He placed it on the stovetop and lifted the lid.

"Pot roast and veggies!" Quinn proclaimed, appearing rather proud of himself.

Jack's mouth watered. "Looks great. Let's get it out before I dive in with a knife and fork, right here."

Quinn smiled, and grabbed a large platter from the cupboard. He manhandled the roast out then scooped out the potatoes, and an assortment of vegetables. "Here, you make the gravy while I slice the roast." He handed Jack the makings.

The meal was ready in no time. They ate while sitting side by side at the table facing the ocean view and making small talk about the coming wedding. Between them, they managed to polish off a healthy percentage of the roast, and most of the greens.

When he couldn't eat another bite, Jack laid his cutlery across his plate and leant back in his chair.

"You *were* hungry," remarked Quinn a moment later when he, too, put his knife and fork down.

"Lunch was a long time ago. Maybe I'm still a growing boy," Jack chided.

"Growing," Quinn remarked, his eyes going from Jack's face down to his crotch. "Maybe."

Jack's face grew warm, but he didn't look away. He loved the banter they shared. "Need some help clearing the wreckage away?"

"No, I want you to go get cleaned up and meet me in the bedroom. I'll be there in just a few minutes."

Jack didn't need to be told twice. He got up and turned towards the two doors he'd noticed in the living room. He assumed one was the bedroom, the other the bathroom. Looking over his shoulder, he asked, "Bathroom?"

"The closest."

With a quick nod, Jack was on his way. The sharp slap on the ass from Quinn hurried him along with a yelp of surprise. He got to the bathroom door and turned to look at his sexy lover, who'd just begun clearing the dishes from the table. A surge of feeling swept over Jack, and he sighed before heading into the more than adequate sized room for a quick shower.

And quick it was. Getting the water just right took but a moment. He stripped off his clothing and jumped into the old-style tub, drawing the semi-transparent curtain around himself. It was as if he'd stepped into his own little world of mist and water. He drew the soap over his skin, and was just rinsing off when he heard the door close.

Jack drew the curtain aside, careful not to let the water stream out, and looked towards the door. Of course it was Quinn. But a Quinn he hadn't expected to see, at least not so soon. The man was naked, his erection thrusting out from a nest of dark curls.

"I was just about to get out," Jack said in a deep, husky voice. "Or, I could stay in here and scrub your back, or your front." He waggled his eyebrows suggestively and grinned.

"Yes, I'm sure you could." He took a step closer and reached inside the curtain, his fingers gripping Jack's hard-on. "But, I've only got a small tank here and I know we'd run out of hot water before we run out of...steam. So, why don't you dry off and I'll hurry?" He gave Jack's erection five or six long, luxurious strokes then withdrew his hand.

Jack bit back a groan of disappointment and fought to control the urge to thrust his hips forward, pushing his cock through the opening Quinn's hand had left. Forcing himself to focus on the man's words, he replied, "Yes, do hurry. Or I'm liable to start without you." He shut the water off and flung the shower curtain aside, pausing for a brief moment, as if to give Quinn one last chance to change his mind.

With his hand on his cock and a glint in his beautiful eye, Quinn winked and said, "Bedroom's across the hall. The sheets on the bed are clean, there's lube and protection in the bedside table drawer and I expect you ready for me."

Jack's mouth dropped open. His hand seemed to have a mind of its own and slid around the shaft of his cock. "Right," he croaked and stumbled out of the tub.

Quinn pulled a bath sheet from the rack and wound it around Jack, then kissed him on the nose. "You okay?"

Giving himself a shake, Jack said, "You bet. You're amazing. You do know that, right?"

"Oh yes, I'm smart too," quipped the sexy reverend, who proceeded to hop into the tub. He pulled the curtain closed, but poked his head out and added, "I'm psychic, too." He closed his eyes and raised a finger to his forehead. "I see...yes, I see it clearly now. You, in my bed, ten minutes from now...on your hands and knees." He opened his eyes and grinned wickedly. "Am I right, or what?"

For a moment, Jack didn't know what to say. The man was crazy. Finally, he chuckled and said, "Might be you on your hands and knees, but the rest sounds right. Wow, you are good."

"You know it." The face vanished and the rush of water soon made further conversation impossible. Jack shook his head and dried himself quickly with the towel. His cock refused to go down, but under the circumstances, he simply made sure he didn't smack it into anything on his way out. One last glance at the showering man made him shudder. Quinn's lower body pressed against the curtain. His cock, hard as nails, pulsed against the plastic.

Jack swallowed the gush of saliva suddenly filling his mouth. The temptation to just walk over and drop to his knees, take the man's cock in his mouth nearly won. But, he'd said he'd be on the bed, and that's where he'd be.

He strode from the room, the damp towel slung over his shoulder, his cock leading the way.

Chapter Five

The bed took up about half of the room. A dresser, an old steamer trunk and a chair filled the rest. A window faced the ocean, and when the partially opened curtain billowed out, Jack realised it wasn't shut. He padded across the hardwood floor and crawled onto the bed. Quinn had turned back the covers, so he headed for the top of the bed, and the side table on the right.

Opened, the drawer offered up the promised tube of lubricant and a brand new box of rubbers. He broke the seal and dug around inside, pulling out a foil pack. He tossed it on top of the table and flopped over on the bed. Lying on his back, he took a dollop of lube and slid his hand over his cock, smoothing the clear jell into the firm flesh.

His heart raced. He clenched his ass cheeks and shuddered. That's what he needed to work on. He rolled onto his side and cocked the upper leg towards his chest. His buttocks spread naturally. He took another gob of lube onto his finger and reached back, carefully sliding the digit around his hole. He pushed and his index finger slipped inside. The sensation was almost more than he could bear. He ached to simply fuck himself until he came, but knew he had to wait. Quinn wouldn't be long. *He'd better not be.* Jack eased his finger in deep, wiggling it against the tight inner muscles to loosen them.

Once he was satisfied they were relaxed, he pushed another finger inside himself and bit his lip to keep from groaning out loud. With his fingers halfway inside, he spread them slowly and twisted his wrist, stretching his hole wider. He didn't dare let his thoughts wander or he was sure he'd wind up shooting. He was that ready.

"Hey, I said ready, not ready to come," Quinn's voice came from the doorway.

If Jack hadn't been expecting the man, he'd probably have shot straight up and run. As it was, he simply rolled onto his back, making sure his fingers remained deep inside his ass, and spread his knees.

Quinn's gaze shifted instantly from his face to his wide spread crotch. The sexy reverend gripped his cock at the base, obviously squeezing it tight.

Jack's cock lay flat against his belly, for a moment. Then it pulsed, bouncing inches high and stretching a long string of clear pre-cum from the tip to just below his navel. His balls shifted in the suddenly cool surroundings.

"Oh my…" Quinn mumbled, apparently unable to find the right words to end the sentence.

Jack continued to spread himself, the sensation sending jolts of sheer bliss from his hole to his balls. He wanted to leap at Quinn and drag him onto the bed, but he forced the desire down. *For now.* "Oh my…what?" He shifted his hips, making his cock slide across his lower stomach. "You see something you like?"

"Oh yeah, like a lot," Quinn murmured, finally clambering onto the bed. "Hope you don't mind if I join you."

"I'd be disappointed if you didn't. I've been getting ready for you." He gripped the base of his shaft with his free hand and gently drew the skin upwards until his fingers hit the rim of his cock head.

Quinn tore his gaze away from Jack's cock and looked up into his eyes. A moment later, he smiled, then laughed. "Can I have it?"

"Yes, please."

Quinn scooted over until he knelt between Jack's legs. With no ceremony at all, he simply leant forward and engulfed the tip of Jack's cock in his mouth.

The suction came close to sending Jack over the edge. The warmth amazed him. Quinn's satin-soft tongue lapped across the head and around the rim. His teeth nipped ever so gently at the skin of the shaft. The man sucked gently, then with more determination, taking more and more of Jack's erection in. He didn't stop until the tip touched the back of his throat.

Jack moaned continually in a low, deep sound of desperate need. "Yes, fuck yes. Yes, like that. More, Quinn, more. Harder. Suck me. Fuck me. Please, I need to come." Jack had forgotten the finger buried in his ass. He'd simply let it slip out and wrapped it around his balls in a frantic effort to keep from spewing too soon. He pulled, gently at first, more firmly when his pleasure soared even higher. The slight touch of pain did the trick, helping him delay the inevitable.

The head of his cock bumped the back of Quinn's throat again, and he whispered, "Ease off. I don't want to choke you for crying out loud." Jack released his balls and gripped the sides of Quinn's face, pulling the man off him.

Teeth scraped along the shaft of his cock and he thrilled at every millimetre of the delicious sensation. Quinn didn't stop sucking, so the pull also sent Jack's excitement higher. When teeth met the ridge around Jack's cock head, he very nearly cried out and lost it all, but bit his lip to keep control. With a determined push, he got Quinn's mouth off him and he sighed.

"I want more," Quinn growled, his voice harsh with passion. He looked up and blinked, his beautiful eyes bright with what Jack could only think of as longing.

"I do too, but I'm going to come if you keep that up."

"That's the idea," Quinn said, and chuckled.

"My turn," Jack said and, grabbing his lover's shoulders, spun him around, then let him fall to the bed.

Quinn landed on his back, and immediately shifted his feet, so one lay on either side of Jack's body. "Taking turns is good," murmured Quinn, who instantly let his knees fall to the sides.

"Grab your knees and pull them up to your chest."

"And I thought I'd get the upper hand." A moment later, Quinn's knees bracketed his chin, his entire genital area exposed for both his and Jack's enjoyment.

Jack licked his lips. Positioned carefully below his lover's body, he leant forward and hooked his hands and arms under the man's thighs. He lifted Quinn to reposition him, then bent forward just a little more and ran the flat of his tongue from the base of the throbbing cock to its leaking tip.

"Sweet Jesus!"

Quinn's hips fought Jack's grip, trying to thrust upwards. Jack held on and repeated the long, languid lapping, until the man's shaft literally leapt up to meet his lips. Jack didn't touch it for several minutes of the sweet torment. Only when Quinn's balls rose, and nearly vanished into his body, did Jack relent and take the head into his mouth. He sucked the entire length deep. He licked along the heavy vein, dragged his teeth carefully over the sensitive flesh and did everything he could think of to make the experience the best ever.

When he knew the man was about ready to shoot, he eased back, letting the pulsing rod sway between them. He didn't stop there. He simply lowered his sights and slipped his fingers into the man's well-spread ass. His mouth and tongue followed. He licked and jabbed at the pucker with his tongue, prying the clenched muscles open with his fingers. A finger sank in easily, another went in just as readily. The third took a little time.

He reached for the lube and squeezed a large dollop onto the soft crinkled opening. Using his index finger, Jack pushed as much of the lube into Quinn's ass as he could. Twisting and turning his fingers seemed to spread the goo the best and also got the most amazing audio results from the supine man. Groans and whimpers filled the room, and Jack thought it was a really good thing there were no close neighbours around. Satisfied, he pulled his fingers out and wiped them on Quinn's inner thigh.

"Ready?" he asked in a deep husky voice.

Quinn looked up at him. Sweat covered his face, his eyes shone and his mouth moved, but no sound came out. The man closed his eyes then tried to speak again, with better success. "Ready? For what?"

"Fucking. I'm going to fuck you until you beg me to stop." Jack winked down at his lover.

"You're kidding. Stop, never. Yes, ready. More than ready."

Jack needed no further urging. He climbed to his knees and gave his cock a few healthy strokes before reaching for the condom packet. Once he'd ripped it and pulled the rubber out, it took him only a few seconds to roll it on. He squeezed a little lubricant onto his palm and worked it along the length of his cock, giving Quinn a momentary picture of him masturbating.

"You do realise, I'm going to get even for this torture, right?" Quinn glared up at him, mock anger in his voice.

"I'm counting on it." Jack smiled back and wriggled forward, positioning himself just right. "Take a deep breath," he said quietly. He reached under Quinn's thighs and lifted the man into the perfect position, his cock kissing the entryway to heaven. He waited for Quinn to take that breath.

When Quinn complied, Jack pressed the tip of his cock against the outer ring of anal muscle and gently shoved forward. The tension lasted an instant. Then he was inside. Warmth surrounded the tip of his cock and held it like a satin glove. Jack leant forward and groaned as his shaft entered. Slowly, he eased in. Quinn's body accepted his, spasmodically clenching and sucking at him until Jack was balls deep and sweating like a trooper. He dared not squirm or withdraw right away, for fear of coming. He was that close.

It took only a few deep breaths for Jack's excitement to calm enough for him to move, but he knew he wasn't going to last long. By the looks of the pre-cum pooled on Quinn's belly, he realised he wasn't the only one close, and smiled.

Shuffling ahead a tiny bit, he began the age-old seesawing motion that would bring both of them the most amazing pleasure. His hips swung as if they were on a pivot, tirelessly, increasing their speed when Jack thought Quinn seemed ready, and he could do so without spewing. He forced his thoughts to mundane things, the laundry, the window he'd seen that needed fixing at the inn, anything and everything to keep from coming too soon.

It worked for a while. But when Quinn's anal muscles clamped down on him as if they were sucking him off, his groan came loud and long, and his own rampant erection pulsed in response. He stopped fucking his man in a desperate attempt to prolong their pleasure.

"Come with me," Quinn whimpered from beneath him. He reached up and tweaked Jack's nipples before lightly scratching his chest. "Come with me. I want to feel you."

Jack looked down and saw Quinn's cock throb when he resumed his fucking. Pre-cum dangled like a thread of silk, touching both his flesh and his lover's. Releasing one of Quinn's legs, he wrapped his fingers around that beautiful smooth cock and jerked it. "Together."

"Yes," growled Quinn, who thrust his body up and down on Jack's shaft.

It took less than a dozen strokes for the two of them to climax. Jack beat Quinn by a stroke, but as soon as his cock pulsed inside his lover's ass, it was like a signal for the man to join him. And join him he did, spraying white spunk all over them both—chest, belly and thighs. Jack even got some on his chin.

Jack shoved forward one last time and felt his dick pulse weakly then begin to deflate. He collapsed, but didn't stay sprawled across Quinn's body for long. Rolling off the man, he made sure he had the condom on. When he was free of his lover, he continued rolling until he could sit on the edge of the bed. "Back in a flash," he said and headed for the bathroom.

He tossed the used rubber in the trash and cleaned himself up. Taking a clean washcloth, he wet it and returned to the bedroom.

"Here, just stay put." He rolled Quinn to the side and cleaned him up, giving him a kiss on the back of the shoulder when he was done. He took the cloth back to the bathroom and while he was there, took a good look at himself in the mirror over the sink. *Is this the guy? He's so perfect it scares me.*

Making his way back to the bedroom, he said to Quinn, "I've got to set an alarm. It's going to be a killer to get up and leave you in the morning, but I can't be late."

"Yeah, I know. It's going to kill us both, but we'll do it. I guess quickies in the a.m. are going to have to wait for days off." Quinn opened his arms and folded them around Jack when he climbed back in.

* * * *

They slept for a while, and somewhere around midnight found the energy for another round. Afterwards, Jack slept like a dead man, rousing only once when Quinn pulled him close.

When the alarm went off, Jack grudgingly dragged himself out of bed and into the shower. He mentally kicked himself for not bringing a change of clothes, but knew it'd just take him a minute to change once he got back to the inn. He dressed and met Quinn in the kitchen.

"You hopped out of bed fast," the reverend teased.

Jack raised his hands in defeat. "Had to. No other way to do it. If I'd stopped to take a look at you, we'd still be there now."

"That's for sure." Quinn's eyes twinkled.

Standing there, in boxers and a ratty old T-shirt, Quinn was still the sexiest man Jack had ever laid eyes on. "Damn, you look good."

Quinn smiled and took a few steps forward, stopping in front of Jack. "Good morning to you, too." He placed a light kiss on Jack's mouth then retreated a pace.

Pangs of regret thumped in Jack's chest. "You know I'd really like to stay, don't you?"

"I'd love for you to stay. Last night was incredible, but I understand. Duty calls." Another mischievous expression crossed his face. "Besides, there's always tonight."

"Oh, yeah?" Jack's breath caught. The man was taking a lot for granted, assuming they'd get together again that night. *Which is exactly what I want, too.* His heart soared. "Tonight sounds good. Do you want to meet at the inn, like we did before? You don't have to cook me dinner, we could grab something easy."

Quinn gave him a quick once-over. "I'll be grabbing something, all right. Don't worry about that. It's too early to talk dinner. I haven't had my coffee yet. Why don't we firm up our plans when I drop by the inn later under the pretext of discussing the wedding with Ethan and Cade?"

Jack smiled. "We can do that. You should go back to bed. I'll see myself out."

"And I'll see you later. Have a good day." He kissed Jack again with feeling, then they parted and went their separate ways.

"You, too. Later." Jack headed out into the still-dark morning.

The roads were deserted on the short drive back to the inn, and the parking lot looked as empty, with only one car. *Cooking should be a breeze today.*

His eagerness to return to the inn surprised him a little. The place obviously had something going on with ghosts or spirits, whatever the entities were. Strangely, it didn't really bother him. Jack found the whole thing rather intriguing.

He glanced at his watch, pleased to be so early. When he'd set the alarm, he'd allowed some extra time in case saying goodbye took longer than expected. He'd gotten out right on time, Quinn had made sure of that. The man was amazing—sexy, fun, and responsible, all rolled into one.

A goofy grin still niggled at Jack's face when he entered the inn, but seeing Logan behind the registration desk caught him off guard and he stopped in his tracks. "What are you doing here?"

Logan offered a weak smile that didn't quite reach his eyes. "Last I checked, I work here."

Jack glanced at his watch and shook it to make sure it was running. "Am I late? Oh, jeeze, I'm sorry."

"You're not late. I've been here since about three. There was an...*incident*."

The expression on his face was something Jack hadn't seen before. His blood ran cold but he had to ask, he had to know what had happened. "What kind of *incident*?"

Logan exhaled a tired sigh and ran a hand through his short, messy hair. "That ghost bride you mentioned? The one you saw the first night you were here?"

"Yes," Jack replied tersely, urging Logan to continue. "I know who you mean." He hadn't told anyone about his dream the next night, but after seeing her twice, felt almost as if he did know the bride.

"Apparently, she appeared to the lone guest we had, that travelling salesman guy with the bad comb-over."

Jack nodded. The guy had a thankless job, and a lousy haircut, but he was a decent fellow. "Is he okay?"

"He's fine. He called the front desk screaming. I guess Ethan went running, with Cade a minute behind him. Ethan got to the landing at the top of the stairs and the ghost pushed him. He tumbled down the entire flight, head over heels, backwards." Logan grimaced. "Cade saw it all, but couldn't do anything to stop it. Apparently, the whole scene was pretty violent and bloody."

"Oh my god!" Jack stumbled back and sat on the arm of the first chair he bumped into. "Is Ethan all right? What happened then?"

"Cade called an ambulance then phoned me. I got here just as they were leaving. Ethan lost a lot of blood from a deep gash on his head, but he'd regained consciousness, so we're hopeful. I cleaned up the mess, and the salesman packed his bags and left."

"God," Jack repeated, feeling horrible and helpless at the same time. "Is there anything I can do?"

"No, but thank you." Logan shook his head. "Cade asked us to stay here and man the place. I told him we would. He'll let us know when there's any news."

"Okay, then." Jack stood. "I'll bake a few muffins to have out today, but if no one's here except Delia, I won't need to set out the buffet. I'll cook whatever she wants to order."

Logan nodded. "Sounds good. I'd take a cup of coffee when you get some made. I'm going to look over the wedding guest reservations and see when we can expect folks to roll in."

"You bet. Give a yell if I can do anything." Jack strolled into the kitchen and flipped on the lights. It felt as if he should be doing something more, but really had no idea what that might be. It was easiest to set about doing the familiar, making coffee and baking.

While stirring the batter, a thought occurred to him and he glanced at the wall clock. *Six-thirty*. Too early to call Quinn. He'd wait until seven-thirty then phone the reverend and let him know what had happened.

The hour passed interminably slowly. Jack forced himself to wait it out, but at the stroke of seven-thirty had the phone in his hand. "Sorry to call so early," he replied to Quinn's 'hello.'

"I'm not sorry. I'm just lying here thinking about you. Thinking that if—"

"Quinn, there's been an accident." Jack hated to interrupt, but his lover needed to know.

"Accident?" The deep voice changed tone immediately. "What happened? Are you all right?"

"It's Ethan. It seems the ghost bride appeared last night and got nasty. She frightened a guest and when Ethan went to help, she pushed him down the stairs."

"The ghost bride? Jack, are you jerking my chain? Because this isn't a very funny joke."

"It's no joke. Ethan's in the hospital. Cade's with him."

"Well, I'll be…" He grew quiet, and seemed to digest the information. "I don't have a whole lot of experience with ghosts. I know they exist, and I've heard stories from the inn, but this is new territory for me."

"You and me both! I've never seen anything like this, either. But the bride appeared to me first, and that means I'm involved, somehow."

"You don't have to be, you know. If you walked away right now, people would understand. No one would think a thing about it."

Jack hadn't considered leaving. For some reason, the inn already felt like home. He chose his words carefully and spoke in a low, clear voice. "I couldn't do that. The people here have been so good to me. I care about them and this place. I'm staying, Quinn."

A rush of breath sounded on the other end of the line. "I'm so glad you said that. Not that our relationship has anything to do with your job there. I'd just hate for you to leave town when we've barely begun to explore the — possibilities."

"I'm not going anywhere, my friend. You and I have plenty of things to explore. But we might have to put that on hold, for now. Ethan and Cade need us."

"Let me grab a quick shower and I'll be right over. Have you gotten an update on Ethan's condition?"

"No. Cade asked Logan and I to stay here and take care of the inn."

"Hmm. As the family chaplain, it's my responsibility to pop in and see if there's anything I can do for them. I'll run by the hospital first, then be over."

"Thank you." Jack breathed a sigh of relief. Quinn had already made him feel better. "See you soon."

"You bet. Bye."

The call ended. Jack squeezed the counter until his fingertips ached. He realised what he was doing and let go, pacing back and forth a couple of times. A quick glance into the dining area assured him there was nothing to do. Some days, the lack of work might give him a nice break. Today, it merely gave him time to worry about Ethan, and wonder about the ghost — and what the hell was up with her.

He strode into the other room and saw Logan looking intently at the computer screen behind the counter. *Probably trying to make the time pass, same as me.*

Jack spoke up, "I'm going to run up and check on Delia. See if she wants anything."

"Great," Logan replied without looking up.

Jack entered the hall with trepidation, slowing more when he approached the stairs. Logan had done a thorough job of cleaning. There was no evidence of the accident — *incident* — other than a damp chill hanging in the air.

He climbed the steps and hurried to the last door at the end of the hall. He knocked twice and waited.

"Who is it?" Delia's voice sounded creakier than normal.

"It's Jack, Mrs. Nelson. From the kitchen? I, uh, wondered if I could bring you anything."

The door opened a crack, and the petite woman peered out. "I didn't call for room service," she said suspiciously.

"I know. It's just really slow right now. The one guest we did have left in the night, so I'm sitting down there twiddling my thumbs."

She opened the door wider and nodded. "I heard him go. How's Ethan?"

"No word, yet. I spoke with Quinn Stevens, the reverend who's officiating at their wedding. He's going to swing by the hospital, then come out here and give us an update."

The old woman's face crinkled with concern. "You will let me know, won't you? Ethan is special. He's one of the few—" She paused mid-sentence, and seemed to steel herself. "Just haul your hiney up here when you get any news."

"Of course, I will. In the meantime, can I bring you breakfast? I could whip you up a big omelette with pancakes and bacon on the side." Jack smiled.

She hadn't eaten more than a muffin on the mornings he'd been there so far, but he was really bored.

Her eyes twinkled for just a quick moment before she rolled them. "A muffin and tea will be fine. You might put your energies into figuring out why Catherine did this, and what you can do to see that it doesn't happen again—to anyone."

"Catherine." Jack blinked, surprised Delia knew the ghost's name. "What do you know about her?"

Delia scowled and closed the door. Through the door, she yelled, "Make that a bran muffin, and see that it's warm! The last time it was cold as a lump of lard."

"It was right out of the oven," he called and turned to leave. "You old bat," he added under his breath, but didn't really mean it. There was something he liked about the cantankerous, white-haired old gal, but he also sensed something infuriating. She didn't like to answer questions outright. *That would make life too easy, I guess.* He trotted down the stairs, remembering Ethan when he got to the lower landing.

Jack hurried past the spot where 'it' had happened, down the hall and back to the kitchen, his domain. He set about preparing a piping hot muffin and tea. *Ought to kill a good five minutes.* He sighed.

After delivering Delia's meal, he returned to the dining room and saw Quinn walk through the front door. Jack changed directions and went to meet him. "Hey."

"Hey there." Without hesitation, Quinn drew Jack into his arms for a quick hug. "How you guys doing here?" He let go and took a step back, glancing from Jack to Logan.

Jack took a second to bask in the intimacy. *It feels really good to have someone who cares.* "I'm okay." He finally found his words. "How's Ethan?"

"Were you able to see him?" Logan inquired.

"No. He's unconscious again, seems he slips in and out. I did talk to Cade for a few minutes. He appreciates all the concern, but says there's nothing to do, at this point, but wait."

"They don't know anything?" Logan blinked. His emotions were obviously close to the surface.

Quinn shook his head. "They're waiting for him to wake up properly. Once he does, they'll know a lot more."

"The wedding's in three days." Logan murmured. "What are we supposed to do?"

Quinn stepped forward and squeezed the distraught man's forearm. "Exactly what we've been doing, waiting and praying. This is all going to be fine, you'll see. Ethan's a strong man. I have faith he'll pull through this with flying colours."

Nerves battled each other in Jack's stomach. "Wait and pray," he repeated, and a thought struck him. He glanced at Quinn with hesitation. "I've never been a very religious type."

"Me either," Logan mumbled sheepishly. He seemed to realise Jack's revelation might be more important to Quinn.

"Takes all kinds." Quinn smiled at both of them. "When I was growing up, no one would have pictured me as a reverend. Even now, I feel I'm more the spiritual type. I try not to be too preachy."

"You're not preachy at all," Jack insisted. As he spoke the words, it occurred to him that he had no idea what kind of a reverend Quinn was, because he barely knew him. Embarrassment and a twinge of guilt tweaked his gut at how fast they'd fallen into bed.

"Thanks. But you might want to reserve judgement until you've heard one of my sermons." Quinn went to an overstuffed chair in the lobby and perched on the edge. "I figured I'd hang around here for a while if it's all right with you two. I only have one appointment this afternoon, and it's not until later."

"Sure." Logan spoke up first. "I'm still not sure what I should do. Should I call anyone? Cade's brother, or any of the wedding guests?"

"Why don't you call Alex?" Quinn suggested. "Seems like you could use him right now. At least talk to him.

Then I think you should carry on with the wedding plans. We'll keep good thoughts that it's going to happen on schedule. I'll man the phones and the desk out here if you like."

Logan nodded, his face registering appreciation. "You're right, I should call Alex. And I was going to start baking today."

"I'll help you." Jack was grateful for something to do. "I should run up and tell Delia about Ethan, though. I promised we'd keep her informed."

"I'll do that before I make my call." Logan headed for the stairs. "Thanks, guys. Jack, I'll meet you in the kitchen shortly."

Jack watched him go, suddenly uncomfortable being alone with the man he'd spent the night with. "I should go get things ready."

Quinn approached him. "This has hit you harder than you want to admit. It's okay to feel bad, Jack. Just know, you don't have to do it alone."

"Feel bad?" Jack blinked. "I feel like shit! All this horrible stuff happened last night while we were..." He didn't finish the sentence. Quinn knew as well as he did what they were doing for a good part of the night.

"You think if you'd have been here it would have made a difference? Like maybe you could have prevented the accident?" Quinn's words oozed disbelief.

"Maybe!" Jack spouted back. "Catherine might have appeared to me instead of that idiot salesmen who freaked the hell out. Ethan might not have been involved."

"We'll never know, will we? But it's ridiculous to blame yourself, Jack. Ethan owns this place. He's fully aware of the spirits and the havoc they wreak. He wasn't just some innocent bystander."

"That doesn't make it better." Jack knew he sounded petulant, but didn't care. He felt increasingly rotten and wanted to make sure Quinn knew it. He took a couple of steps towards the kitchen.

Quinn grabbed his arm. "Jack, listen. I know—"

Jack spun. "You *know* what? That I can't sleep sometimes at night so I watch old movies until dawn? You know that I hate broccoli and used to feed it to the dog under the table when my mother served it? Did you know I can't stand the colour yellow, but I like most shades of blue? What do you know about me, exactly, Reverend?"

Jack took a breath and went on. "We're two guys who fell in the sack *hours* after meeting each other, and I don't think either of us has stopped to think about much else since then."

Shock registered on Quinn's face. "Wow, where did *that* come from? You could knock me over with a feather right now, babe. I had no idea you felt that way."

"Neither did I!" Jack snarled, and immediately after, wanted to crumple into the other man's strong arms, but resisted. "It's just all happening so fast, and now this business with Ethan, and Catherine." Thinking about the bride tore at his heart. He softened his tone and added, "I've got to try and help her. She appeared to me first for a reason. I don't understand why, but I feel this in my heart. I have to do something."

Quinn stared at him for a moment before answering. "Whatever you have to do, I'll help you. I can see you're hurting, so we'll put any other conversations on hold until later. But know this. I hate broccoli, too, and if I'd had a dog growing up, I'd have tried to feed it to him. I also hate runny eggs, maybe because they're that putrid shade of yellow. My favourite colour is sky blue, accented by navy, which you might have spotted in most of the rooms in my house last night. If you happened to notice, that is."

"Can't say that I did," Jack admitted, a pleasant warm sensation replacing the anger in his gut. "Course, I was preoccupied with you."

"And I, with you," Quinn said firmly.

Jack looked at the floor then back up into the reverend's beautiful light-brown eyes. "So, do you like old movies?"

Quinn shrugged. "I can take them or leave them. But I promise you this, I have better ideas on how to pass a sleepless night."

Jack's heart melted and he grinned. "And *that* is a conversation best saved for later. Thanks, Quinn. I'm sorry I snapped at you."

"Forget it. I have big shoulders. I can take anything you dish out, my friend."

Jack waggled his eyebrows. "Thought we agreed to save that talk for later."

"Get busy." Quinn swatted Jack's butt and shooed him into the kitchen. He helped himself to a muffin before shooting Jack a quick smile, and heading to the front desk.

* * * *

Mid-afternoon, Jack and Logan had just taken the last tray of a double batch of cookies from the oven when Cade arrived. Clothes rumpled and ponytail askew, he paused at the desk to talk with Quinn. Logan and Jack joined them.

"Hey!" Logan gave the tired-looking man a quick hug. "How is he?"

Cade sighed. "He's awake and seems to be staying that way. He's still in serious condition, and probably has a concussion, but he doesn't seem to have any memory loss, which is a very good thing."

"It is," Jack agreed, and they all murmured assent.

"What's his prognosis?" Quinn asked.

Cade shook his head. "The doctor is running some tests, so I came home for a quick shower. We'll know more once we get the results."

"Let me make you something to eat," Logan offered.

Cade waved a hand. "I had a bite at the hospital, and about a gallon of coffee. I'm okay." He sniffed. "Although, if those are chocolate chip cookies I smell, I could eat a couple of those on my way to the shower."

"I'll get some." Jack headed to the kitchen.

He heard Logan tease their boss. "We baked them for the wedding, but I guess we can spare some for you. But only you."

Jack returned with four warm cookies wrapped in a napkin.

"Thanks." Cade accepted the bundle and walked towards the room he shared with Ethan. "We appreciate everything you've done, fellas, but right now, I don't think there's going to be a wedding."

"What?" Jack's jaw wasn't the only one to drop.

"At least not this weekend, and not here. I doubt Ethan will be up for it. And besides..." He glanced around and scowled. "I'm not sure I'll be bringing Ethan back here."

Chapter Six

Jack stood speechless, and his friends didn't seem any better. He glanced from Quinn to Logan. They all simply stared at Cade.

The dubious groom popped a cookie in his mouth and retreated to his room without another word.

"Oh my god," Jack murmured.

"Fuck me," came Logan's much harsher retort.

"Hang on, guys." Quinn raised his hands. "Remember, Cade is functioning on very little sleep and a great deal of worry. Let's not take anything he says right now as gospel."

"We've got to do something." Jack paced the lobby, mind racing.

"I have an appointment in town, but I'll be back as soon as I'm done." Quinn stepped in front of Jack and caught his eye. "Maybe we can grab a bite to eat and talk this out over dinner?"

"Yeah, sure." Jack nodded.

Quinn squeezed Jack's arm before heading out. He called over his shoulder, "You up for dinner when I get back, Logan? I could bring something."

"Don't bother," Logan replied. "We have enough food here to feed an army." He gazed at each of them wryly. "Or, a bunch of wedding guests. Anyway, we'll come up with something. See you later."

Quinn nodded and left.

Jack sauntered closer to Logan and scratched at a small piece of tape stuck to the front counter. "What do you think Cade's going to do?"

"Hard to tell. Guess we should give him some time, like Quinn said." Logan caught Jack's eye. "He's a pretty smart guy, that one. Seems to have a good head on his shoulders. Plus a few other nice qualities." Logan smiled.

"A few," Jack agreed nonchalantly, as if it didn't mean much to him. His face grew warm and he chuckled. "Okay, more than a few. I think he's a really great guy."

Logan laughed and patted Jack's arm. "I do, too. So, shall we go clean up the kitchen, then decide what we can rustle up for dinner?"

"Yeah." They'd reached the dining room when Cade reappeared, freshly showered and changed, a small suitcase in his hand. He'd pulled his damp hair back into his usual neat, smooth ponytail.

"I'm going back to the hospital. If anything changes, I'll let you know. The nurse brought in a roll-away bed so I can sleep there."

"That was nice." Logan seemed to want to say more, but held back.

"Later, guys." Cade headed out before anyone could speak again.

"Later," Jack repeated, disappointment welling in his chest. When he heard the sounds of Cade's truck driving off, he added, "I really hoped he'd come out and say he'd made a mistake. That he'd said those things in the heat of the moment, but didn't mean them."

"He still might." Logan shrugged. "Let's give him that time we talked about."

"You're right." Jack sighed. *Patience is not my strong suit.* "Say, one of us should run up and tell Delia the latest developments."

"I can do that." Logan started for the hall, but paused when the front door opened again. They both faced it.

A tall, good-looking man with thick, shaggy hair and a rumpled suit jacket over jeans smiled at them. "This place looks the same as I remembered it."

"David!" Logan's face lit up. He retraced his steps and drew the man in for a quick bear hug. "How the hell are you?"

"Great, Logan. Just great." He hugged back then took a step to the rear. "I was on my way to the lighthouse, but I had to stop in and say hi to my old friends, first." He glanced around. "Where are the lucky grooms?"

Logan cleared his throat. "Not here, I'm afraid. There's been an unfortunate incident with Ethan and one of our 'otherworldly inhabitants.'"

Jack was surprised that Logan mentioned the ghost so quickly to the newcomer. He was shocked again when the man's expression beamed with interest.

"No!" David glanced from Logan to Jack and back. "What happened? Is Ethan okay?"

Logan motioned to Jack. "Oh, sorry. David Sanderson, this is our new cook at the inn, Jack Donner. He'll be taking over for me after this weekend. Jack, David is an old friend and former guest here."

"Former?" Jack thought the wording sounded strange.

"David stays at the lighthouse keeper's place when he comes to town these days." Logan answered in a sing-song tone. "He and Hunter are an item."

David grinned. "Yes we are. I've no shame in admitting it, you dork." He punched Logan lightly in the arm then extended his hand. "Pleased to meet you, Jack."

Jack stepped forward and shook hands. "You, too. So what line of work are you in, David?" He'd seen Hunter, the light keeper, just once. The man was a hunk and a half. Jack didn't know their circumstances, but it seemed if the keeper was his fellow, he'd certainly live closer than someone who 'comes to town' occasionally.

"I'm a paranormal investigator." David's eyes sparkled. "And I'm dying to hear what happened with Ethan and, who was it? Angry Annie?"

Jack's heart leapt. *A paranormal investigator!* What the fuck kind of good timing was that?

"Oh, no." Logan shook his head. "Annie loves Ethan. She still likes to stir things up, but she'd never hurt him. This was a new ghost. A bride ghost." He raised his brows.

"Catherine," Jack added, and together, the two men pieced together what they knew of the story.

The ghost chaser shook his head when he'd heard all the details. "Well, what do you know about that?"

"Not nearly enough," Jack replied eagerly.

"Yeah, I wasn't talking literally." David smiled and paced around the lobby. "Seems to me, you need to try and figure out this Catherine's problem. Although Mrs. Nelson might tell you, not all ghosts have problems, and not all of them want our help. But it sounds like this one might." He looked at Logan. "Is she still here, Mrs. Nelson, I mean?"

"Oh, yeah. Can't budge her out of the place."

"I'll have to say hello. Oh, and I guess I'll see her at the wedding."

Jack and Logan exchanged glances. They'd left the wedding being questionable out of their story with a mutual, unspoken agreement.

"About Catherine." Jack changed the subject back, desperate for help with their situation. "Any suggestions on how we go about learning her story?"

"A couple of possibilities." David nodded. "One, there used to be a bunch of records boxed up in Ethan's office. There's a lot of the inn's history there. It took me a couple of days to get through them all. There's also a font of information at the courthouse. Logan, would you have any idea if Barbara Trent still works there?"

"Last I heard she did. She guards those records like a mother and her cubs, though."

David smiled. "I might be able to help you out, there. But, I need to get to the lighthouse now. Hunter's expecting me. I should have some free time tomorrow, if you decide you need something looked up." He shook hands with both men and headed out the way he'd come in. "You know where to find me."

"Yeah, thanks." Logan waved. "Have a good night."

David grinned. "You know I will."

"Nice to meet you," Jack called.

David waved over his shoulder and left.

Jack glanced at Logan. "What kind of good timing was that?"

"No shit!" Logan chuckled. "I'd sort of forgotten about David because he's not registered to stay here. We might be able to use his help."

"No 'might' about it, far as I can see. He said it took him a 'couple of days' to go through those papers in the office? We don't have that long. But with the three of us, Quinn included, and David makes four, we can possibly figure this thing out before the wedding day."

Logan clamped a hand on Jack's shoulder. "Let's get busy in the kitchen, and after dinner, we'll start digging through those boxes."

"Yes!" A surge of excitement hit Jack. For the first time, they had a plan. With Ethan lying in a hospital bed, and not much they could do about it, doing something constructive felt good. He couldn't wait for Quinn to get back so he could tell him the details. *I can't wait for Quinn to get back for a lot of reasons.* Jack smiled.

* * * *

"That's the last box." Jack stood and stretched his weary limbs. He'd been crouched over, searching through papers, for the better part of the last five hours. Quinn had been enthusiastic, and after dinner the three men dived into the task with gusto.

Now, it was nearly midnight. They were all obviously worn out and had found very little new information. Catherine's maiden name was Montclair. The groom's name was Charles Nelson.

"Come on Quinn, I'm exhausted. It's long passed my bedtime and yours, too." Jack slipped his arm around his lover's shoulders and pulled him close.

Logan took the hint and after a spine cracking stretch, said, "I'm going to crash on the sofa in here, you two. If anyone rings for a room, I'll get it. It's going to be a long day tomorrow. Guests will begin arriving and I'm dead sure we're going to have some explaining to do before the day's out." He got to his feet and shook the kinks out. "I'll see you in the morning. Get some sleep."

Quinn climbed to his feet and groaned. "Feels like I've been sitting here for hours." He checked his watch and grimaced. "Oh wait, I have. Come on you. Let's get out of here." He grabbed Jack by the hand and pulled him towards the door. "Your room tonight. I'm too pooped to go home."

"I didn't want to leave here tonight anyway," Jack said, feeling a little sheepish. "I still feel like this was my fault somehow. If I'd just been here, she...Catherine, would have come after me instead of Ethan."

Quinn's grip on Jack's hand tightened. "I thought we'd already sorted this one out. There was nothing about this that could be considered your fault."

Jack looked at his lover and tried to smile, unsuccessfully. "Yeah, I know that in my head." He tapped his forehead with his index finger. "But I can't seem to get it through my heart. I feel like I could have kept it from happening."

"Yeah and if Ethan knew who was causing the ruckus, he wouldn't have gone up the stairs. If that guest had known who it was, he wouldn't have yelled for help." Quinn stopped them both and spun Jack to face him and said, "Hindsight is pretty much always twenty/twenty. Agreed?"

Jack's face grew warm and knew he was blushing. *Damn!* "Yes, I guess so."

"You guess so?" Quinn gave him a stern look.

"Uh, okay, you're right. But it's still not easy." Jack turned and headed for his room, Quinn's hand again in his.

"So, you really made your dog eat broccoli?" Quinn asked when they stood outside Jack's door.

Jack couldn't help but chuckle. "Yeah, he didn't seem to like it much more than I did. But, he ate it if I dipped it in the gravy." He pushed the door open, flipped the light on and stepped aside, allowing Quinn to brush past him. Even that slight touch made Jack's blood race, like no one else ever had. He thought of the harsh words he'd said earlier and regretted them all. Of course, they didn't know each other's likes and dislikes. They'd only known each other a few short days. But, the attraction couldn't be denied.

"Sneaky little devil weren't you?" Quinn stopped just inside the door and spun around to look at Jack, that bemused smile on his face again.

"Yeah, I guess I was. Mum saw right through me, though. She'd always make sure I ate at least some of the wretched stuff."

"Mums are like that."

Jack shut the door and strode towards Quinn, stopping only when his chest came close to touching the other man's. "I'm really sorry for being such an ass earlier."

"You weren't an ass. You've got a lot going on right now. New job, relocating to the inn. The boss getting hurt. A wedding to help plan…a lot. You really don't need a new man in your life adding pressure."

"But, you weren't." Jack reassured.

"Why don't you sleep well?" Quinn asked out of the blue. He raised his arms and let them rest on Jack's shoulders.

"No idea," Jack said, his voice rough with the beginnings of passion. "Even when I was a kid, I never slept really well. Mum and Dad used to fight and I'd hear them."

"Ah, that's rough."

"It happened a very long time ago, too. You'd think it would pass. I'm a big boy now."

"True, but we tend to hang onto things like that, even when we're older. Kids learn from what their parents teach them, or the example they set." Quinn pulled Jack closer and kissed him on the cheek. Not a passionate kiss, but one to show he cared.

"Yeah, I know that, too," Jack said in a soft voice. He remembered the nights he stayed up into the wee hours watching the old movies. *The ones with happy endings.* Maybe that's what the sleeplessness was all about.

"Hey, it's pretty late. If we both don't get some sleep, we're going to be bagged in the morning." Quinn released him and looked around the room. The bed was made up, the bathroom door was open and everything seemed all right.

"Get into bed then. I'll be right with you." Jack strode into the bathroom and did his business. Standing in front of the sink, he washed his hands while looking at himself in the mirror. What on Earth could Quinn see in him? He really wasn't 'all that' and knew it. He smiled, just glad the reverend had zeroed in on him.

He ran his fingers through his unruly dark hair as he left the bathroom, shutting the lights off on the way to the bed. There was just enough natural light to see Quinn laying under the covers, curled up on his side, his face towards Jack.

Jack stripped quickly, his jeans and t-shirt landing in a heap, his underpants and socks on top. His cock, while not fully hard, did show signs of an erection but he ignored it and climbed under the covers.

Quinn snuggled in closer and pressed his mouth to Jack's in a soft kiss. With their lips still touching, Quinn said, "I hope you feel a little better about you and I being together now."

"You mean after my rant today?" Jack replied softly. He slipped his hands around Quinn's body, each coming to rest on a firm buttock.

"Yes," Quinn sighed, then groaned when Jack tightened his grip.

"I'm feeling much better, and a little horny." He alternated the tight grip with a slow rotation, which spread the man's glutes apart. "You?" As he said it, Jack slid the forefinger of his right hand between Quinn's cheeks and grazed the tip across the man's anus.

"Oh, yes," Quinn whispered in a tone barely loud enough for Jack to hear. An instant later, the man's lips found his, and Quinn's tongue pushed its way past his teeth.

Their lips locked together as Jack eased his digit into Quinn's eager hole. The tube of lube lay in the bedside table drawer, which, at the moment, he couldn't reach. The snug clenching of his lover's ass around his finger turned him on tremendously. His cock pulsed to its greatest girth in a matter of seconds, pushing its way upwards between them.

Industriously, Jack fucked Quinn with the single finger, until the man was actively humping back.

"I need to get some lube, babe," Jack said into Quinn's mouth. "Don't want to hurt you."

"If you insist," Quinn panted.

"Hang on." Jack slid his finger free and rolled away, reaching for the drawer. A moment later, he had the large tube in his hand and a condom covering his erection. A dollop of the clear goo clung to his fingers. When he turned back, Quinn had risen to his knees and laid his head on the pillow. The sexy reverend's light-brown eyes shone as the man looked up at him.

Jack climbed to his knees and in full view of Quinn, ran his lube-covered fingers over his latex sheathed cock. It bounced and throbbed, eager for the fucking the reverend so temptingly offered. "I'm not going to rush this."

"Please, I want you inside me." Quinn's voice held a note of desperation that surprised Jack, but he refused to be hurried.

So far, their entire relationship, if what they had could even be called that, had been rushed and fitted into moments of free time. Done with that, he positioned himself behind his sexy reverend and placed his hands on the man's hips. "Don't move," he said, and bent forward. He pressed his lips to the warm flesh of the man's left buttock, then moved to the right and repeated the kiss. Back and forth, he kissed and licked, carefully biting and nibbling on each cheek until he'd covered the flesh of each sexy mound. He'd determinedly avoided getting too close to the cleft separating each buttock, but decided the time had come. He repositioned himself, getting more comfortable and again leaned in.

"Tell me something else about yourself. Something I don't know," Jack said and smiled. "If you stop talking, I stop licking." He bent a few inches closer and stuck out his tongue.

"What? Now?" Quinn sounded shocked, confused.

"Yes, right now. I want to know one thing about you that I don't know already. Shouldn't be difficult." He waited, tongue poised above the uppermost part of the man's ass crack.

"Uh, senior prom, I took Janice Be—"

Jack dived in, licking from the top of Quinn's cleft downward, stopping directly over his anus when the sexy reverend stopped talking. Leaning up, he said, "and?"

"And…and, Janice Belinger. Yeah, Belinger. She was two years older than I was, and, and…as big as…"

As Quinn told the tale of his prom date, Jack lavished the man's soft, puckered hole with his tongue. Stiffening his tongue, he pressed the tip into the quivering opening. It clutched and writhed against his lips, exciting Jack to a fevered pitch.

As if from some great distance, he heard Quinn saying, "Janice tried getting…I couldn't get it up…I wasn't…I wasn't…I—I. Oh my g—Please—"

Jack couldn't help but smile, even with his tongue buried in the man's behind. Quinn groaned, but his speech sputtered an end. Unable to find words, it seemed he'd decided noises might suffice, and Jack allowed it.

Using his tongue and fingers, Jack opened the man and lubricated him until three fingers slipped in easily. Still, he wanted to bring the man greater pleasure and reached between his widespread legs for the swaying erection tapping at Quinn's belly. Deftly, he stroked it, taking special care to anoint the entire crown with the pre-cum drooling from its tip.

Backing away, Jack mumbled, "Janice wasn't for you then?"

"Huh?" Quinn had apparently lost his train of thought.

Jack chuckled and released the man's impressive erection, vowing to get to it again later. "Are you as horny as I am?"

"More. You're horrible, you know that, right?" Quinn looked over his shoulder and smiled.

"Yeah, but you're enjoying this, too, or you wouldn't be playing along." Straightening up, Jack took hold of his cock and aimed the tip at the soft entrance to Quinn's backdoor. "More? You did ask for more."

"Yes, more. I need your cock inside me." Quinn reached back and grabbed Jack's hip, pulling him forward.

Jack bent forward and kissed the man's back between his shoulder blades. "More is a good thing. Slow." He let Quinn pull him in, but only a tiny bit at a time. He knew he'd come if he entered too quickly, and from the way Quinn's cock had throbbed, he knew he wasn't alone.

Sweat popped out on his forehead and ran down his face. Jack groaned and whispered how much he wanted the man to care for him, how much he cared for Quinn already. The words came easily, and to his great surprise, they felt right as he said them, even if they sounded like gibberish.

Fully encased in Quinn's ass, Jack rested for a moment before he made any other movements. Slick sweat coated his lover's back, and Jack slid against him. The warmth of the man's hole clenched around his cock made his head spin. The beauty of their joining amazed him.

Jack eased out, nearly pulling his cock free of the clamping hole, before pushing back in, balls deep in the fluttering depths. A slow rhythm of gently pulling out, then driving back in, had both of them gasping for breath in no time.

"Jack, yeah, that's it. Grind your hips around." Quinn worked his ass up and around, trying to get Jack to follow his lead.

"Like this?" Jack asked as he rotated his lower body, hoping to give Quinn the pleasure he sought.

"Oh yeah, just like that. More, yes, more. Please."

Quinn seemed beyond making sense and Jack loved it. He'd never been able to enrapture a lover so much or as quickly before and it really boosted his ego.

From then on, Jack fucked the man five or six times then rotated his hips while holding Quinn's flanks. Once or twice, he reached beneath the reverend and stroked his erection, but soon realised if he continued that move, he'd end their session much too soon. As it was, he knew it couldn't last a lot longer anyway. His cock throbbed almost continually with the need to spew its load. The only way he managed to keep from coming was to think of how much he wanted to make it good for his lover.

It didn't matter. His need to climax rose, soaring with each passing moment until he couldn't control it. He slammed into Quinn's butt and growled, "Gonna come!"

Quinn yelled, "Yes, yes, now. Come with me." He pushed his body back, clamping his ass tight around Jack's erection and whispered, "Yes, yes!"

Jack reached beneath the man and held his dick, feeling it pulse mightily as the man's orgasm shook them both. Quinn shuddered and Jack gulped in a huge lung full of air, his own climax stopped a thrust short. Yet, he knew it would come, and soon. He waited, heart racing, sweat pouring from him, as his lover gyrated on his steely hard cock.

When Quinn relaxed, Jack leant forward and whispered, "Hold still. I need to come."

"Damn! Yes, do me." Quinn spread himself as if eager for Jack to renew the onslaught.

Jack moved as gently as he could, not willing to hurt the man with his wild pumping. Three or four deep thrusts later, his orgasm rose and he sent a stream into the condom buried in Quinn's bottom. Another followed and another, sending shivers of ecstasy from Jack's head to his toes.

When the last spasm died, Jack collapsed across Quinn's back and lay there, spent. He shuddered one more time then sighed.

"That was amazing," Quinn said, still breathless from his climax.

"Uh huh, it sure was," Jack agree, less interested in speaking just yet. He reached around Quinn and held the man tight to him, rolling to his side. "I'm afraid we're made an awful big wet spot."

"No kidding. I don't think I've ever come like that before. What did you do to me?"

"Don't know, but when I get it figured out, I plan to do it again, okay?"

"Oh yeah, I'd be disappointed if you didn't." Quinn turned his head and grinned back at Jack. "Thank you."

"For what?"

"For asking me to come with you. For sharing your bed. For giving me more pleasure than I've ever had before. I could think of a few other things, but I'm exhausted," the reverend said and as if to emphasise his statement, he yawned.

"I'll be right back," Jack said, slipping free of Quinn's bottom and sliding out of bed. He went into the bathroom and got rid of the condom, then cleaned himself up. Grabbing a towel and another dampened facecloth, he returned to the bedroom.

Quinn lay as Jack had left him, more asleep than awake. Jack carefully wiped him down then stuffed the towel beneath the sheet, to save the mattress from being stained. He tossed the facecloth into the sink then rejoined Quinn. Cuddled behind Quinn, Jack pulled the man close and kissed the back of his neck. "Good night." And to himself, he added, *lover*.

From somewhere close by, a woman cried softly. Jack turned his head, but couldn't see anything or anyone. Yet, the crying continued.

"Quinn," he whispered. "Hey, you awake?"

"Umph," came the man's less than enthusiastic response.

"Can you hear something? Someone crying?" Jack sat up and peered into the darkness. He flipped on the bedside lamp, but there was nothing. The crying stopped.

Quinn sat up and rubbed his eyes. "What's up? Can I hear what?"

"Someone crying. A woman?" Jack got out of bed and checked in the bathroom, but again found no one, nothing out of the ordinary.

"No. I didn't hear a thing." Quinn pulled the covers aside and patted the bed. "Just you. Now, come on. You need your sleep."

Jack climbed back in and snuggled up to Quinn, listening for...*what?* The next thing he knew, half-asleep, he heard Quinn murmur, "I'm falling for you, Jack Donner. Sleep well, my sexy man."

Sleep took him then, his dreams were filled with Quinn and Catherine, and a big girl named Janice.

* * * *

The next morning, Jack fingered the one newspaper clipping they'd discovered the night before that shed some light on their dilemma. "James and Etta Montclair announce the engagement of their daughter, Catherine Grace, to Charles Spaulding Nelson, son of Scott and Marion Nelson." Something niggled at him, but he couldn't put his finger on it.

There was no question they were the right people. In her engagement photo, Catherine looked exactly as she had when she'd appeared to him, sans the bruises. The man, Charles, definitely owned the face that'd appeared in his mirror.

He'd already called David Sanderson, the ghost hunter, and asked if he could do further research into whether or not the wedding had taken place. Quinn left for a full day of counselling appointments.

He and Logan busied themselves preparing wedding food as if there were no doubts the ceremony would take place. The inn remained quiet until late afternoon, when the front doorbell finally sounded.

At loose ends again, Jack followed Logan to the lobby. A tall, rugged man with shoulder-length brown hair wrestled two large suitcases through the door.

"Welcome to Whiskers'." Logan stepped behind the desk.

The man glanced up and his dark eyes crinkled. "Hey. I believe you have a reservation for me. Dylan Wyatt's the name."

Logan's eyes widened. "Cade's brother?"

"And best man. That's me."

He grinned and Jack noticed the family resemblance. "Best man," Jack repeated softly.

Logan said, "Great to meet you. I'm Logan Emerson and this is Jack Donner. We cook. Here, at the inn, I mean."

Dylan's smile widened. "Good to know. Listen, I've spoken with Cade several times so I know what's going on. I just got into town, and wanted to drop my stuff here before I go to the hospital. Although, I'm not that keen on staying here anymore. I fucking hate ghosts, and Cade knows it. First sign of trouble, I'll be checking into the nearest Regency Hotel."

"Which is a long drive from here," Logan replied, "So think about that before you go running into the night."

Dylan's smile tightened. "I didn't say I was *afraid* of ghosts. I just said I *fucking hate them*. Didn't used to believe in them at all, but Cade changed my mind about that. The man has some stories."

"More now," Jack agreed.

Logan held up his hands. "Sorry to offend. Since you've talked to Cade, I have to ask. Did he mention anything about the wedding being on hold? That's the last we've heard from him, but we're hoping he'll change his mind once things calm down."

"No offence taken." Dylan waved it off. "Don't you worry. There'll be a wedding. I'll see to that. As long as Ethan can handle it. If I have to wheel him up the aisle in a fucking wheelchair, I'll do it. He's the best thing that's ever happened to my brother, and by God, there's going to be a wedding."

Jack grinned.

Logan's face beamed with relief as he answered, "Thank you. We were really hoping things would work out." He reached under the counter for a key card, and scanned it through the computer. "You're in room two, just down the hall. We'll get your bags, just leave them there."

"Thank you." Dylan accepted the card and nodded. "I'll let you do that. I'm anxious to get to the hospital. I'll see you both later."

"Nice to meet you." Jack watched the tall man leave. To Logan he said, "Wow."

Logan chuckled and turned so his back faced the door. "He's something, isn't he?"

The front door opened again, and a big man in a stylish black suit appeared. He held the bell so it didn't chime. He looked at Jack and pressed a finger to his lips for quiet.

Jack bit back a grin.

Logan crossed his arms and leaned against the counter. "I thought Cade was hell on wheels. He's a pussycat compared to that guy."

The handsome newcomer leaned close to Logan and murmured, "What guy? You making time with someone behind my back, handsome?"

Eyes bulging, Logan spun around. "Oh my god! You're here!" He threw his arms around the bigger man's neck and hugged him over the counter.

"Where else am I going to be? I got here as soon as I could get my schedule cleared, babe. I'm sorry you're had to go through this alone."

Logan pulled back and wiped at his eyes. "I, uh, haven't been alone, Alex. I told you about the new cook Ethan hired?" He nodded towards Jack. "He's been here, and he's been great."

"Sure, Jack, isn't it?" Alex smiled enormously and extended his hand.

He mentioned me. Jack blinked with surprise, but shook the proffered hand. "Logan's spoken highly of you, sir. It's a pleasure to meet you."

"It's Alex," he corrected. "Unless you appear before me in court. Then Judge Brookfield will do."

"Yes, sir, er...Alex." The bear of a man intimidated the hell out of him, but obviously had a different effect on his co-worker.

Logan slipped around the counter and back into Alex's arms. "I'm so glad you're here. Thanks for coming early."

"Anything for you." They gazed into each other's eyes.

Jack took a step backwards. "I'll just go and leave you two—"

Alex raised a hand. "You'll do nothing of the kind." He placed a light kiss on Logan's forehead and pulled away. "I didn't intend to chase anybody off. We'll have time later."

Logan fished in his pocket for keys, and yanked one off his ring. "You can go on over to the cabin if you like."

Alex tugged at his necktie. "I'd like that very much. Do you have a lot left to do today?"

"Just dinner, but there's almost no one here."

"I can take care of dinner," Jack spoke up. "Alex can come back here to eat, or you can take something home for the two of you."

Alex and Logan gazed at each other. "Taking something home sounds real good," Logan murmured. He glanced back at Jack. "Thanks."

"You bet. I'm going to haul Dylan's things to his room." He hefted the two big bags, and grabbed a master key card. "Again, it was a pleasure to meet you, Alex."

"You, too, Jack."

Suitcases in hand, Jack slipped down the hall and pretended he didn't see the necking taking place in the lobby. The men may have wanted to wait until later, but obviously couldn't. He smiled. That kind of love was hard to find. *Ethan and Cade found it.* A fleeting thought of Quinn passed through his mind but he tamped it down. *Too early.* Still, butterflies flitted in his stomach. He couldn't wait for Quinn to return, and he liked that feeling very much.

After Logan and Alex left, Jack puttered around in the kitchen, planning a meal for himself, Quinn, Delia, and whoever else might show up. He had no idea if Dylan would be back in time to eat, but wanted to make enough so there'd be food if he did.

Someone rapped on the back door and Jack jumped. He glanced up and spotted David. For some reason, the hair on the back of his neck bristled. He beckoned the man in. "Hi."

"Hi there." David grinned. "Thought I might find you back here. I'm just returning from town, and figured you'd want to know what I found out."

"Absolutely!" Jack wiped his hands on a towel and tossed it on the counter. "So, you found something?"

"Four somethings." David grabbed two stools and pulled them to the counter. Both of them sat, and he spread out some copies of newspaper articles. "First of all, the announcement of the engagement. The wedding was supposed to be here, at the inn."

"That one, I've got." Jack pulled a similar clipping from his pocket and laid it next to the copy. "But that's it. No word on whether the wedding ever took place."

"It didn't." David pointed to the next article. *Groom Killed in Automobile Accident.* "Local businessman Charles Nelson was killed when he lost control of his automobile and careened over the side of High Meadow Road. Nelson was en route to Whiskers' Seaside Inn, where he was to marry local debutante Catherine Montclair. Constables at the scene determined brake failure to be the cause of the nearly new vehicle's demise." David stopped reading and looked at Jack.

"Wow," Jack breathed. "This was, what? 1898? I didn't even know they had cars back then."

"Most people didn't. Only the very wealthy, or the well connected, did. After the turn of the century, cars became much more prevalent."

"Well connected?" Jack inquired.

David shrugged. "Maybe he didn't own it. He might have borrowed it for the wedding. Not sure we'll ever know. I searched several months after that, but didn't find anything else about the accident."

Jack pointed to the other two papers. "But you did find something else?"

"Oh yeah." David waggled his brows. "This is where it gets interesting. Check it out. Two weeks later. A very small announcement of marriage, between one Catherine

Montclair and a Mr. Theodore Nelson. Same last name. Coincidence? I doubt it."

"Two weeks later?" Jack scratched his forehead. "What could that mean?"

"I had one thought. Perhaps someone in Charles' family offered to step up and take care of Catherine. Maybe it was a marriage of convenience."

Jack's eyes widened. "You think she was…" He held a hand in front of his stomach to indicate pregnancy.

Another shrug. "Once again, we might never know. Last thing I found, and I have to say, this is where it gets freaking creepy. Read this." He pointed to the final, small article.

Jack leaned in to read the fine print. *Local woman dies in unexplained accident.* "Catherine Nelson was found dead late Saturday night along the side of High Meadow Road. No cause of death was given, and no foul play was suspected." Jack looked at David. "High Meadow Road again? Is that a huge coincidence, or what? Are you kidding me? Those jokers had to have seen her face. How could they say no foul play was suspected?"

"This was over a hundred years ago, man. I doubt they had the crackerjack forensics officers we're used to. I'd imagine they did the best they could under the circumstances."

Jack hopped up and paced the kitchen. "I'm not sure that was enough—for Catherine."

David stood. "I wish I could offer to help you dig into this further, but I've got an article of my own to write, with a looming deadline. I really need to get busy on it."

"You've been a lot of help." Jack shook his hand vigorously. "Seriously, thanks so much, David."

"Glad to do it. Guess I'll see you Saturday, at the wedding." He screwed his face into a nervous expression. "Hope this one takes place."

Chapter Seven

Jack knew David was kidding, but the joke was closer to the truth than the other man could know. "Me, too," he murmured, and smiled.

David left and Jack rustled up some pork chops and fried potatoes. He took a plate up to Delia, who asked him through the door to leave the tray. When he returned to the dining room, Quinn was there.

"Hey, good looking." The reverend greeted him with the sexiest smile Jack thought he'd ever seen.

"Get over here." Jack motioned to his lover. "We've basically got the place to ourselves. You can do better than that."

"Oh, yes I can." Quinn drew Jack into his arms and bent him backwards for a soul-searing kiss.

"That's what I'm talkin' about," Jack teased breathlessly, when they separated.

"I missed you today. Sorry I couldn't be here for you, but my counselling appointments are scheduled well in advance. I freed up my calendar for tomorrow, though, so whatever you need done, I'm all yours."

Jack grinned. "I'll start a list. The first thing on it is going to be more kisses like that one."

Quinn's eyes sparkled. "Plenty more where that came from. So tell me, how was your day?"

"Unbelievable." Jack wasn't sure where to begin. From Cade's brother to Logan's beau, and now Catherine's story, it had been a fascinating day. "Let's eat and I'll fill you in."

"Sounds good." Quinn followed him to the kitchen. "Anything that needs to be done after dinner?"

"Oh, yeah." Jack glanced over his shoulder, scanning up and down his lover's body seductively. "A couple of big things."

"Perfect." Quinn swatted Jack's ass.

* * * *

Jack padded down the hall in his pyjamas, ostensibly to make sure the inn was secure for the night. He'd left Quinn snoring like a buzz saw, a sound that didn't bother him one bit. The reverend seemed to have no trouble sleeping, especially after a bout of raucous sex. But even heavy-duty fucking hadn't helped Jack's insomnia. He'd tried talking to Quinn as they lay in the dark, but ultimately sleep had won out for Quinn.

"Why hasn't Catherine appeared the past two nights?" he whispered as he entered the dining room. "Where are you, Catherine?"

The inn remained dark and quiet. Dylan had phoned saying he'd be in late, and would use Cade's key.

Jack checked the kitchen and spotted a plate and glass in the otherwise spotless sink. He smiled. Dylan had apparently made it back. He double checked all the locks and headed back into the dining room, where he ran smack into someone in curlers and an old pink robe. "Shit!" Jack jumped back then grabbed Delia, who he'd nearly bowled over.

She straightened her robe and heaved a sigh. "In a hurry young man?"

"I'm sorry. Are you okay?"

"If that hunky reverend was waiting for me, I would be," she replied.

Jack smiled. He'd never met anyone her age who seemed to care less about whether anyone was gay or straight. She pestered everyone equally. "Yeah, well, I can't sleep. This business with Catherine and Ethan has me worried. You know, Cade still hasn't told us if there's going to be a wedding."

"Of course there will be," Delia scoffed.

"I'm not so sure. Ethan was badly injured, and Cade is flat-out pissed. You didn't see him. He talked like they might not ever come back here."

"They'll come back!" she insisted, but her voice faltered. "Oh, damn it all to hell!"

"Wow, tough talk from you, Delia—err, Mrs. Nelson. *Mrs. Nelson?*" Jack blinked as the connection hit him like a ton of bricks. "As in Charles Nelson, Catherine's would-be groom?"

The old woman scowled. "Whatever are you talking about? I don't know any..." Her bravado deflated. She took a breath and exhaled. "Charles. Poor Charles." She gazed up at Jack. "He was my great uncle."

Jack's heart leapt. "Your uncle? Oh my God! Then you know all about the clippings I read today. His car accident, and why Catherine married someone named Theodore Nelson just two weeks later."

Delia's scowl returned. "Uncle Theo was a horse's ass. Everyone in the family agreed on that. He tricked Catherine into marrying him, and then never treated her properly."

"He tricked her? We thought maybe she was pregnant, and he was helping her out."

"Of course not!" Delia snapped. "Catherine was a respectable young woman. She loved Charles very much. They would have been so happy together." She shook her head sadly.

Jack watched the plastic curlers bob, unsure of what to say. "The accident was unfortunate."

"It was no accident!" Tears streamed down the old woman's face. "Theo did something to the automobile, cut the brakes, or some such thing. Cars were a novelty then. Charles was an inexperienced driver. He probably never knew what happened."

"He cut the brake lines? Why on Earth would he do such a thing?"

"Catherine," Delia whispered. "He wanted her for himself, but she'd refused his advances. Then she met Charles. Theo was livid at the thought of them marrying."

Mind racing, Jack tried to straighten out the details of the story. "So Theo kills Charles, and then, what? Convinces Catherine to marry him instead?"

"Yes. They had a small, civil ceremony at the courthouse. Catherine tried to be a good wife to the cad, but he mistreated her cruelly. Some say he was haunted by Charles' ghost, and would never find peace. I don't know if that was true, but he acted like a tortured soul. He went so far as to admit to Catherine what he did. When she found out that Theo had purposely killed his brother, she went crazy and tried to kill him."

Jack realised he'd been holding his breath. "What happened?" He hated to ask, because he knew the eventual grim outcome.

Delia stared at the wall. "Theo beat her to shreds. Catherine escaped, drove their horse and buggy to the spot where Charles had died, and threw herself off a cliff. She died that night. Uncle Theodore, unfortunately, lived a good many years after that. He died alone, an unhappy man, with an ugly spot on his soul."

"Oh my lord." Jack rested his back against the kitchen door. "What a sad story."

Delia focused on him. "I come from a very fine family, young man. You can see why I'm not particularly proud of that bit of history."

He shook his head. "No one has to know about this. But Mrs. Nelson, Delia…if I can use this information to somehow help Ethan, wouldn't you want me to do that?"

Her face crinkled. "Ethan. Yes, please, do what you need to for that sweet boy. But I beg you, be judicious in the retelling of those events. People don't need to know the details."

Jack nodded. "I understand, and I agree. I'll keep the story under wraps as much as I can."

Delia's head tilted and she gazed at him quizzically. "What story?"

He blinked. He stared into her eyes, and honestly couldn't tell if she was yanking his chain or not. "Delia?"

"*Mrs. Nelson* to you, young whippersnapper. But, say, do you have any more of those chocolate chip cookies you baked earlier? And maybe a glass of warm milk?" She smiled sweetly.

Jack sighed. On the other hand, cookies and milk didn't sound like a bad idea. "Right this way, Mrs. Nelson."

* * * *

Jack, Quinn, Logan and Dylan were sipping coffee the next morning in the dining room when Cade exited his bedroom.

"Morning, all."

"Cade!" Logan greeted him. "Dylan told us you'd wandered in sometime in the night. How's Ethan?"

"Better." He grabbed a cup from the nearly empty buffet table and poured himself some coffee. He took hold of a chair from the next table and pulled it up to join them. "He's still suffering from headaches, and he's got a big ol' white bandage wrapped around his head. Good news is, we were told he might be able to downgrade that to a smaller one by tomorrow."

"Tomorrow?" Jack raised his eyebrows hopefully.

Dylan smiled over his cup of steaming brew.

"You knew!" Logan teased Cade's brother. "And you knew we were all sitting here wondering if we should continue with the wedding plans or not. You dog."

"Not my place to say." Dylan replied. "But yeah, I knew. I told you there'd be a wedding."

"Thank god." Quinn breathed a sigh of relief, which everyone seemed to identify with.

Cade smiled. "Here's the deal. I'll bring Ethan home in the morning. We'll just be here long enough to change for the wedding, and have the service as scheduled. We'll stay for the reception, and after that, Dylan has graciously agreed to let us stay at his place in Montana."

Jack smiled and the others nodded and grinned. "Sounds nice."

"I'm glad you decided to take a honeymoon after all," Logan said. "I always felt bad that you weren't going anywhere because I was leaving, too. No one to run the inn."

Cade blew on his coffee and shrugged. "That was part of it, but we've solved that problem. We're closing down the inn. Takes the pressure off worrying about when we have to get back. We'll stay as long as we frigging want."

Jack's jaw sagged.

His boss must have noticed because Cade added, "We'll pay you for two weeks, of course, and evaluate after that. Meanwhile, if you find another job, we'll understand."

"I don't want another job!" Jack protested. "I really like it here. I could keep the place open for you." He knew as he said it, no one in their right mind would leave a business in the hands of a man they'd known five days.

Logan placed a hand on the table. "I'll stay and run the inn. Alex will understand. What's a couple more weeks when we have a lifetime together ahead of us?"

Cade shook his head. "We'd never ask you to do that. It's time for you and Alex to get on with your lives. Where is the judge, anyway? I heard he was here."

"*The judge* only recognises one five-thirty per day when he's on vacation. I let him sleep." Logan frowned. "I wish you'd let me do this for you."

Setting his cup on the table, Cade pushed back, stood, and smiled. "You're cute when you beg, kid. But it's been decided. Ethan and I will contact guests with reservations in the next few weeks. For now, I'm off to the hospital. Don't you have some wedding business to attend to?"

"Yes." Logan got to his feet, still appearing decidedly unhappy.

"You guys could do one more thing for me. I laid out the clothes we're wearing for the ceremony. Personally, I don't care much one way or the other, but I'm sure Ethan would like it if they were neatly pressed."

"I'm hell on wheels with an iron," Quinn spoke up. "I'll handle that task."

"Thank you." Cade's eyes sparkled with obvious appreciation. "You all have been just great. Ethan and I can't thank you enough."

"Anything we can do, just ask." Jack felt deflated, as if he hadn't been able to do nearly enough.

Cade started to leave, then paused. "Oh, Logan? You might throw some clothes in a suitcase for us. I think the bags are downstairs in the storage room. Casual stuff, you know what we like to wear. I'd ask my brother to do it, but we'd end up with two toothbrushes and a g-string."

Everyone chuckled and Logan winked. "If I find a g-string in there, I'll be sure to pack it."

"Yeah, right. See you later." Cade left.

"Wow." Logan paced the room. "I guess we have plenty to do now."

"And there's going to be a wedding." Dylan stood. "I'll head down to the basement and dig up a couple of suitcases."

"Thanks," Logan told him. He turned to Jack. "Not exactly how I'd hoped this would turn out. I'm sorry, man."

Jack shrugged. "Not your fault, but thanks."

"I'll go get those wedding clothes." The blond-haired man went into their bosses' bedroom.

Jack and Quinn stood and faced each other. "Actually, this sucks." Jack frowned. "I was really starting to get comfortable in this place."

"I know you were. I'm sorry, babe." Quinn drew Jack into his arms.

Jack nestled his face in the crook of his lover's neck and inhaled the now-familiar scent. "I'm getting pretty comfortable with you, too. Definitely not ready for this to end."

"It doesn't have to end." Quinn squeezed him tight. "I told you last night. I want you to stay with me, regardless of what happens at the inn."

"I know." Jack sighed. He hadn't wanted to act in haste. Now, it felt as if time was running out.

"I love you, Jack." Quinn whispered.

He pulled back and looked into those magical, light-brown eyes. Before he could speak, Logan returned.

"Here are the wedding clothes." He stopped in his tracks. "Oh, sorry."

"It's okay." Jack stepped back, eyes still locked on Quinn's. "We'll talk later. We all have plenty to do."

Quinn nodded, and they got to work.

* * * *

Jack couldn't believe how fast the inn returned to full capacity. By the end of the day Friday, every room was full, and he was cooking for a full house again. Quinn stayed until the dinner service had been completed, but both of them had been so busy they hadn't found a minute to talk. He'd left shortly after, deciding it'd be more proper, as a reverend, not to spend the night.

The lobby and dining room were overrun with the grooms' family and friends, chatting and socialising with Dylan and later, Cade. Jack slipped off to his room and fell asleep as soon as his head hit the pillow.

He woke to his alarm the next morning amazed he'd slept soundly through the night. He prepared breakfast for the rowdy crowd, most of who seemed to have no idea about the events of the past week. Everyone knew Ethan had had an accident, but the mood was festive with him returning that morning.

Just as he finished the dishes, the catering team Logan had hired arrived to take over for the rest of the day. Jack was off duty. He just had to change into his best blue suit, and he'd be ready for the wedding.

With every hair slicked into place and a rarely used tie securely around his neck, Jack entered the dining room about thirty minutes prior to the service. The weather had cooperated, providing the perfect sunny day for an outside event. He saw guests congregating around and under the large white canopy in the garden. There were more faces than he'd imagined. A large number of townspeople had turned out, which pleased Jack. Ethan and Cade were good men. Folks liked them.

The wedding party remained inside. Dylan, Logan and Alex stood in the dining room. The door to Ethan and Cade's room was open, and Jack heard laughter from within.

"They made it," he commented.

Logan turned to Jack and blinked. "Wow, look at you! You didn't have to get so dressed up. Even the grooms aren't wearing ties."

Jack noticed Logan's open-neck shirt and slacks. Dylan was dressed the same. Fortunately, the judge wore a suit like he did. Jack shook his head. "I just assumed…"

"You know what they say about assuming, boy," Dylan teased.

"Leave him alone." Alex smiled, and brushed a speck from Jack's lapel. "He looks very nice. It never hurts to dress formally."

"Thank you." Jack grinned. He started to add something when a blast of wind blew through the dining room.

"Son of a bitch!" Cade muttered loudly.

He backed Ethan out of the bedroom, one arm around him possessively. They were both dressed in black trousers and nice white shirts, open at the collar. Ethan sported a large white bandage on his forehead.

Jack turned to see what they were staring at, and there she was. Catherine, in full bridal regalia, stomped towards them. She looked much the same as she had that first night Jack saw her. A filmy veil covered her face, but he recognised the bloody bruises beneath it.

"Where's *my* groom?" she shrieked.

"Listen, sister," Ethan spoke in soothing tones. "We know you're upset about something, but this isn't the best time."

"This is a fucking lousy time," Cade retorted.

"Shhh!" Ethan squeezed his arm. "Lady, look. We're just about—"

"Where's my groom?" she repeated, her already shrill voice rising a notch.

"Catherine!" Jack stepped forward.

All heads turned in Jack's direction, including the bride's.

He gulped, and tried to steady his voice. "You're looking for Charles. You were supposed to marry him here."

She cocked her head at Jack quizzically. "Charles is late. Where is he?"

Before Jack could decide what to say next, a series of doors slammed. The noise started deep inside the inn, grew closer, and ended with Ethan and Cade's bedroom door blowing closed with a loud *thud*.

Another pale-haired vision in white appeared, a beautiful woman with an ugly scowl on her face. Like a twister, she circled Ethan then paused in front of Catherine. "Leave him alone!"

"Angry Annie," Logan murmured.

"Get out of my way," Catherine snarled at the other woman. "It's my wedding day. If I can't have Charles then another groom will do, and this one I'll take to the grave!"

She rushed Ethan but Annie held her off, the two women struggling, floating and spinning in circles in a filmy white haze.

"A ghost chick fight!" Jack murmured in awe.

"Somebody *do* something," Logan said under his breath.

Dylan took a step back. "Like sell the inn? Good idea."

Jack scanned the room. Delia stood at the back in a fancy, flowered dress and ridiculously huge hat. She seemed mesmerised and almost glued to the wall. Everyone else was still outside.

"Alex," he whispered. "Can you make sure everybody stays out, please? And find Quinn. I might need him."

"You got it." The judge slipped out quietly.

The ghosts didn't seem to notice. They continued their noisy wrestling match as Cade slowly backed Ethan away.

Jack stepped forward. He mustered up his loudest voice and as much courage as he could manage. "Stop it! Annie, Ethan's fine. Catherine! Look, there's Charles. Your groom is here." He crossed his fingers, hoping the trick wouldn't backfire.

"Charles?" Catherine glanced up hopefully. She spun around, looking for him.

Annie paused and looked around until she spotted Ethan. She planted herself between him and the bride, and folded her arms across her chest.

Come on, Charles. Jack didn't know much about ghosts, but he hoped the late groom was somehow listening, and would be as glad to see his bride as she was anxious to find him. *Come on, Charles!*

"Where is he?" She screamed, focusing her anger on Jack.

"There!" Logan pointed.

Jack spun around, heaving a huge sigh of relief when he spotted the hundred-year-old groom.

"Charles!" Catherine gasped, and the couple came together in the centre of the room. "I missed you, so!"

"And I, you, my love. I'm sorry I wasn't here for you."

They joined hands, clasping them at their chests. When Charles released her, he took the edge of her veil and lifted it up, over her head, uncovering her face.

In the blink of an eye, Catherine's face became beautiful and unmarked. Again, she looked as she must have on her wedding day. The couple gazed into each other's eyes.

Jack viewed the emotional scene with amazement, then inhaled and glanced around. Quinn watched from just inside the door. "Reverend, you're up."

"What?" Quinn raised his hands.

"Say the words," Jack urged. "You know, dearly beloved…blah, blah, blah…but maybe you should skip to the important part."

"Oh!" Quinn stepped forward, following Jack's lead. "Um, do you Charles, take Catherine to be your wedded wife?"

"I do," the groom said lovingly to his bride.

Jack grinned at Quinn, and the reverend went on.

"Do you Catherine, take Charles to be your wedded husband?"

"I do." She beamed and without another word, the couple kissed.

Quinn cleared his throat. "I now pronounce you husband and wife. You may now kiss the bride. Which, you're obviously already doing."

The couple separated and smiled at each other once more. Catherine glanced at Jack and mouthed, *thank you*.

To Ethan she mouthed, *I'm sorry.* The bride and groom vanished.

Angry Annie twirled like a dervish where they'd been standing and called out, "You certainly are sorry! Don't you ever come back here!" She paused and when she noticed all eyes were on her, giggled with embarrassment. "My territory, you know." She whooshed in a circle around Ethan and straightened his collar. "Go get married. And put on a tie, for heaven's sake." Annie evaporated in a puff of smoke.

Everyone in the room let out a collective breath. "Oh, my god," Jack was the first to speak.

Dylan shook his head. "I shouldn't have polished off that bottle of whisky last night."

Cade smiled at his brother. "Yeah, it was the whisky. None of this ever happened."

Ethan gazed at Jack. "That was something, kid. How'd you know to do that?"

Jack smiled and shrugged. "A little research, and a lot of help from my friends. I can't explain why, but this inn feels like home to me already. I'd do anything to keep it open. I don't want to leave."

Ethan smiled. "That's the way I felt when I first came to this place. Whiskers' *is* home. We're not going to close the place."

Cade spoke up. "If I can convince Dylan to stay and help you out, would you be willing to run the inn while we're gone, Jack? I'm sure Logan can go over some details with you before he leaves. And it'll only be a couple of weeks. It's not like we could leave this place for long."

Jack knew his smile stretched from ear to ear. "Absolutely, sir. I'd be honoured."

Everyone looked at Dylan, who threw his hands in the air. "I might need some more whisky, but what the hell?"

The crowd cheered, and Jack noticed even Delia was smiling from her corner. He gazed at Quinn and saw all the happiness he felt reflected in the man's eyes. *I love you,* Jack mouthed.

I love you, too, Quinn mouthed back, and both men swiped at their eyes.

Jack cleared his throat. "Judge Brookfield, would you be so kind as to show Mrs. Nelson to her seat? We have a wedding to attend."

"Certainly." Alex took Delia's arm and led her out the door. The other guests found their chairs.

Quinn said, "We didn't have a chance to practice this, so we'll have to wing it."

"It'll be fine," Ethan assured.

The reverend opened the door. "Cade and Dylan, follow me."

"I need to help Ethan," Cade protested.

Ethan touched his lover's hand. "Logan and Jack can get me down the aisle. Both of them can stand up there with me, you know, in case I fall."

Everyone smiled and Cade said, "I'd be happy to have them up there as our friends and witnesses. But if you fall, I'm always going to be the one who catches you."

Ethan beamed. "You got it. Let's do this thing."

Jack's heart brimmed with happiness. He watched Quinn, Cade and Dylan file up to the front of the crowd and take their places. Standing on one side of Ethan with Logan on the other, he proudly walked down the aisle, smiling at the happy faces of the large crowd.

They made it to the front and handed Ethan over to Cade. Logan and Jack stepped to the side.

"Dearly beloved," Quinn began. "Our friends Ethan and Cade welcome you here today to celebrate the blessing of their union. I'd like to start by reading you a passage they've chosen, called an *Apache Marriage Blessing*."

He gazed at each of the grooms. "Now you will feel no rain, for each of you will be shelter for the other. Now you will feel no cold, for each of you will be warmth for the other. Now there is no more loneliness. Now you are two persons but there is only one life before you. May your days together be good and long upon the Earth."

With the soothing words in the background, Jack's mind wandered. *Two persons, one life. Is that how I feel about Quinn?* He glanced at the reverend. Pride, love and a twinge of lust swelled in him. *Damn right it is!* He realised at that moment, there was nothing he wanted more than a life with Quinn. As soon as the ceremony was over, he'd tell his handsome lover that, and a whole lot more. Excitement tingled in his chest and all points south.

Another thought struck him. *For the next two weeks, I'll be running the inn!* The idea made him very happy. He knew by doing a good job, and continuing to do the best cooking he was capable of, he'd have a place here at Whiskers' for a long time to come. *Ghosts and all.* Jack smiled. *I wouldn't want it any other way.*

He returned his attention to Quinn's blessing and smiled. *I'm the blessed one.* Hopefully, Quinn felt the same way. When the reverend caught his eye, the wink Quinn shot him made it clear he did, indeed, feel the same. Jack winked back, and his heart soared.

About the Authors

Jenna Byrnes

Jenna Byrnes could use more cabinet space and more hours in a day. She'd fill the kitchen with gadgets her husband purchases off TV and let him cook for her to his heart's content. She'd breeze through the days adding hours of sleep, and more time for writing the hot, erotic romance she loves to read.

Jenna thinks everyone deserves a happy ending, and loves to provide as many of those as possible to her gay, lesbian and hetero characters. Her favourite quote, from a pro-gay billboard, is "Be careful who you hate. It may be someone you love."

Jude Mason

Jude's imagination frequently leads her astray and she eagerly follows while trying to keep out of trouble, or at least, not get caught. For those of you who know her, you'll know that's not always easy. A picture, a smell, an unexpected glimpse of flesh, or a load of soil in the back of a pick-up, are all fodder for her writing. Her male characters run the gamut from the dominant male ruling his women with an iron fist, to a simpering purple-clad boy-toy whose only desire is to please. As diverse and as richly depicted, her women find themselves in a myriad of exotic and erotic situations.

Jenna and Jude love to hear from readers. You can find their contact information, website details and author profile pages at http://www.total-e-bound.com

Total-E-Bound Publishing

www.total-e-bound.com

Take a look at our exciting range of literagasmic™
erotic romance titles and discover pure quality
at Total-E-Bound.